# COVER STORY

## Carol Burns

First edition published in 2015 by Heddon Publishing.



ISBN 978-0-9932101-4-3

Cover design by Catherine Clarke



Book design and layout by Heddon Publishing.

www.heddonpublishing.com
www.facebook.com/heddonpublishing
@PublishHeddon

For Ewen

# ABOUT THE AUTHOR

Carol Burns grew up in the Midlands and trained in regional newspapers before going freelance and undertaking a second degree and MA in Fine Art. She now lives in Cornwall with her husband and son. She is editor of *Cornwall Life* magazine.

# COVER STORY

# In the beginning

*It was the tattoo she recognised. Badly written by the barely literate, presumably with the age-old application of several cans of cheap beer, the ink from a crushed biro and the heated point of a compass. The letters were still legible despite the dried blood, spelling the word 'HATE'.*

*"Fucking hell." She said it loudly but the reporters housed in nearby cubicles didn't stir. Swearing was an art form in newsrooms up and down the country, more highly regarded by many than the sub-editor's ability to wring a pun out of stories so thin they were practically anorexic. She would have to come up with a more original epithet if she wanted a response.*

*She moved towards her desk for a closer look. The day's post sat unopened on her chair. She slumped down onto it, her legs suddenly unable to take her weight. The noise of bubble wrap popping under her failed to raise a smile, though her neighbour cast a smirk in her direction as he talked loudly into the phone jammed between his left shoulder and ear.*

*The news editor had recently outlawed spikes, the old-fashioned wires vertically protruding from a cork base traditionally used in newsrooms to file paper after a story went to print. Despite their existence for more than a century, it was only now that someone considered having a sharpish wire on a desk a Health and Safety hazard. "You could have someone's eye out with that," her editor had said, replacing it with a sharp-cornered box file some weeks before.*

*Now her spike had been reinstated – placed where her computer keyboard usually sat - with a human hand impaled on it.*

*"We wondered where you got it from, it looks real enough." Having finished his call, her neighbouring reporter got up and wandered over, stained coffee cup in hand. "Very funny. I'd have gone for an eyeball. Spotted it when I got in this morning, but it didn't fool me for a second. Lizbet was very unamused." He gestured with a tilt of his head towards the Features desk.*

*"It is real," she answered, her voice husky. She coughed before continuing. "And I know who it belongs to."*

*Before he could respond, she leaned over and emptied the contents of her stomach into the unused box file at her feet.*

# CHAPTER 1

It was the curse of every successful man to face the disinterest of his progeny. Sir Jesper Donaldson was no different. He looked across his mammoth desk, created from a single slab of highly polished walnut, and sighed at the man sitting opposite. The movement caused his frameless glasses to tilt slightly, hiding his small grey eyes and shooting a reflective glare from the lamp on his desk.

The younger man fought the urge to wince as his retinas came under attack. It was hard to tell if the glare was unintentional, or a well-rehearsed move to put visitors at a disadvantage.

No computer marred the clean lines of Sir Jesper's desk. A classic green glass shaded reading lamp sat angled at one corner of the ancient desk, which had once sat in his great-grandfather's library. At the centre sat a pristine copy of the latest issue of *Compagne* magazine.

A slender telephone sitting in a silver dock provided him with his only link to the outside world, via a competent secretary who guarded his inner sanctum. A man of his stature had no place behind a keyboard. Computers were for his minions.

Behind Sir Jesper's head, the walnut-panelled walls held hunting prints from the past two centuries and a smattering of miniature oils of long-dead Donaldson relatives who were only identifiable via the engraved brass plaques incorporated into the overly ornate frames. The room looked more like a gentlemen's club than the nerve centre of a publishing empire, and Sir Jesper liked it that way. His family had never had to work, but to do so in this setting added to the aristocratic air so important to the look of his magazine.

Sir Jesper had made his money – or rather his family had – through land. His was one of the few families to increase their fortune in the early 20th century when so many ducal families were forced to sell their land off cheap. Sir Jesper's grandfather had used his cash to buy up land from his unexpectedly impoverished neighbouring peers – not allowing family ties to get in the way of a bargain – and as a result Sir Jesper was now sitting on a sizeable chunk of prime land overlooking the Atlantic coast of North Cornwall.

For the young Jesper, a favourite bedtime story had been that of a particularly unfortunate Cornish duke left penniless by some bad investment decisions during the American depression and who had taken his remaining prized possession, an early James Purdey & Sons 12-bore shotgun, into the woods he no longer owned to end his life. The duke's country seat now made up the ancient nerve centre of *Compagne*, The Lodge.

Originally created as a 17th century hunting lodge, the old building was rumoured to have welcomed more than one royal guest to rest on its ancient four-poster beds. Today it had been sympathetically converted into an editorial suite befitting one of the country's most revered lifestyle magazines for the aristocracy and its hangers-on. The ancient hall served as the reception area and housed a conference room. Its imposing boardroom table was once used as the dining table of the ancient home. Sir Jesper's suite of offices sat in the former library.

Sir Jesper had arrived early to work, as he had a full diary of meetings to discuss the sudden loss of their editor and the need to appoint a replacement as soon as possible. Sir Jesper was a man in the prime of his life, he felt, and his room reflected this success. It was furnished with a range of pieces of furniture and art from his Grade I listed home, The Glades, which had been in his family for more than six centuries.

A selection of Sèvres on display behind him was still used at board meetings as a reminder of the rich heritage that those around the table were privileged to be a part of. A complete set to all but the most careful of eyes; a side plate had been lost back in the 1980s, when Sir Jesper threw it at the then Finance Director for his unfavourable report of the financial performance of his father's last years in office. Fortunately Sir Jesper's aim was off due to a shoulder strain sustained during a lengthy session of cunnilingus with his London-based mistress of the time and the Finance Director had lived to tell the tale, but not within the halls of *Compagne*.

Today it was the man sitting opposite Sir Jesper who was eyeing up the priceless china, wondering vaguely how much the collection was worth. Mathieu Durrant Donaldson was better known as Matt to all but his father. He had been summoned to The Lodge to discuss his future. At that moment, if he was totally honest, he wasn't feeling like he had one. His uncut hair failed to hide the cut above his right eyebrow.

"I walked into a door," he had told his father when he entered the room, in response to the raised eyebrow. His father had sighed disbelievingly; it was further evidence that it was high time his only son looked to the only possible future on his horizon – as heir apparent of *Compagne*.

The irony was that the door story wasn't far from the truth. Uri, the debt collector's PA, had knocked on Matt's door at 9pm a couple of nights previously. Matt had opened the door with the chain on and, once Uri had identified himself, had half closed it in order to take the chain off. Uri, assuming it was being closed in his face, pushed the door violently and Matt ended up sprawled on the floor of his hallway, the sight in his right eye temporarily obscured by a steady flow of blood from a cut above.

£47,000… £47k… the numbers kept reverberating around in Matt's head until they made no sense. He needed to get the money together within 72 hours, the debt increasing hourly; the interest rates made payday loans look like a fire sale. His father was his only chance. He knew it would come at a price but couldn't afford any other option.

"Dad. I've got into a bit of trouble," Matt began, working out that since he had got up that morning, the debt had increased by £300.

"What kind of trouble?" Since his son had reached puberty, Sir Jesper's daily worry was that he would get a girl knocked up and they would be stuck with someone unsuitable to carry on the family name.

"I need some money."

Images of a heavily pregnant teen evaporated. "Money?"

"Yes. Money. I've got into a bit of debt."

"Debt? What kind of debt?"

"The worst kind – with a loan shark."

"Betting?"

"In a fashion. It was part of my Master's."

"Part of your education? We gave you plenty of allowance to keep you debt-free."

"This was extra-curricular."

"So how is betting part of your education?"

"I've been researching betting websites." Matt knew it was going to be a hard sell, but the truth was he had become fascinated with the world of online gambling, and had borrowed money in order to research how the sites worked. It wasn't that he wanted to set one up himself, or that he particularly wanted to close them down, repugnant though they were. He was fascinated by the idea of people sitting in front of laptops and tablets getting off on betting. Gambling was the new online porn. And the more he watched, the more ideas he got.

Matt scratched his head vigorously, lifting his dark hair up to reveal a striking widow's peak; the only thing he had inherited from his father so far, although he lived in hope of a large settlement. This would free him up from the publishing world, which didn't inspire him, and release him into the world of games design, which did.

His Master's degree in software design had managed to keep him out of a full-time job with his father but now, at the age of 24, he was running out of time. The request from Sir Jesper for a meeting to discuss his future had come at a good time, the need to get hold of money to ensure he actually had a future foremost in his mind.

"Mathieu. If you've got yourself into debt gambling, then admit it. Be a man and we can work something out."

"But I was doing research – and I think I've come up with a brilliant idea for a new game."

The aim of Horseface was to create the perfect virtual horse through genetic breeding with other virtual horses, which would then race other virtual horses online, with players able to trade and buy horses, breed and race. Matt had spent enough time around the equine-minded to know that Horseface could occupy the time they weren't able to spend in the stables or become an online substitute for the real thing for those who couldn't afford it. Of course, he would need to come up with a better name for it before it was released.

Sir Jesper stretched his hands out and tapped his left index finger on the desk in front of him, thinking. On one hand, his son would learn his lesson better if he had to borrow the money and work to pay it back but on the other hand he didn't want a son with broken legs.

Turning 60 in a few years, Sir Jesper found himself thinking more and more of his ancestors. How his grandfather had launched the magazine, which had gone on to become such a success in publishing. Sir Jesper had only intended to stay until his own business – or businesses – took off. But like many sons of incredibly successful men, he had struggled to crawl out of his father's shadow. Throughout his life, he had been forced to endure all those powerful and successful men he met through business who clasped him firmly by the shoulder, relating tales of the great parties they had attended at his home, hosted by his grandfather and then later by his father, Sir Jesper Senior. Only in recent years did the men in his boardroom not remember his father at the helm, but only because those who did were dying off. Cold comfort to a man who himself was reaching retirement age.

His grandfather, the first Sir Jesper, had been a dazzling hero on the social scene. He and his wife Jacinta had become the toast of the 1930s as a young couple then Sir Jesper ran off to become a hero in the Second World War before returning to his wife and her largely uninterrupted social life, which provided the inspiration and much of the content for his first issue of *Compagne.*

From the first, *Compagne* had charted the social life of every peer of the realm, helping to remind those coming back from the war and facing a newly impoverished England of what had made Britain great, and by extension would do again, while injecting a little of the French elegance Sir Jesper had witnessed in the early years of the war, before France fell to the Germans.

It could so easily have backfired while people were eking out their existence on powdered egg and home-grown turnips, but they lapped it up. *Compagne* might have been perceived as tasteless; a magazine recording the house parties, weddings and interiors of the super wealthy at a time when the everyday woman still faced meat and sugar rations but as it turned out, people were in desperate need of a little glamour, even if it could only be obtained vicariously at two-pence a month.

Just as no one had questioned Sir Winston Churchill's right to swill Pol Roger champagne and chew endlessly on Romeo and Juliet cigars, the public seemed willing to accept that the elite shouldn't go without just because the rest of the country was still eating bread made from sawdust.

The current Sir Jesper's father had taken over the magazine during the 1960s, until his son was old enough to take over. During his reign, the magazine had expanded to cover the social life of some of the 'nous-nous' that were desperate for a guest role on the coffee tables of the ruling classes. These newly rich families not only had more to prove, but often more to spend, hosting some of the most glamorous events while older families struggled to make ends meet and hold the National Trust surveyors at bay.

Now it was time to expand again. *Compagne* was going digital, if only Matt could be convinced to stay and do it.

Sir Jesper reached for a chequebook from his desk drawer, his mind made up. It was time his son joined the publishing milieu. "I will pay this debt, but you will have to pay it back."

"I will Dad, thanks. But can you transfer it into my account – I need to put the cash into his hand by Monday morning."

Sir Jesper nodded. He would get Jo, his secretary, to transfer it later from his private account.

"You will work the debt off. We need help developing our online and digital issues. And you clearly need something to keep you out of trouble." Sir Jesper realised that would make it a business expense and he could pay Matt from the company account. He scribbled a note to himself to get a contract drawn up.

"For how long?" Matt recognised he had little choice but if he had to spend a few months at The Lodge, it was going to slow down the development of Horseface.

"I will take half your salary back each month. It will take you about two years to pay it off."

"Two years! But if I got a consultant IT job it would only take me about six months to pay it off."

"As you wish." Sir Jesper had spent too long in the boardroom to be intimidated by his son's transparent attempt at blackmail.

"But I need the money now."

"Well." Sir Jesper stared down his frustrated son.

"I could move back home; that would help me pay you back more quickly."

Sir Jesper frowned. It would be nice to have his son back under his roof, but he would rather have him at The Lodge, indefinitely.

"You start on Monday." Sir Jesper turned away, his mind immediately focused on the next problem: *Compagne's* sudden lack of an editor.

Matt left the office. He waited until the solid oak door was shut before kicking a rust-red sofa.

"Fucking bollocks," he snarled as his foot connected with the solid leg of the ancient Chesterfield. His father's secretary ignored his outburst, instead responding to Sir Jesper's buzzer and making herself scarce, pad and pen in hand.

Matt headed outside, limping slightly. The ancient sofa was more solid than it looked. Horseface would never get developed by the end of the year if he had to spend every day at The Lodge hunched over a computer screen, sorting out their non-existent website.

"Fucking bollocks," he said again, with less volume but more venom, as he passed the receptionist who had smoothed her blonde hair and refreshed her lipgloss on his approach. Her making-up went unnoticed by Matt, who continued to mouth abuse under his breath. This time the abuse was aimed at himself. How could he have been so stupid as to put himself exactly where his father wanted him? He knew Sir Jesper would do everything in his power to keep him at *Compagne* forever but he was fucked if he was spending his life behind that oak desk, no matter how nice the view.

# CHAPTER 2

Sir Jesper's secretary could have been chosen simply to wow guests. Her perfectly sized pert breasts stuck out at just the right angle underneath her baby-blue cashmere sweater, while two strands of pearls hung at just the right length, grazing the collarbone just visible above her neckline. Her make-up was subtle in a way that required an hour every morning to achieve, and her soft ash-blonde hair was brushed smoothly down to her shoulders, with one side carelessly tucked behind a petite ear to reveal the hint of a diamond glint of just the right size in her lobe.

It was a look that took a lifetime of breeding to achieve, but fortunately for Josephine Caruthers (who was born Jo Clark) it could also be bought through an intensive online course at *www.snagapeer.com*, a kind of online Professor Higgins, which taught clothes, make-up and styling for young budding not-quite-ladies looking for a rich husband with a title. Although hailing from Mansfield, Josephine had learned to lower her voice, in both tone and volume. The real secret lay in silence; Jo had learned that it paid to speak as little as possible. As well as helping to avoid any slip-ups in conversation this also gave just the right impression of obedience that the landed gentry had come to rely on in their womenfolk as much as they had their fertile loins to provide the next generation.

To Victoria Manders, prospective editor, arriving two minutes late – which left her no time to wash her hands and avoid handing over a sweaty paw at the start of her interview – Jo appeared the very image of a lady. She stood up from behind her desk, rising in one fluid movement as Tory entered the room, and held out her hand. Tory responded by stretching out her own to shake it, before realising that the woman was simply offering to take her coat. Handing it over awkwardly, Tory inwardly thanked her mother for encouraging her to invest in the rich red designer mac, which felt reassuringly expensive.

"Thank you," Tory said with a smile, surreptitiously wiping her damp palms on the coat's fabric as she handed it over.

Jo pressed a button on her sleek console. "Victoria Manders has arrived, Sir Jesper," she said in a husky lilt into the speaker before adding in a more forceful tone to Tory, "Please take a seat."

Tory sat on the low leather couch, taking care to smooth down her tailored dress before sitting and crossing her legs daintily to show off her designer shoes. She placed her small cream Mulberry handbag on her lap, and leaned her battered black leather portfolio case against the sofa leg. Copies of the latest *Compagne* sat on the low wooden table in front of her. She leaned over, picking one up to flick through it. She had her own copy secreted in her portfolio case but it was riddled with sticky notes, to give her easy access to those parts of the magazine she wanted to discuss. A weighty tome of some 300 pages, the magazine combined an excess of millionaire interiors with millionaire faces, squeezed between a smattering of horsey debs at social gatherings raising money for such varied good causes as children's cancer and retired racehorses.

Within a few minutes she was led into an office where Sir Jesper Donaldson rose from behind his giant desk and reached over with his hand outstretched. Tory, despite her five-foot, eight-inch height, found she struggled to bend far enough over the monstrous desk to grasp it. Whilst she smiled a hello, an image popped into her head unbidden, of being pushed against the desk, skirt around her head, knickers to her ankles, being entered from behind.

Mentally shaking her head, Tory's eyes followed where Sir Jesper was gesturing to two ancient Chesterfield sofas upholstered in soft oxblood leather, sitting at right angles to each other, a carafe of water and two crystal glasses set out on the highly polished rosewood table in between.

"Please do sit," Sir Jesper said.

Tory determined not to drink the water; she was bound to leave a watermark on the table.

"Thank you," she said, trying to sound both confident and posh.

Sir Jesper clearly felt he didn't need to introduce himself but his eyes shifted to a man sitting at the side of his desk, whose presence Tory had not registered.

"This is Mathieu, our newly appointed Digital Editor."

Tory turned, a ready smile forming on her lips, then immediately reddened, the practised smile dropping from her face. The hand now coming towards hers she had last seen on her breast about 12 hours ago, precisely three hours after she had first met the person it belonged to. She wondered if *Compagne's* Miss Manners columnist had a section that dealt with situations like this. Her immediate response was embarrassment, quickly followed by anger, and swiftly returning to embarrassment.

"Nice to meet you," Matt covered up his surprise better than Tory, but he was under less stress. The well-bred gentleman in him blocked out the vivid memories that came to mind of his last view of her, lying curled on her hotel room bed, crumpled sheets wrapped around her lower body, Hollywood soft focus style, as he had crept out of the room.

They had met in When the Bell Tolls, the pub where Tory had gone for a late supper and Matt had gone to settle his nerves. She had mentioned an interview, for a job that she was desperate to get, but he hadn't been overly interested in her career ambitions. Today, he hadn't thought about her much, beyond wondering if she would be back in the pub again later.

It had been one of those nights. They had met, made polite conversation, admitted a powerful attraction that had only a little to do with the wine they had consumed, and ended up back in her hotel room.

Tory didn't make a habit of picking up handsome, well-spoken men with facial injuries in pubs, but she had been afraid of spending the night alone after her previous night's flit from London. Now she plastered a less genial smile on her face. She had put their encounter down to a good use of the nervous energy that always preceded these kinds of events and had yet to have time to fully explore her feelings about it or him. After all, she had more important things to worry about.

Next to possibly being stalked by an unknown assassin from the Baltic Mafia, a one-night stand with a potential boss's son was *petit pommes de terre*. She just wished he wasn't sitting in the room, smiling benevolently at her as if to reassure her that last night was another country.

"I thought it would be a good start to go through some of your ideas and thoughts about the current magazine," Sir Jesper said, unaware that *Compagne* was far from the minds of both of his companions.

Tory turned her attention back to him; after all, if she did survive the possible stalking by said Baltic Mafia maniac, she would need a job. Her 'to do' list when she woke that morning had been simple: stay alive, get a job and find a place to live. There was no room for a romantic entanglement worthy of a straight-to-download movie.

She wasn't fooled by Sir Jesper's gentle entreaty. After all, it was clear from her CV that she was qualified. What he wanted to know was if she was a good fit for his beloved title.

"I don't want to put you on the spot," Sir Jesper added, although he clearly relished the idea.

Tory opened up her well-thumbed copy of *Compagne* to the first of her rapidly scribbled notes. She knew it was important to strike just the right balance of awe and criticism. She needed to make him think she admired him as well as the magazine, and all it stood for, despite having never picked it up before 7am that morning, while explaining how she could improve it through small, seemingly insignificant, changes that would make all the difference.

Her friend Lyle had set up the meeting for her the previous day, while she had been sleeping off her midnight journey. He had mentioned that the former Managing Editor had left at short notice and that as long as Tory didn't turn up to the interview drunk, she would probably get the job. He'd had a copy of the latest issue delivered straight to her hotel along with details of the interview so that, when she awoke, she was able to start her preparation.

"It's an incredible magazine — the real benchmark for any aspiring magazine journalist," she began. "Your features are incredible, but the photography needs more careful editing; *Compagne* should be winning awards for its garden, homes and portrait photography. The interviews are often the things that attract people to a magazine. These should be high profile, written by celebrity writers with their own fan base. Arts tourism is a real growth area, and the Arts section should have its own editor; someone knowledgeable, who can get profiles, not only of the important artists but also the collectors, who are just dying to show off their collections when they're not lending the work out to national galleries to gain tax rebates."

Sir Jesper nodded encouragingly. He had just lent some works to a new touring exhibition for exactly that reason.

Tory turned to the Social pages. These spreads she knew helped ensure the magazine sat on antique coffee tables up and down the land, as Mr and Mrs double-barrelled name were keen to expose themselves across its pages.

"Your Social pages are a key element of driving traffic to the new website," she said, warming to the subject. "It is as easy to take 50 photos at one of these occasions as it is to take the 16 needed to fill a double page spread. The complete coverage could be shown in exclusive online society galleries," she smiled in Matt's direction without looking him in the eye.

"The company should also be exploiting sales of these photographs, on canvases, as screen savers, mugs, t-shirts…" she trailed off, trying to think of something suitably high class to splash a society photograph across. "Or simply in a silver frame for one's desk."

Sir Jesper smiled. It was a great way to increase their coverage – and the bottom line. He knew that on more than one occasion the Social Editor had complained that some important guest had been excluded from coverage of an event and even he had faced a frosty reception at the golf club from someone who felt they had been slighted by exclusion. He uncapped his Mont Blanc fountain pen and ostentatiously wrote a note to himself. This girl had ideas. She was attractive, bright – and seemed at home in the surroundings. She looked presentable, but he would rely on Jo to assure him of the suitability and quality of her outfit after she left. A subtle nod from his secretary could decide one way or the other.

"*Compagne* has built up an incredible reputation as a magazine, but we haven't really broached the internet," Sir Jesper said.

More than anything, he needed someone who could start straightaway. It wasn't yet generally known that the previous editor had suffered complications during a liposuction procedure. The surgeon, unable to find an ounce of fat on her carcass, had accidentally sucked out some muscle mass from her thighs instead. She had lost twice as much weight as expected, muscle weighing more than fat, which she had been delighted with, but with it had gone her ability to walk, at least temporarily. She was now under a strict physiotherapy regime to try and rebuild the lost muscles.

"The internet is vital in today's publishing," agreed Tory. "You need to offer daily content, email newsletters and online subscriptions which send out e-copies of the magazine on the same day every month. Driving readers to your site provides advertisers with two bites at the cherry, as it were. And you will find you gain a growing number of exclusively online readers who may differ in profile from your traditional readership." She felt rather than saw Matt nodding in agreement.

"Newspapers are probably ahead of magazines in this," she

continued. "My last newspaper had more hits online than readers of the paper copy. Every writer had an online profile and blogged, tweeted and Facebooked stories. Extra content was added to the website on a minute-by-minute basis."

There was a pause as Tory caught her breath.

Sir Jesper smiled, "The website will take some time to develop, and I think it's fair to say our editors are not fully cognisant of the latest information and communication technology."

Matt smirked; this was an understatement. The brief look he'd had at the IT systems showed storage was at capacity as emails were rarely read and even more rarely deleted. How they would cope with an editor who wanted them blogging, tweeting and Facebooking... he would make sure he didn't miss that meeting.

"It's obviously an area you want to develop, and it will need to be done alongside all the other social media. One of the first things I would do is set up Twitter accounts and get people following us. The Social Editor in particular will prove popular if she can tweet her diary, maybe even take a few snaps to add to her posts."

Sir Jesper nodded. Lyle — a favourite photographer and occasional pulling partner - had said that Victoria was perfect for the job. She would shake things up. His staff were getting a little too comfortable in their roles. "Do you have any questions for me?"

"Tell me about the staff."

"You have editors for each of the major sections of the magazine: Food, Society, Homes and Interiors and so on. They like to run them pretty independently, so your role is to bring them all together, manage the pages in each issue and work with the advertising and design teams to create each issue."

"And will there be a handover from the current editor?"

Sir Jesper shook his head. "I understand from your email yesterday that you are available to work at quite short notice?"

He was relieved to get to the only real vital question he had to ask.

"Yes, I'm available immediately."

"See you on Monday, then." Sir Jesper stood and held out his hand. He was too relieved to question why she was available so suddenly. Lyle had vouched for her and he was a good judge of character. For now at least, the vacancy was filled, even if they had to find someone more permanently at a later date.

# CHAPTER 3

Tory walked carefully out of The Lodge, smiling to herself. That was the first thing to strike off her 'to do' list. Next was somewhere to live. Not such a big problem now she had a confirmation letter, with a monthly salary that almost matched her annual income from the *Post*. She smiled at the receptionist as she signed out of the visitors book, which sat on an ancient breakfront, and fought back a slightly hysterical giggle as she spotted the half-full umbrella stand in the corner by the large oak door and a row of well-used green rubber boots: not a black welly in sight.

Tory praised herself for parking her decrepit Ford Focus out of sight. It had an oil leak that could fund an independent Scotland and although she wanted to leave an impression at *Compagne* she hadn't wanted to leave a stain in the car park. What kind of company car could the new editor of *Compagne* expect? A Bentley? Whatever it was, she planned to feed the Ford Focus all the oil it could drink and then abandon it somewhere suitable where it would make a welcome plaything for the locals.

It was strange to think she was in Cornwall. Although she had only been to the county once, when she was in nappies, it had seemed like a good hiding place.

She strapped herself into the car, slipping out of the navy Manolo Blahniks, and stripping off her 'barely there' tights before easing her hot feet into a battered pair of Birkenstocks kept in the passenger-side foot well. The temperature had risen to more than 25° and it was only June.

Cornwall was well-known for its great light, as the sun reflected off the ocean that surrounded it. Tory thought she would need to invest in some decent sunglasses. Although journalists are supposed to dress to be prepared for anything, for Tory being dressed to impress would take some getting used to. She allowed herself a large swig of the warm water from the bottle on her dashboard and unwound her window to enjoy the non-existent fresh air before setting off back to the hotel.

A good lunch awaited her with Lyle and she was hoping his sofa bed would be available until she could track down a more permanent residence. There were some incredible seafront apartments to choose from, or a fisherman's cottage by a quaint harbour might be the answer. Realistically, she knew she would settle for what she could get.

Pulling into the traffic after inputting the address of Ramsden's restaurant into her satnav, she finally allowed herself to think about Matt. Was this a sign of things to come? Was she moving to a part of the world where you kept bumping into the same people? In London you could sleep with someone and be pretty confident that you would never see him or her again. Ever. Even more so if you actually wanted to. She had only been in Cornwall one day and already the mistake of the night before had reared its head in the most unlikely of places.

Last night he had seemed gentle and polite. He hadn't seemed the kind of... She scrunched up her eyes and fought the urge to smack her head against the steering wheel.

"I really enjoyed meeting you," those had been his last words to her as she left Sir Jesper's office. Spoken without a hint of irony. Last night there had been no last words, more of a last grunt. Oh god, oh god, oh god! What had she been thinking?

She cleared her head and did a double take as the glittering Atlantic Ocean came into view. This place was like California, she thought, turning her concentration back to following the instructions of the automated satnav voice, which was taking her along something called the Atlantic Highway and on to her lunch date.

"No need to ask how it went," Lyle had already arrived and was sitting at one of the corner tables of the restaurant, poring over the à la carte menu, his back to the picture window which offered a view of an old fishing quay where a few sailing boats bobbed up and down in the water. The boats were pristine and looked as though the only fish they had ever hauled onboard were of the ready-smoked variety that lay between two slices of buttered brown bread.

Ramsden's was one of a handful of new boutique B&B restaurants along the north Cornwall coast. A former Methodist chapel, it had an open plan dining area pressed up against large clear glass windows, the kitchen in the place where the organs had once stood. Lyle watched Tory take in her surroundings as she took a moment to think about the number of people who must have taken the pledge in the very spot now displaying an impressive array of wines. Sometimes progress could be a good thing.

"The scallops here are tremendous," Lyle said. "And I've ordered a bottle of each, you can stay over at mine." He spoke casually, not wanting to make it sound like a seduction.


Tory and Lyle had met on their first job on a weekly free newspaper in East Finchley. Lyle was an accomplished and ambitious photographer with an eye for a juicy celebrity story and accompanying shot while Tory held onto her aspirations to investigative journalism long enough to become his editor and help him decide what was a real story. At that time, the weekly newspaper had a readership of 6,000 and nothing could compare to the thrill of her name on the front page.

From the weekly *Star*, Lyle quickly went off to the nationals, hanging out in all the right clubs to spot the stars and get exclusives. He made piles of cash and loved his job. Now, at the age of 28, he was close to a celebrity in his own right. He had chosen his home away from the celebrity-laden streets of London, although it was in one of Cornwall's most exclusive enclaves. His riverside house came with its own mooring, and he was one of only a handful of people with a season ticket on the Paddington to Penzance sleeper.

Tory still considered the news a serious and important business. And when the opportunity came up for her most recent post as editor of a Saturday supplement, she felt it was a good fit. There was time to allow stories to ferment, although rigor mortis had quickly set into her last would-be splash. Tory had managed to get in too deep with the story that had forced her out of London with only time to pack an overnight bag and her laptop.

She owed Lyle. Aware that she was unhappy already with her existing job, he had got into the habit of passing news of any suitable vacancies on. Generally Tory barely paid any attention to his messages but this one – spotted just when she had been talking to the police about making herself scarce – had led to an immediate firing off of her CV to Sir Jesper. Without waiting for his response, she had headed for the M4.

Despite her slightly sarcastic take on it all, she knew she was lucky. *Compagne* was a venerable publication that at least didn't have its journalists rummaging through the rubbish bins of Chelsea in search of the next cover story. Liposuction complications not withstanding (she had heard the receptionist muttering the latest gossip into her phone on the way out of the building), Tory guessed the editors weren't generally risking life and limb.

"They offered it to me on the spot," she told Lyle as a waiter came over to fill their wine glasses. "I can't believe places like that exist. It will be like working in a stately home. Sir Jesper didn't ask me one difficult question. The last time I was interviewed the editor tried to make me cry."

Lyle smiled knowingly; he wasn't surprised by the turn of events. Sir Jesper was an old ram and the prospect of sitting opposite his beautiful friend at editorial meetings was bound to win him over, even if her extensive CV and his own excessive compliments hadn't. Lyle felt hopeful that he finally had Tory within his grasp.

As if feeling Lyle's change of mood, a wave of unease rolled over Tory. Being chased by murderous criminals had put her far out of her comfort zone and now the job ahead suddenly seemed beyond her. Perhaps she was being ungrateful; it was like complaining the lifeboat that scooped you out of the sea smelled of fish. But it had been a bizarre day on top of a quite frankly terrifying 48 hours.

# CHAPTER 4

Despite a few undertones, Lyle's company soothed Tory and after a long lunch and nothing else to do, she took a walk along the harbour. The sea sparkled in the sun and she discovered that the yachts moored out in the water which she'd seen from the restaurant window were reassuringly mixed with enough battered fishing boats and tugs to convince her she was looking out onto a real fishing harbour. She had heard the stories of how most of the fishermen were long gone by now, but if her lavish lunch of Cornish seafood had been anything to go by there was still a fishing industry out there somewhere.

Taking a seat, she stared out to sea, enjoying the sound of the surf hitting the harbour wall, the boats gently swaying with the tide, and thinking of all the places she could end up if she set off in a boat – apart from the bottom of the ocean.

In the end, Tory had turned down Lyle's offer of his spare room. She didn't want to get too reliant on company to keep her fears at bay and, after the previous night's disastrous one-night stand, she didn't want to find herself crawling into Lyle's bed one night for some companionship only to wake up the next morning having ruined a friendship.

Strangely, now she had a job, she felt more fearful of the future. Like a refugee whose life is in danger, she had seemed to cope, to get through the escape; it was only when the danger had started to dissipate and she was beginning to feel safe that the depression began to sink in. And the vision of Craig Smith's severed hand stabbed through her spike kept reappearing.

She checked her voicemail again but there was no message from Sergeant Donovan telling her all was well and that she could return home. Her last conversation with him had simply confirmed that the severed hand had belonged to the reviled and presumably recently deceased Craig 'Cracker' Smith. He hadn't been seen since her interview with him and a search of London's A&E departments had failed to turn up anyone answering to his description. There were, however, a surprising number of people in the capital missing their right hand, the sergeant had told her conversationally.

The story had started out as a straightforward interview. Cracker Smith was a leading light in the London-based Neo Socialist

Party, the latest in a long line of vicious thugs posing as politicians, who no one took seriously until the success of a few right-leaning organisations in a few parliamentary seats inspired all kinds to crawl out of the woodwork. It was only when she met Smith that she understood his curious moniker. His waistline did bear an uncanny resemblance to Robbie Coltrane's in the titular role, but turned out to be incidental. Smith had actually been renamed for his constant knuckle-cracking; a nervous habit, rather than a menacing manoeuvre, which had led to early arthritis in his hands, now so gnarled it was difficult to read the green-tinted lettering staining each finger between his top and middle joints. These hands had become his trademark. Strange to think that one of them was now sitting in a cold storage drawer at a morgue waiting for the rest of him to be found so it could be reunited.

Cracker had wanted to come across as smart in his interview and, like all politicians, as having all the answers. This catchall worked best if you kept things quite vague; that way whatever answers a listener, or reader, is looking for, whatever ideology they subscribe to, they can identify and align themselves. This was the reason Tory was sitting opposite Smith in the Starbucks on Hammersmith High Street to discuss the finer points of his life thus far. She had followed her interview with a brief conversation with her editor who had decided on a series of articles revealing the stories behind the right-wingers. He even had an apocalyptical header ready: *The Rise of the Right*.

The following day, Cracker's right hand had turned up on her spike.

As Tory replayed their final words to each other she realised it was the same hand she had shaken as they said goodbye. The thought activated her gag reflex even as she sat looking out to sea. She dropped her head, closed her eyes, and did some deep breathing, taking in deep lungfuls of the warm, fresh salty air and trying to empty her mind. In the end she opened her eyes and thought back to how her journey to Cornwall had begun.

"The lights are on and nobody's home." The sentence had reverberated again in her head. It was her editor Gatsby's highly unoriginal comment about the man who had sawn off a hand from an already deceased body, according to the scene-of-crime officers who eventually called in to collect it.

However, if it hadn't been for that sentence bouncing around in her head, she possibly wouldn't have thought about the fact that her own light was on when she arrived home. She had stepped out of the taxi and looked at her building then done a double take. It was already getting dark and she could see her bedroom was illuminated, but she knew she hadn't put the light on that morning.

The block of flats were basic, thrown up to house the necessary workers of London without the frills of balconies. Standing on the kerb, staring up conspicuously, she thought of Jamesy who lived upstairs. She would ring him and ask him to have a look. Her meeting with the police in the office had left her a little shaken but just because she was paranoid didn't mean they weren't after her.

"Ms Manders?" The voice had carried much further across the newsroom than it needed to. Since the find on her spike, the room had been abnormally quiet as a slew of uniformed police trampled through. Tory had looked the middle-aged man over. He looked tired and was carrying a little too much timber, like the cops on TV shows, but the clincher was the police ID card he held up in his left hand announcing him as Sergeant P. Donovan.

She led him through to the interview room-slash-store cupboard and sat down expectantly.

"Tell me about the hand," he sat down heavily and pulled out a notepad, which he flicked his eyes towards from time to time throughout the interview, occasionally scribbling a note.

"I think I recognise it."

"So do we," he answered.

"Craig Smith."

"Yes."

"I understand you met with Craig Smith yesterday at the Starbucks in Hammersmith High Street?"

Tory finally found her voice. "I did."

"What did you talk about?"

Tory shrugged. "He said he wants to share his story, we set up the interview last week."

"What did he tell you?"

"All kinds of things, nothing headline-grabbing. What happened?"

"Tell me what you talked about – did you record your conversation?"

"How did he die?"

"We won't know until we get the post mortem results – if we get any. It's been a while since our pathologist had so little to work from. All we know at the moment is he was dead when the hand was cut off."

"How do you know?"

"Something to do with blood coagulation."

"But killed? By who?"

"Well," Sergeant Donovan shifted in his seat. "The list is marginally shorter than the Greater London phonebook, but the fact that he met with a journalist, in a public place the day before he died, is highly suggestive. I need to look at those notes."

"I need to talk to the editor." Tory had never had any interview notes requested by the police, but she remembered in the distant past that there was some protection against having them forcibly taken away. Hadn't some journalists gone to prison to protect this inalienable right? It was a hell of a way to prove your mettle. Especially at the *Post*, where management seemed to go out of their way to show how little the journalists meant to them.

She stood and together they headed over to the glass cube that contained Mark Gatsby. He looked up on their approach, more than happy to put aside the most recent circulation figures that had landed on his desk that morning.

The *Post* had survived two centuries, two world wars, several depressions and 19 editors. Its current incumbent was more than aware of those facts. Now it was limping into the 21$^{st}$ century and the paper was dying. There was no official diagnosis that it was terminal but you didn't need to be a member of the Royal College of Physicians to know that haemorrhaging of any kind was never a sign of rude health.

And they were haemorrhaging readers. Every month the circulation figures dropped. It was like being parachuted onto the *Titanic* after it had hit the iceberg and then being blamed for the collision. But Gatsby hung on because he still thought he could make a difference; like one of those women who married men on death row he still thought he could change it.

He looked out of the dusty glass windows that separated his office from the rest of the newsroom. Too many of his journalists were sitting on their arses re-writing press releases. Begging images to go with the stories from smug PR professionals who were being paid twice as much as them. Gatsby remembered a time when only the best stories went into the paper – reporters would be fighting each other for assignments. Today the newspaper's philosophy was like a World War Two housewife: nothing gets wasted.

Now a real story had landed on his desk. Well, one of his reporter's desks. Over the years readers had sent in many things, from a half-eaten burger containing a false eyelash to a carefully removed cow's ear, but never a human hand. He didn't know whether to be horrified or relieved they finally had a real exclusive front page. Happily they had managed to get a few pictures of the hand in situ before the police had turned up and broken out the stripy tape.

Tory, still pale, walked into his office. "Sergeant Donovan has a request."

"I need to see Ms Manders' notes from her interview with Craig Smith."

"Cracker?" Gatsby interrupted. "Is she right then?"

His news antennae immediately pinged; the more information they could get, the better the story.

Sergeant Donovan nodded. "Can we talk off the record?" At Gatsby's slow, begrudging nod, he continued, "This is in connection with a murder; Cracker Smith's murder. It has been suggested that the reason for his demise may have something to do with his meeting with Ms Manders."

Gatsby looked over at Tory who was keeping quiet. He was already off the record; he guessed he would have to capitulate fully. "As an employee of the *Post*, we own anything that is done on our behalf by staff so if there is a problem here, I can order Vicky to hand over the notes to you."

"I wasn't refusing," Tory said quietly, even now bristling at the use of her much-hated nickname. "I was checking."

She was surprised at how easily Gatsby had agreed to speak off the record. A splash on the news of Cracker's death combined with a trailer for her in-depth feature in the Saturday supplement could get the *Post* sales out of the slump.

"Okay. Vicky, you will need to copy all your notes for Sergeant Donovan. The originals should stay here. We may want to run the interview in a future edition."

Tory looked at Gatsby. He had managed to score a major point without being remotely antagonistic. Maybe she had underestimated him.

"I've transcribed my shorthand notes, so I can just print them off."

Gatsby nodded his agreement and she went off to get her notepads. Most of the interview had been transcribed onto her computer and sat within a folder for stories she was still working on. She set the ancient printer going and pulled out her shorthand notepads, dropping them into a bag. She would need to read through them again and see if there was anything she had missed.

In Gatsby's grubby glass box ten minutes later, Sergeant Donovan got to his feet, hand held out for the raft of printed sheets.

Tory handed them over, along with a memory stick. "I thought you might want an electronic copy as well." She wanted to show that she was more than happy to be helping the police with their enquiries.

She followed Donovan out of Gatsby's office and headed for the stairs. At the top, the sergeant turned. "I'll want to talk to you after I've been through these. See if there is anything else you remember." She nodded and he turned away.

"Ms Manders?" He walked back towards her. "There is a possibility, a remote possibility, that these notes might be of interest to more than just me." He pulled out a business card. "This has all my contact details on. You might also want to take extra precautions."

Then there she was, standing outside her flat, a light in her bedroom that hadn't been on when she had left that morning.

Typing in Jamesy's number, praying he was in, she bit her lip, wondering if she was being ridiculous.

"Hi Tory, what's up?"

She paused. If there was some crazy murderer in her flat, should she really be sending her neighbour to investigate?

"Are you trapped under a wardrobe?"

"Huh?"

"You must be really lazy, ringing me when you're only a floor away," Jamesy, unaware of her moral quandary, continued.

Her mind raced. Jamesy assumed she was in the flat below. Why? "What makes you think I'm home?"

Jamesy laughed. "I can hear you. Have you been re-arranging

the furniture? Thought you might have got yourself stuck."

"Jamesy, sorry. Are you saying you can hear furniture being moved around in my flat?"

He paused. His voice suddenly became serious. "Shit. That's not you in there?"

Tory's pounding heart dropped into her stomach. "No."

"Seriously? You're not shitting me? Where are you?"

"I'm outside, I pulled up in a taxi and noticed my bedroom light was on."

"Are you outside now?"

"Yeah." She spoke more quietly. Standing outside her building shouting into her phone about burglars in her flat was probably not a good idea. "Can you still hear noise?"

Jamesy was silent for a few seconds while Tory walked further down the street, out of view of her bedroom window. "Can't hear anything. I can go and have a look."

"No!" Tory shouted into the phone, before checking herself. "Look, it might just be a burglar, but something weird happened today at work – and I don't want to take any chances."

"At work?"

"Yeah. Someone I was doing a story on died, and the police think it might have something to do with the story. Only I've not written it yet."

Jamesy paused to think. "Okay. I've got a plan. Come in and come straight up to mine. Pretend you live here. I'll wait by my door to let you in, but get your keys out so it looks like you've unlocked the door."

Tory nodded agreement before realising he couldn't see her. "Be there in two minutes."

Holding onto her keys in a tight fist to hide her tremble, Tory entered the building. She vaguely remembered a self-defence class for women at university, which had advised holding a bunch of keys in your hand to pack a bigger punch. It had also advised shouting 'fire' if being assaulted, but hopefully it wouldn't come to that.

She pulled her blonde hair from behind her ears and fluffed up her fringe to cover as much of her face as possible. It was impossible to know whether, if they were after her, they knew what she looked like.

She headed for the stairs, fighting the urge to stare at her front door; instead taking a quick peripheral peek as she passed. It stood slightly open, but it was impossible to see if anyone was behind it waiting to jump her. Fuck. If they were in there waiting, there was no point tiptoeing past as it would only arouse suspicion. She decided to be obviously loud; act as if there was no reason not to be. Pulling out her phone, she began a conversation loudly as she stepped onto the bottom stair. "Lou, it's Claire, yeah, just got back from work, heading in." Tory paused as if listening to the non-existent Lou respond. "Yeah? That would be great, I'll need to invite Lindsay as well. Let me get in the house and… hang on, just going up the stairs, two flights up nearly kills me every time."

She safely reached Jamesy's front door, and loosened the keys in her hand with some difficulty, pulling out a random one and slotting it into the already open door as she put her phone away.

"Jim, you home? It's Claire!" she called as she pushed the door shut and, ignoring Jamesy, continued along the laminated floor of the hall to the quieter carpeted living area. She knew from experience that you could hear footsteps above from her flat. If there was someone listening below, it might seem strange to go home and then stand by the front door.

Exhausted by her performance, Tory collapsed onto Jamesy's leather sofa, dropping her head to her knees and trying to control her breathing. Jamesy followed her into the room after locking the front door. Without saying a word, he headed for the freezer in the kitchen area and pulled out a bottle of Stolnyka vodka. He poured a healthy slug into two mugs, leaving the bottle uncapped on the kitchen counter before walking over to put one of the mugs into Tory's already outstretched hand.

"Bad day at the office, dear?" he asked, sitting down on the sofa opposite.

The bad joke was enough to get Tory to lift her head and look at Jamesy but it took several sips of vodka before she said anything. "Did you hear anything more from downstairs?"

Jamesy shrugged. "Other than my wife coming home? Not sure. I tried to listen, but with the street noise and the tap dancing lesson going on upstairs, it's hard to say. What about you, did you see anything?"

"I couldn't swear to it, but I thought there might have been someone behind the front door. It was slightly open, which I suppose isn't surprising after a burglary. But it felt like I was being watched as I walked past. Hence the fake phone call."

"I thought that was pretty impressive." Jamesy knocked back his drink and got up for a refill. "We'd better call the police."

She nodded in agreement. "Hang on, though; the policeman who came to see me at work today, he gave me his number. He was the one who warned me I might be targeted." Tory pulled out her bag, looking for the card. She prayed it might only be a burglar, thinking things must be bad when a burglar is your best option.

Her hands were shaking, which wasn't helping. Jamesy grabbed the bag and refilled her mug. "Take a minute."

She slugged it back, reclined, and closed her eyes for a minute. "Thanks."

It took five minutes to connect to Sergeant Donovan, and another five to explain who she was and why she was calling. Donovan didn't waste time but spoke briefly to Jamesy to gather some information about who might still be in the flat – or, she wondered, was he checking to ensure she wasn't some hysterical paranoid? When she came back on the phone he seemed convinced. "We will get a team in place and approach as quietly as we can. Stay where you are, no matter what you hear, until I or one of my officers comes up to find you."

"Okay."

There didn't seem much else to say.

It was more than 30 minutes before they heard any more noise downstairs. Jamesy had moved from vodka to beer, pulling out an open container of pistachio nuts and slowly working his way through them as he drank.

After waiting for it for so long, the raid was over very quickly. The front door was smashed in without preamble, there was a rush of feet up the stairs and a sudden entry into the flat below followed by muffled shouts, a window smashing and the noise of people being dragged down the stairs.

Tory stood up, overcome by a sudden urge to see who it was. She had to know what they looked like. She knew she wouldn't rest without knowing who the fuck had been sitting in her flat. Maybe if she saw them she would get an idea of who they were and what they had planned to do to her. Perhaps they would look harmless and it would put her mind to rest.

She rushed out, ran down the stairs and towards the front

door, which now hung broken off one hinge.

"Wait," she half-yelled, half-screamed as four black-clad police officers pulled two men towards a police van.

All six stopped and turned. Tory focused on the two men being manhandled into the van. Both were shaven-headed and dressed in dark clothes, and looked about 30 years old. The first appeared pretty ordinary. Not like the men Cracker usually associated with. Her eyes were caught by the expression of the man on the left, however. He looked like the kind of man you might cross the M25 at rush hour to avoid passing on a dark night. He didn't look scared or cowed, as you would expect when you had a pair of storm trooper-like police escorting you into an armoured van. Instead he looked at her with a smile.

"Gotcha," he mouthed as the police officers dragged him towards the waiting vehicle.

Tory continued to stare at the space he had occupied long after the van had pulled away, sirens blazing.

A voice behind her pulled her out of her self-induced coma. "I really wish you hadn't done that."

She turned. Donovan was looking down at her, rubbing an open palm across his close-cropped skull before pulling the hand down over his eyes and pinching the top of his nose. He walked away without further comment.

A hand on her arm brought her back to the present and she meekly followed Jamesy back into the building. She walked behind him, matching each of his steps. She knew she was moving but something about it felt unreal, like taking ecstasy but without the good bits. She heard snatches of conversation around her. Someone; Jamesy, she thought, was talking about her and she overheard him say 'in shock'. Yes, she thought, that's what it is. Someone had probably tried to kill her tonight; not surprisingly, she was in shock.

Sitting in Jamesy's flat, she felt better. Someone handed her a mug and she lifted it to her mouth to take a huge slug of the vodka it had contained earlier, only to scald her lips on the hot tea that had replaced it. She ignored the pain and took a large swallow. The liquid burned its way down her throat, into an empty stomach, and she enjoyed the welcome feeling of heat, and the sweat it produced on her upper lip.

Tory sat still, drinking the tea, waiting for normal feeling to be restored. It would come, she knew. She just had to be patient.

After an hour, a uniformed officer had escorted her down to her flat, under strict instructions not to touch anything.

"Who would have thought the old lady had so much blood?" Tory had muttered when she saw the mess. Only in her case, instead of blood it was stuff. Unlike Jamesy's, her flat was little more than one big room and everything she owned was now sitting in a big pile in the middle of it: every single item of clothing, all the books, old records, CDs and the cheap IKEA crockery that had been tidily sitting on the shelf of her kitchen area when she went to work that morning now lay in a tangled and smashed heap. Tory's first thought was that she would simply leave it all there and move house. Buy new stuff.

"Do you have anywhere to stay?" Donovan was looking at her from his position at the door, unknowingly mirroring her own thoughts. She instinctively looked to Jamesy who had already opened his mouth to offer her his sofa.

"I was thinking of somewhere a little further away." Donovan beckoned her out of her flat. She had been allowed in to try and ascertain if anything had been taken. Her laptop, of course. Other than that it just looked destroyed.

Sitting back upstairs in Jamesy's living area, she was handed more tea by a police officer who had remained behind. By that time Tory had replayed the conversation in her head.

"What do you mean, 'further away'?" she had finally asked Donovan.

Donovan accepted a mug of tea and sat back in his chair. "The men in your flat weren't known associates of Craig Smith. They are of a rather more serious breed."

"I know."

"You know? How?"

"I saw them."

Donovan sat up abruptly, tea spilling from his mug. "Of course. Did they see you?"

Tory nodded. "One of them even spoke to me."

She tried to explain her sudden need to see who had been in her flat, her flight down the stairs, the scary blond intruder who had mouthed 'Gotcha' at her.

Donovan sat back down. "That's what he said? You're sure?"

Tory replayed it again in her head. Yes, she was sure.

He sighed and repeated his earlier words. "I really wish you hadn't done that."

"Why do you say that?"

"They saw you."

"So? You've got them."

Donovan shook his head. "These aren't 'them', these are 'their' men. 'Them' are still out there."

Tory thought of her missing laptop. "There must have been someone else there. My laptop is missing."

"I know."

"But they will tell you what this is all about?"

"Well, the word so far is that neither one speaks English."

Tory sat back. "He didn't seem to have any trouble with 'gotcha'. So what happens now?"

"We need to get you out of London, go somewhere safe."

"Witness protection?"

"No, but this might be a good time to take a long holiday in the country."

Tory turned pale. She hadn't left London in several years. "I have a job, my home... I live in London. What do you mean go to the country?"

Donovan shrugged. "Look, I can't tell you what to do, and I can't make a case for giving you a new identity – or police protection," he added as she opened her mouth to voice the suggestion. "But I am advising you to get out of London for a while if you can. This case is far from over."

"When?"

"Those guys will be in custody for the next 48 hours. After that they may want to find you again and find out what you know."

"And what do I know?"

"I read the notes, and nothing jumps out – but it may be that Smith never told you whatever it is they think you know."

Thinking beyond Cracker, Tory sat back. "There's been some talk of clashes with drug dealers. This NSP group that he belonged to were making noises about links to immigration and organised crime."

Donovan pulled out his notepad, balancing it on his knee. "And what was he doing about it?"

Tory shrugged. Remembering the interview, Smith had seemed to blame immigration for pretty much everything, so the focus on drug dealing had hardly seemed headline-grabbing at the time.

When she did interviews she always had a hundred questions lined up, in case the interviewee had nothing of interest to say. They could be anything from childhood pets to how they voted in the last election. Now she had just one. "Is my life in danger?"

Donovan shrugged. "It may be. If they want to know something you don't know, the conversation may not end well for you. On the other hand, they may soon realise you don't know anything and you will cease to be of interest."

She nodded, a thought occurring: Lyle. She could go and stay with Lyle. He lived in the middle of nowhere and was always offering her a holiday. She could hole up there and wait for all this to blow over.

"Okay. I'll need to let my boss know."

"I can do that," Donovan stood up. "Save any awkward questions. PC Maloney here will stay with you while you pack a few things."

"How many pairs of pants will I need?" Tory hadn't meant to sound sarcastic. She adjusted her tone; after all, none of this was his fault. "I mean, how long will I be gone for?"

"Honestly?"

"Yes."

"I don't know. I would recommend at least until we find the rest of Mr Smith."


It was then that her mobile had pinged. Donovan reached for it first; looking at the screen, checking it was not some kind of threat.

"Well it could be worse," he said, a small smile lifting the corners of his wide mouth.

Tory took the phone and stared at the text message that had come through, thinking that Lyle must be telepathic: 'Pack your bags babe, I've found you the PERFECT job – and it's in Cornwall.'

# CHAPTER 5

Tory's wardrobe was empty. She had shed her clothes into a pile of basic black and still she stood in her newly bought Marks and Spencer bra and knickers, wondering what to wear. It was her first day at *Compagne* and she'd had just a weekend to prepare. Not having had a month's notice to wander the streets of designer London for some workday classics, she had spent two hours in the best boutiques Cornwall's capital city had to offer to find something suitable to wear.

She had rather liked Truro. It had a modern piazza set around the River Fal, and some beautiful buildings tucked away down alleyways which all seemed to lead to the prepossessing neo-gothic cathedral. There were cobbled streets and even an old-fashioned tearoom where waitresses in Edwardian monochrome served up pots of tea, plates of delicately made sandwiches and Cornish cream teas – always with the jam on first, apparently.

Eventually Tory settled for the least creased of her wardrobe, a green silk blouse with a pussycat bow, and a grey pencil skirt that fell to her knee. She finished off the look with a pair of barely-there tights and beige designer high-heeled shoes that still had the outlandish price sticker on their virtually unworn soles.

After she had received the text from Lyle, she had stayed only briefly in her flat in London with her uniformed minder. Fortunately Constable Maloney had patiently sat in her tossed living room, drinking coffee provided by Jamesy as Tory piled all her clothes into cases, overnight bags, and, when they were full, black bin bags. The problem was that she didn't know when or even if she would ever return.

Maloney had been vague about it; a brief telephone call with Donovan an hour after he left her had confirmed that they were no further along in questioning her burglars. One of the hardest things to get her head around was that she wasn't sure if she was running for her life or merely being hysterical.

PC Maloney had politely but firmly confiscated her mobile phone after replying to Lyle, 'Set it up! I'm on my way, proper call to follow.'

She had headed off with her car piled high with clothes, favourite books and her ancient laptop, which resembled a slab of concrete and weighed about the same.

After a long drive, she had arrived at a small but pretty hotel on the North Atlantic coast, with exquisitely designed rooms that made the most of the nearby former home of Daphne du Maurier. It was far earlier than the official check-in time but she had made an early morning call to the proprietor, explaining her lengthy journey and important job interview and he had assured her that he had a vacant room and they were happy to break the rules for her. They would even provide a home-cooked breakfast in her room on arrival.

Despite her nerves, Tory found she was ravenous by the time she arrived so the breakfast was very welcome, as was the immaculately made bed which she settled into and promptly fell fast asleep.

Waking in the afternoon, it took a moment to take in her situation. She re-lived her escape from London and the job offer from Lyle. She had called him from the road and told him where she would be staying, asking him to set up the interview ASAP. He had been as good as his word; she looked towards the hotel room door and found a copy of *Compagne* pushed under it along with details of her interview the following day and how to get to The Lodge and she knew it was real.

After several cups of strong coffee and a few hours' careful examination of the magazine, scribbling frantic notes, she had headed along to the nearest pub for a bar meal and a glass or two of wine, which is when she had met Matt.

After her interview and lunch with Lyle – which she insisted on paying for as a thank you for finding her the job – Tory had managed to call an estate agency in nearby Fowey and accepted a month-by-month rental on an unfurnished cottage, unseen, in a nearby harbour. It was a holiday let that had been done up ready to go up for sale, and its owners were happy to earn a few quid while the mass of summer holidaymakers peered in the windows and dreamed of making a permanent move. At least the promised sign-up bonus being offered at *Compagne* would take care of the two months' advance rent required, although having a flat in London and a cottage by the coast was still not sustainable in the longer term.

Sub-letting her London flat didn't seem a good idea. She could see the advert: '*Studio flat, one careful owner, possibly being staked out by murderous members of the Balkan Mafia. Council tax inclusive.'*

When she found it, her tiny cottage was empty except for a bed which was too big to fit through the bedroom door; it must have been built in situ, an overstuffed tartan chair, and a makeshift desk created from a wallpaper-pasting table that had been left behind by the decorators who had re-plastered and whitewashed the walls. Tory needed furniture, but that could wait. She was hoping that if she left it long enough, maybe she wouldn't need it. Anything she bought for this cottage, small though it was, would be too big for her flat. But it was easy to be seduced by it all, especially with several glasses of wine drunk whilst sitting on the cottage's tiny deck, the ocean glittering in the distance. She could spend weekends on the antiques trail and fill the house with piles of battered old suitcases; serve afternoon tea on mis-matched china in the tiny flower garden.

Alternatively she could make it more modern – filled with lacquered red furniture, bare floors and white walls. Donovan was right, it could be a lot worse. But, given the choice, what she really wanted was her flat – and her life - back.

Donovan had promised to keep her up-to-date and had passed on a message to Gatsby that she was taking a leave of absence.

A quick call, via her new pay-as-you-go phone, which she had picked up at a surprisingly well-stocked service station on the A30 en route to the South West, revealed there was nothing to add. So it looked like she really was the new editor of *Compagne*, at least for today.

On Sunday she had closed down her social networking accounts and emails. Even though she had promised not to use them, Donovan said it would prevent anyone from contacting her with any threats. Instead she had set up an anonymous webmail. "You can contact me at hiddenaway@webmail.com," she had told the policeman. He took down the address without comment.

Now that she was dressed for her first day, the next order of business was coffee. There was no kettle in her kitchen nor was there a Starbucks anywhere in the vicinity. Dressed to impress, her hair piled up into a simple, hopefully elegant, chignon, Tory grabbed her battered but beloved Mulberry and headed out of the house.

Her little cottage was in a quiet, narrow street, and she had slept surprisingly well. The peace, the sea air, and probably the bottle of Camel Valley wine she had found in the fridge, had proved surprisingly effective at putting her into a deep, mercifully dreamless, sleep.

During a short drive into the pretty town in the new Audi that had turned up the previous afternoon as part of her resettlement package, Tory spotted just what she needed. Rhubarb, like many rural businesses, was a master of multi-tasking. It began the day as a gentrified truck stop, serving big mugs of tea and hearty bacon sandwiches, served up elegant salads for lunch, and went into the afternoon producing pots of Earl Grey and home-made scones with locally-made clotted cream and jams for visitors, finally finishing the day as a bistro serving fresh pasta, seafood and tapas. That morning, the tea and bacon sandwich sounded perfect.

"Not too much ketchup," Tory called as an afterthought to the owner as he headed into the kitchen to fry up a fresh batch — she didn't want any spills on her silk.

Arriving 15 minutes later at The Lodge, she found to her delight that a space had been designated for her in the ample and mostly empty car park, close to the door with the rubber boots. She swung the shiny new sports car into its space, noting regretfully that the new car smell had already been replaced by the aroma of fried bacon. She filled her mouth with the last of the roll and slurped the last of her tea as she stepped out of the car, cheeks bulging.

"Good morning," she heard a quiet voice behind her as she pulled her bag from the passenger seat. Covering her mouth as she turned, hurriedly swallowing the remains of her breakfast, she saw Matt leaning on a battered road bike.

"Morning," she locked the car and strolled with attempted insouciance towards the grand porticoed entrance to The Lodge. Not easy on gravel in her unfamiliar heels.

Matt wheeled his bike alongside her. "First day."

"Yes," Tory struggled to reply. The remnants of her breakfast seemed to have taken up residence halfway down her throat.

"No, I mean it's my first day," he watched her discomfort with a *schadenfreude*-tinted smile and followed her past the gatehouse. For some reason Matt couldn't fathom, Tory's understandable embarrassment at their flagrante seemed to be manifesting itself in malevolence.

She decided to clear the air. "Look, I never would have done what we did if I'd known we were going to end up working together. It's not going to happen again and I think it would be better if we forgot it ever happened at all." Tory stopped, the effort of speaking leaving her breathless. She really needed to get inside and find some fluid to push the undigested bacon buttie down her throat. She wondered if the editorial kitchen stocked Gaviscon.

He looked at her for a beat, his dark eyes opaque as he pondered a suitable response. His eyes dropped to her lips and for one second Tory was convinced he was going to kiss her. Before she could decide if she wanted him to or not, his gaze moved back towards her eyes.

"You've got ketchup on your chin." He wheeled off ahead of her, pausing to lock his bicycle by the door.

Tory swore softly to herself and rubbed at her face, harder than she needed to, successfully removing the ketchup but failing to clear the stain of her blush. This was not the start she had hoped for. Fuck it; she had much bigger problems to deal with. She squared her shoulders and headed for the doors.

"Good morning," she walked towards the reception desk, only to find she was talking to an empty chair. Strike two. Fortunately there was no one to witness it this time. She was early, she knew. There hadn't been time for a tour on Friday so she set off up the stairs to explore.

The staircase seemed similar to those she had seen many a debutante ascending in the pages of *Compagne*. In fact it was the very same – the offices were often used for photo shoots where the deb's home was deemed too suburban. Climbing carefully as her heels sank into the carpet, clinging to the ancient oak banister, Tory reached the first floor where she faced a central corridor. Originally it would have led off to bedrooms but it was now home to the various staff required to produce the magazine each month. The offices belonged to Society, Food, Equestrian and Fashion, the latter's back wall hidden by towers of shoeboxes featuring the names of famous designers. Tory filed this information away for future use.

At the end of the corridor a single larger room, which once belonged to the master of the house, now housed the more junior editorial team who sat together in a huddle of desks, although they too were empty.

Tory headed back along the corridor and found her way to a large room in the corner with her nameplate attached to the etched glass door. *Miss Victoria Manders, Editor*. Opening it up, she found an exquisitely furnished room almost the same size as the *Post*'s entire newsroom. She remembered Gatsby's small makeshift glass box; its grubby glass walls that didn't even reach the ceiling. Here there was slightly faded green and pink Liberty print wallpaper, obscured occasionally by framed covers of *Compagne* from the past 60 years. The desk featured a very large flat computer screen, a stack of fresh business cards with her name and contact details embossed beneath the famous *Compagne* masthead, an iPad mini, an iPhone, and a bowl of freesias, which lent the room a heavenly smell. Somebody had been busy over the weekend.

The keyboard to her oversized computer was hidden beneath a stack of paperwork relating to the next issue. She picked up the pile and headed for a cream sofa behind a low table, situated by the long windows, which looked out onto an Area of Outstanding Natural Beauty that stretched towards the coast. Tory noted a slight haze sitting over the horizon that suggested they were in for another punishingly hot day. The table was furnished with several copies of the current issue of the magazine, alongside a folder of pages for the upcoming August issue. She opened it up and started to read.

On the other side of the building, Jo Caruthers shared an illicit cigarette with the rotund and dapper Food Editor. Harry Hampton had been poached many years ago from the world of food publishing when it was a tiny portion of the giant smorgasbord it had become. Few people knew that Harry had turned down a slot on TV that had eventually gone to Keith Floyd. But he wasn't bitter about it. He loved food which, he liked to joke, came second only to sex. That Harry, a gentle 60-something, still had sex was beyond the imagination of most of the young women he met. But Harry's seduction technique was surprisingly successful at getting these unsuspecting young women into the sack.

"So what's she like?" he asked, taking a deep drag on his cigarette.

"Young, attractive – just your type," Jo joked.

Harry had succeeded with Jo in her first week, but once Jo

realised he wasn't marriage material, despite the wealth accumulated through his shares in the food arm of a small publishing company, their fling had developed into an unexpectedly genuine friendship, fed on regular secret fag breaks and work-related gossip.

"Good work ethic, great bone structure," Jo added. "Take her under your wing — or those lot will ravage her." She nodded towards the building.

Harry took a deep final drag on his cigarette and threw it with impressive aim into the rose garden. Years of bowling for his house at school had its uses. "What about me, am I allowed to ravage her?" He rolled his 'r' dramatically.

Jo smiled. "Give her a week or two to settle in, at least. Although I had heard that Matt has already been there, so she obviously likes them younger."


Harry walked up to Victoria's office and popped a mint into his mouth.

"Knock, knock!" he called heartily as he poked his head around the door.

Tory held her index finger up to indicate one minute as she finished reading an uninspiring interview with the wannabe Tara Palmer-Tomkinson currently gracing the cover of the next issue.

"Yes?" she smiled at the bespoke-suited, slightly ruddy-faced man leaning against her door frame.

"Lunch, I thought," he said. "A little place I know, off the beaten track — which means we won't bump into any of this shower." He indicated with his head towards the corridor.

"They have the best *moules marinières* this side of the channel." He paused dramatically. "In fact, don't say so in Paris, but probably better than on that side too."

Tory opened her mouth to voice a refusal. The work was piling up; she really didn't have time to swan out for a long lunch break. At the same time she needed someone to give her the lowdown on her staff.

"A little clichéd for a lunch date in June, but they add a splash of brandy and tarragon to the classic mix. Delightful. I'll pick you up at one." Harry paused, taking her silence as assent. "I'm Harry, by the way; Harry Hampton, Food Editor. Toodle-oo."

Tory returned to the folder of the August issue. Her sticky notes were now so numerous the pages were beginning to fan out under the weight of them. Eschewing a pile of posh notebooks, she pulled out a reporter's pad from her handbag and scribbled down her day's to-do list. She had half expected to have a meet and greet with the staff, but a quick walk through the editorial floor at 10am had shown there were few people populating it that morning. Even Sir Jesper was absent. She sincerely hoped this wasn't business as usual.

And at 1.30pm, Tory found herself sitting opposite Harry, a crisp white tablecloth set with silver flatware and endless glasses between them. Clearly Harry was well known at Clancy's restaurant, which sat in the heart of a small hotel on the South Cornish coast, which the countryside had made its own. Walking down to the restaurant, Tory had spotted a glorious stretch of sand beneath them. Harry had noted her smile of pleasure at the view.

"You are never very far away from it in this part of the country," he had told her. "The ocean has a very seductive quality."

Tory had enjoyed the brisk walk to the restaurant. Her morning had been fraught, but quieter than she had expected. At eleven, she had headed out to meet her junior editorial team, all suddenly in situ and busily working on the small features and stories that would fill the magazine. A quick hello and introductions all round and she had let them get back to work.

"Perhaps we can all have a drink after work and get to know each other better," she had said to the shocked faces; they were clearly more used to having orders barked at them. Tory made a note to ensure a fresh basket of fruits and pastries was delivered to their kitchen each morning. Not only to show appreciation for their work - it might also encourage them to get in to the office on time.

Having then identified the Editorial Assistant, she had asked her for a proper tour. Laura led Tory downstairs where a receptionist now sat, flicking through a rival magazine usually found on a lower shelf to the regal *Compagne*.

Laura introduced her as Melissa, adding, "She's one of the Flowers of Medieval."

Tory shrugged her question. Laura smiled in reply, heading behind the reception to a cave-like entrance. Inside sat a dozen staff, all women, sitting in cabals and sporting matching Bluetooth headsets.

"This part of the building is the oldest bit, dates back to medieval times," Laura explained. "The copy-takers and advertising bookers are based here. They got their nickname because of the building rather than their sexual orientation. If the air conditioning ever breaks down, head down here; its thick stone walls will keep you cool."

Tory stood and watched the staff for a few moments, trying and failing to catch someone's eye to say hello. They were busy taking advertising orders while typing up the details, occasionally wandering away from their desks to file paperwork and grab cans of Diet Coke and Red Bull from a well-stocked fridge, all the while talking into their headsets.

"The orders are then sent to the design team to create artwork for ads, which the clients approve before we go to print," Laura continued as Tory stood and took it all in.

Heading into a newer part of the building, which sat to the right of the reception area, Tory noticed the windows were bigger and the walls thinner.

"This is the old morning room," Laura said as she pulled open a set of heavy wooden doors with some difficulty. "It's been kept in its original condition and used to great effect as the backdrop of photographic shoots."

Tory paused to look out of the large South-facing floor-to-ceiling windows which offered uninterrupted views of carefully tended rose gardens, a seemingly endless lawn and, in the distance, the sea.

"Last night I dreamed I went to Manderley, and now I'm here," she joked.

Laura smiled again, showing dimples on either side of her freckled face. "You'll no doubt get a chance to visit Fowey during their literature festival held in Daphne du Maurier's honour. It's a beautiful place. The houses are a bit rich for my salary – but it's a great place to go sailing."

Tory nodded. The last boat she had been on was a rowing boat on the Serpentine the previous summer.

As they headed back to the reception area, Melissa looked up from her magazine, finger on the page so she didn't lose her place, as she was introduced to Tory.

"There's a drinks reception tonight to introduce you to everyone," she said. "Boardroom, 6pm."

Laura pointed to the boardroom door, made from imposing carved oak, to the left of the reception area and next to Sir Jesper's suite of offices. As they stood looking in at the oak-panelled room, a door opened opposite and a close-cropped blond male head appeared. Laura nodded at him and he closed his door without speaking.

"Fredo Donaldson," Laura said. She blushed and instantly corrected herself. "Freddy, I mean. Sir Jesper's younger brother."

"What does he do?"

Laura and Melissa gave each other knowing looks.

"He's in Advertising," Laura finally answered.

Heading back out of the impressive doors, they walked through the Flowers of Medieval office and towards a back door – only slightly less grand than the front – towards what would once have been an outbuilding.

As they crunched across the recently raked gravel, Tory tried not to think of the leather on the heel of her three-figure shoes being exfoliated. Laura, striding on in her scuffed black ballet pumps, explained that the designers who created the pages were housed in the former stable block. "We call them the donkeys – and not just because they live in the stables; they also seem to work the hardest."

Inside, the block was converted to an open-plan workspace and included the magazine's computer servers. A glass divide had been erected to become the nerve centre of the new *Compagne Online*. This was Matt's domain. Tory made a note to herself to avoid the stables at all costs.

After the tour, Tory headed back to her office, gratefully pulling off her shoes and accepting Laura's offer of a coffee. She would buy herself a machine on the way home. Clearly the previous editor had been caffeine-free as well as fat-free; a shelf behind her desk held a designer kettle perched next to an array of herbal and green teas. Tory had made a mental note to see if Clancy's would do her a takeaway double espresso she could heat up in the editorial kitchen's microwave after her lunch with Harry.


"I am still trying to get my head around who everyone is," she told Harry as she picked up her wine glass and put it to her lips. It was an old trick she had picked up from a PR consultant at a party. Smear your glass with lipstick so it looks in use, but don't drink it; all the better to quiz those less restrained.

Harry watched her manoeuvre, a small smile playing around his surprisingly pink lips. It was going to be fun corrupting this one. "Come on dearie, have a proper drink – and I promise to be indiscreet about your new work colleagues."

The *maître d'* wandered over to say hello. "And who is your delightful dining companion?" he asked Harry, after they had exchanged outlandish pleasantries.

"Allow me to introduce our new Managing Editor, Victoria Manders, hot from London's media mangle."

Tory bit back a grimace at the unfortunate turn of phrase, a vision of Cracker Smith's severed hand floating into her mind. If only he knew.

"Welcome to Cornwall," the *maître d'* turned on his considerable charm. The editor of *Compagne* would have a large expense account and deserved special treatment. "Of course your first lunch at Clancy's must be on the house – unless you are on expenses?"

"Always," Harry assented.

"Well, next time then. I always take great pleasure in reducing Sir Jesper's pile - of cash that is." With a nod to the Cornish lobster bisque on the menu, he walked back towards the door to greet his next important diners.

"Sir Jesper's pile?" asked Tory. "It sounds like a rare intestinal disease."

"Yes, symptoms are a pain in the arse, and verbal diarrhoea."

She smiled and turned her attention back to the menu. "Moules?" She asked.

"Moules," Harry promised.

As the mussel shells rose between them, Tory turned the conversation towards *Compagne*. "So what do I need to know?"

"If you want to survive in this nest of vipers dearie, you need to do what I do." Harry paused to dab his mouth. Really, the moules were incredible and deserved a place in his top ten. Tory found herself leaning forward to better catch whatever nugget of wisdom he was about to drop. "Get something on them all."

Tory sat back in surprise. "What?"

"Listen out for rumours, innuendos and salacious gossip – the more scurrilous the better. Everyone has secrets, darling. Remember, something you may consider trivial may be someone else's deepest, darkest secret."

He paused to scoop up the last of the herb-flecked cream and white wine sauce left on his plate with the remainder of the freshly baked baguette that had arrived with their meal.

"So what's yours?" she asked, sipping from her water glass. Gay, she guessed.

He smiled at her, as if reading her thoughts. "You're the award-winning journalist, I'll let you figure it out."

Perhaps he was straight, she mused; his eyes did alight occasionally below her collarbone. But that might just be appreciation for her pussycat bow-tying skills.

"Of course they will already have started."

"Started what?"

"Finding out your weakest link. And then it will be goodbye," he flicked his hand up in the universal gesture of dismissal. He eyed his now empty glass, wondering if he should order brandy.

She raised an eyebrow. "Perhaps I don't have one."

He leaned back, sated. "That would be disappointing. I was rather looking forward to finding out what it is. I tell you what, in the interests of fair play, I'll even help you start your collection. Your Gardens Editor, Malachy, writes homoerotic fiction. You can have that one for nothing. He's deeply ashamed of it, poor boy, but he's really rather good." He smiled again, a master at mis-direction. Now she would be convinced he was gay – who else would read homoerotic fiction, or admit so freely to it?

Tory smiled, her eyes sparkling in amusement. Perhaps being stuck four hours from London, knee-deep in talentless in-breds, surrounded by this gorgeous coastline, would be fun after all – at least until the trouble had blown over back home.

Harry leaned towards her again, raising his almost empty glass, "To the victor, the fruits."

"Don't you mean spoils?"

He smirked back at her. He knew.


Returning to The Lodge, double espresso in hand, Tory wafted Sancerre fumes throughout the corridors, and made a mental note to stock up on chewing gum. She tried to keep up with Harry as he pointed in turn to a row of closed office doors further along her floor.

"Where are all the staff?" she frowned. Somewhere inside, she had the feeling that The Lodge contained everything needed to run a magazine – except actual writers.

"Lunch?" Harry guessed, pointing to the over-sized Arne Jacobsen Banker's Clock above their heads that showed the time as 2.45pm. "Darling, you come from a world of several deadlines a day; these lazy bastards have one a month – and even that is a struggle for most of them. You'll find lunch generally starts at about 11.30, until they can be arsed to struggle back into the office, if they come in at all. Of course, being the Food Editor, lunch is a big part of my job," he added before she could point out the obvious.

She felt the tightness around her stomach – too many lunches in Clancy's and dinners at Ramsden's and she would be joining them. The sofa in her office seemed extremely enticing. These new working hours were going to take some getting used to.

Timothy Cornell-Johnes was better known, rather predictably, as Gusher. As *Compagne's* Royal Editor, his desk was awash with well-thumbed biographies of the be-titled, complete with his red-penned corrections, and he was well known for his encyclopaedic knowledge of *Debrett's Peerage*. Like Professor Higgins, it was said he could spot a commoner at a hundred feet. His favourite story as a child had been *The Princess and the Pea* and he was currently involved in creating a contemporary take on the story. He felt the queen had been horribly misrepresented – after all, she was just trying to prevent an imposter from entering her castle and watering down the aristocratic bloodline.

As Gusher left his office in search of his assistant to add some dates to his diary, he spotted a commoner at about twenty feet. Presumably she was the new Managing Editor, and being escorted by that shabby alcoholic Harry Hampton. It wasn't just that Hampton had gone to a better school then he – Gusher's parents had been suddenly impoverished after his birth and as a result had only sent their youngest son to a minor public school instead of taking up the family's place at Eton – but that he didn't seem to care. He chose to spend his time with that little fraud who guarded Sir Jesper's inner sanctum instead of his peers, despite the fact that the woman had clearly never seen the inside of a decent school.

State-schooled, he mentally calculated about the new Managing Editor as she chatted with Hampton, unaware of his scrutiny; but at a good one in the royal triangle, he mused. A nice rural village upbringing with a few London scuffs around the edges from her time on a few daily newspapers, perhaps. Looking her up and down, Gusher saw that she clearly knew the importance of dressing well, but had not quite mastered it yet. However, it was too late. As far as Gusher was concerned, she had already chosen sides. Hampton always refused to take him seriously, and he was sure he'd heard himself called Timmo as the pair had passed his office.

Despite being able to spot them, Gusher had nothing against ordinary people. He recognised they had their place; the only problem came when they didn't know it. He returned to his latest copy of *Compagne* to continue his peerage audit – anything below 60 names from ancient families and he would fire off his usual memorandum to Sir Jesper. His invitation to the little drinks thing that evening was sitting on his desk. Perhaps he would go after all.

The Sancerre had worn off and been replaced by a nagging pain in the middle of her forehead by the time Tory got back to her office. She closed the book of pages from the August issue and composed an email to Laura, asking for all the editors to be available for a content planning meeting the following morning. Breakfast would be included, she said, and asked Laura to find a supplier – suggesting Rhubarb – who could provide fruit, bagels, cream cheese, salmon and pastries, alongside some fresh buck's fizz.

The only answer seemed to be rapid rehydration. She headed towards the small fridge that sat beneath the colourful array of fruit teas and grabbed a bottle of Evian, sitting and glugging it straight from the bottle just as *Compagne*'s Society Editor sashayed through the door. Tory hastily pulled the bottle away from her mouth and wiped her chin as water dribbled over it.

She made a mental note to ask Sir Jesper about getting a personal assistant – someone to guard her from unwelcome interruptions. Her predecessor had fired her last assistant for forgetting to order in her lunchtime sushi, before she went off for her pre-summer liposuction. Maybe Jo knew someone suitable. Or perhaps Laura might like the job?

"Hellair," her uninvited guest honked loudly in an accent that could have cut crystal, demanding full and immediate attention. Tory rose to her bare feet, thankful that her toes were hidden behind her desk, before dutifully holding out her face for her cheekbones to be violently clashed with those of the svelte and be-furred vision before her. "I'm Sophie Dexter-Browning, wonderful to have some young blood. My secretary has my calendar and I have highlighted several events you simply must attend."

Tory finally dragged her eyes away from Sophie, who looked not unlike Cruella de Vil, towards a small plump woman standing three steps behind her, waiting to hand over several sheets of printed paper.

"Lovely to meet you," Tory said, arm outstretched to shake hands and trying but failing to make eye contact with the PA. She waited for a proper introduction but instead the woman meekly put the papers into Tory's outstretched hand.

Sophie clearly felt that 'secretary' was enough information. "You may go," she told her in a voice that could have reversed global warming. Tory fought a Pavlovian urge to respond herself by leaving her own office.

"Now, I have five minutes before I need to get ready for the Smyth-Lamington do. Awful people; just bought The Puddles. He is evidently huge in hot tubs or saunas or something. She's determined to throw herself on the mercy of society and has clearly ordered the menu directly from London, including the 'family heirloom' china and crystal it will be served on. Let's hope she remembers to take the John Lewis price tags off them first. Anyway, you simply must do something about my expenses – they are an absolute scandal."

Tory nodded understandingly – the non-existent expenses had been a constant battle at the *Post*. The publisher had always failed to understand the need to reimburse reporters for the drinks they bought interviewees in the pub from their measly salaries.

"I must have a new dress for the National Trust's President's Luncheon - and as a work event I must look my best. I am after all *the* public face of this magazine. I don't want to turn up in some LBD and end up looking like the hired help," Sophie's eyes flickered to Tory's outfit without comment. "Yes, well, perhaps I can give you the name of my dressmaker."

Tory fought back a sudden urge to slap her in the face as Sophie continued undeterred, "I have seen a divine little Oscar de la Renta number, but obviously I only wear them once."

Tory gulped. She had one designer dress, rarely worn, rolled up somewhere in a bin bag - and yes, it was black.

"We once had an editor – went down a storm at the Hunt Ball, until I discovered," Sophie paused and lowered her voice as Tory prepared herself for some terrible blunder; perhaps he had made a pass at the publisher's wife, or urinated in the white soup, "he was wearing a ready-made tie."

Sophie nodded, taking Tory's wide-eyed response as shock and disgust. "Of course, I did try and warn Sir Jesper. I mean, how can you trust a man who doesn't wear hand-made shoes? Anyway, must dash. Sorry to miss your little drinks thing later, but I think we've covered everything we need to."

It wasn't a question. Sophie strode out of the office.

# CHAPTER 6

The Honourable Frederick Donaldson occupied an office slightly bigger than his brother's. In fact it was a half a square foot bigger. Freddy knew this because he had measured it. From his slightly larger office, Freddy had watched the new editor arrive at Reception and smile at the girl from the Flowers of Medieval nominated for reception duty that day.

That had been one of his little improvements. Reception work was exhausting and offering up one of the typing pool on a rota to serve on the desk would help to keep them fresh. It had been a huge success and, with his office sitting opposite, it gave him the opportunity to see all the girls in rotation, providing him with much-needed executive relief. Until recently he would go into the Flowers of Medieval office on the last day of the month to copy their reception rota, so he knew who would be on show when, but these days his jaded palate preferred the element of surprise.

Of course, he had his favourites. There was a petite, demure-looking redhead who favoured long skirts with slits that opened when she sat down, offering a tantalising glimpse of upper thigh – bare and delicately tanned at this time of year. The reception furniture had also been his project. He had opted for a gloss white-topped desk with chrome legs instead of an enclosed console, allowing a clear view under the table. His redhead was not as obvious as the bottle blonde, who wore sheer shirts and short skirts that got shorter when she sat down. But even she had her subtlety. She liked to take her high-heeled shoes off underneath the desk and every so often she would seductively rub the top of her right foot with the ball of her left. As she did it, usually subconsciously, he would sit and imagine himself sitting on the floor at her feet, watching closely but, crucially, not touching.

It was little known around The Lodge that Freddy was in fact Sir Jesper's twin. Although they had a very similar build, Freddy was blond and blue-eyed while Jesper was brown-haired and brown-eyed. Sir Jesper had come out first and Freddy had followed seven minutes later.

Freddy had spent most of his childhood watching Jesper get things first, thinking: *If only I had pushed out a little earlier, this would all be mine*. He had left the fold early, determined to make his mark, heading for London and a freelance job as an A&R man at the heart of the London music scene. But he picked the wrong decade. Being the son of a peer of the realm during the punk revolution of the 1970s had not been a great way to gain respect from the green-teethed, spit-addled teens snarling on stage. For some, a public school background was irrelevant, they had made it work for them, but Freddy found it hard to take these bands seriously and had missed key signings.

After that he headed for an advertising agency, hitting his stride amid the worst economic meltdown of the last century, when no one had money for advertising. He put that one down to bad luck. He lasted eight months in that job. He took a two-decade sabbatical toying with a more libertine lifestyle before heading back to *Compagne.* By accident, he had arrived back in Cornwall around the same time as his father, Sir Jesper Senior.

Now it was that time of the month again; time for a visit with the *paterfamilias.* It wasn't widely known that Sir Jesper Senior was still alive and living at The Glades. His sons had quietly rescued him from his hotel suite in Monte Carlo just over three years previously, where he had been happily planning to live out his final days. However, with his increasingly erratic moods and actions culminating in a skinny dip at his hotel during the wedding of a minor royal (which had earned him a mention in the column inches of *Wow!* magazine), Sir Jesper had quietly popped over and brought his father back to live at his old home, complete with round-the-clock care provided by several hand-picked, well-paid and well-endowed nurses.

This last qualification had been at the advice of the family doctor, who had suggested it might make the old man more malleable. Large breasts seemed to be doing the trick so far, and Freddy was confident his father was happy, particularly as one of the nurses, Janice, was known to moonlight as a lap dancer: this fact alone had secured her the job. Currently Sir Jesper Senior was petitioning for the installation of a pole in his suite.

Sir Jesper Senior's dementia always seemed worse at teatime, when he became distracted and difficult, perhaps due to the end of the day reflecting the passing of his own life and a brief awareness of the affliction that was robbing him of it. Janice the lap-dancing nurse called it 'sun downing'. While for some a game of bingo might suffice, for Sir Jesper Senior nothing short of nurse Janice in full lap dance routine would do it.

Freddy found it hard to criticise his father, having seen Janice hard at it himself. At times he wondered how appropriate it was for a man of his father's stature to be locked away watching a half-naked nurse gyrate around his drawing room, but having seen the glow of pleasure on his father's face during this regular routine, he couldn't help but think that growing old disgracefully had its moments.

It was hard to see his father in such reduced circumstances. There was a time when Sir Jesper Senile – Freddy knew what the staff at The Glades called his dad – had once been one of the most prominent professionals of the realm. He had dined with royalty and was on first-name terms with most of Europe's crowned heads, but the incident in Monte Carlo had put an end to those relationships. Both Sir Jesper and Freddy tried to spend a few hours with him at least once a month. For Freddy it was that time of the month again.

Sir Jesper Senior was still a good-looking man. Now in his mid-70s, he was slender and silver-haired, and thanks to the hard work of those around him, always impeccably dressed. On occasion he shed his handmade suits in favour of the altogether, but it was largely ignored. That a peer of the realm's slide into naturism and dementia remained untold by the gossip columnists was only partly because his increase in nudity was matched by the increases in pay for those witnessing it. In short he was well liked and his staff were well-paid, but they were also that rarest of things: loyal.

Arriving for tea at 4pm, Freddy entered his father's suite of rooms, accessed by a separate entrance through The Glades' kitchen garden. The private entrance had been added to allow staff to come and go without comment or interference from the main house.

Behind the discreet entrance created from a fire escape sat a grand set of rooms, which included a large bedroom overlooking a private terrace, a drawing room and study. Freddy wondered if his father recognised the irony of his bed being placed in what was formerly the nursery. However, if Sir Jesper Senior recognised the room, he never mentioned it, and Freddy never brought it up.

"Hello Papa," Freddy stood waiting for his father to recognise him. Sometimes it happened immediately, sometimes awareness came halfway through his visit, and at other times his father was convinced it was Freddy's slightly older brother sitting there. The latter was something he could never fathom, considering they had such different colouring.

His father stood to greet him. "Have you met this charming lady?" He gestured to his companion, sitting demurely on the green and gold brocade sofa placed at a right angle to his own seat.

Freddy nodded a greeting towards Janice and she smiled before standing and heading for the kitchen.

"I'll get your tea, Sir Jesper," she said.

"We're not old ladies, woman. Get me a malt with a splash of water." Sir Jesper sat back down in his high-backed chair. His tone of voice mixed an irresistible cocktail of imperiousness and humour that meant his requests were often acceded to when they were alone.

Although Sir Jesper Senior rested his left hand on a silver-topped cane, he moved around the room easily. It was one of life's little ironies that his body was in perfect health while his mind was heading rapidly into decrepitude.

Freddy settled into the sofa. "What's been happening, Dad?" His vague opening was carefully considered but delivered casually. When the diagnosis of general dementia had been given, Sir Jesper Senior's family had spent time with a range of experts. All had received some training to ensure he was comfortable, but it was a fine line between creating a comfortable, non-threatening environment and patronising a formerly very important and generally good man into aggressive or erratic behaviour.

"Good, good. Did you meet my new assistant? Janice. Lovely looking woman, got a pair of tits on her you could get lost in."

Freddy looked down at the parquet flooring, embarrassed. Until his illness, his father had never talked about women like this. He had taught his sons to respect and admire strong women. But this way of talking must have been in there all along. And that meant his father was not only no longer the man he had been, but had never been that man at all. That was a painful proposition for a son who had looked up to his father all of his life.

"I'm thinking of marrying her."

"Janice?" Freddy's eyebrows rose to match the pitch of his voice.

"Imagine waking up to that arse every morning. Grabbing her tits whenever you liked without being at fear of a legal writ. Yummy." The last word was spoken as Janice returned to the room bearing a tray of delicately sized but well-filled sandwiches and a dish piled high with chicken salad. Freddy wondered to which his father was referring. He couldn't be sure if he had imagined it, but a slight smile in his father's voice suggested the double meaning was intentional.

"Roast beef and horseradish today, Sir Jesper," Janice said, leaning down slowly to place the tray on the low table in front of the sofa. She stood slowly, winking at Freddy. It told him she knew Sir Jesper's thoughts and didn't mind them, in fact positively encouraged them.

"Yummy," Sir Jesper repeated, this time leaving Freddy in no doubt. Picking up a side plate, Janice piled up sandwiches and draped a heavy white linen napkin carefully on Sir Jesper's knee. Freddy helped himself to a sandwich; it was a ritual to encourage him to eat.

"Jessie, how is your brother?" Sir Jesper Senior asked, using his older son's childhood nickname. Freddy smiled and swallowed the remains of his sandwich.

"Freddy is doing really well." It struck Freddy that his father's confusion offered up the perfect opportunity to boast about his achievements, without it seeming a boast. The fact his father wouldn't remember their conversation an hour later took away only some of the pleasure.

"You must look after him, he's not like you," Sir Jesper Senior began. It was a line of conversation they had travelled down before but it took a new direction when he added, "We had to make a decision about who to put first."

"Dad, its okay." Freddy grabbed another sandwich, only half listening to his father. The sauce was home-made by the cook from fresh horseradish pulled from the kitchen garden below, the roast beef rare and thinly sliced, and both were generously applied onto the freshly baked bread. His stomach grumbled appreciatively.

"You were born five minutes apart," his father continued.

"Seven," Freddy corrected him absently, before filling his mouth with another bite. He had long come to terms with his bad luck in being the second son. There were no prizes for second place in the peerage, and Jesper had beat him to the finish line fair and square, winning the family gold, as well as the family home, the enormous estate it encompassed, and the publishing empire their grandfather had created.

Freddy wondered how many sandwiches his father was going to eat. He had four untouched on his plate and Janice didn't seem to be eating; she had seated herself out of earshot, working her way through a pile of magazines. *Compagne* was at the bottom.

There were three sandwiches left. Freddie picked up another one, finishing it in two satisfying bites.

"We never knew which one was which."

"Our hair colour, Dad," Freddy swallowed the remains of his sandwich and eyed the chicken salad. Fresh salad leaves with hearty chunks of chicken breast had been lightly dressed. "We have different coloured hair."

"But which one came first – do you know?" His father looked at him, a crease of confusion suddenly appearing between his faded blue eyes.

Freddy's hand paused halfway to the sandwich plate; he had promised himself one more before trying out the salad.

"What?" He forgot to temper his voice. Janice looked up, caught by the change in his tone. It was a rule of the house that no one ever raised their voice to Sir J.

"We never knew who came out first."

"Who, Dad?"

"Which came first: the blond or the brunette?" Sir Jesper Senior asked Freddy. Unconscious of the effect his words were having on his son, he turned to Janice, his tone changing. "Are there any more sandwiches?"

"Who, Dad?" Freddy repeated, fighting to get control of his voice. The sandwiches that had so occupied his thoughts were forgotten just as his father's fractured mind seemed to finally fixate on them.

"Sandwiches. I want another sandwich." Sir Jesper Senior's voice rose to match his son's. The sudden irrational irritation was a warning of the possibility of a more extreme reaction.

Janice stood up and came over. Picking up a sandwich from the tray she bent over him slowly, adding it to the sandwiches already balanced precariously on his plate.

"Dad – what is it you never knew?"

Sir Jesper Senior looked up, dragging his eyes away from Janice's ample cleavage, which had sedated his irritation more successfully than any drug could. A smile lit his face as he looked at his son.

"Freddy, when did you get here?" He stood suddenly, his plate of sandwiches falling to the floor. "How wonderful to see you, your mother has just popped out and I'm off out to lunch in a few minutes but sit down my boy, sit down and tell me how things are going in London."

For some reason his father seemed to focus over and over again on Freddy's brief stint in an advertising agency. He stood, stepped over the broken plate and spoiled sandwiches, and shook his father's hand, as though he had just arrived.

Dragging his mind away from the conversation that had just taken place, Freddy attempted a tone of casual pleasure at their meeting. "Hello, Dad. London is good, a lot of new accounts to deal with."

Janice quietly cleared the broken china and sandwiches which were lying on the floor.

"Well it was lovely to see you, Freddy, I'm off to my luncheon now. But your old room is ready for you. I hope you are staying. Only a few of us for dinner tonight, Lord and Lady Nichols are bringing their daughter; she's just come out. Would love to introduce you. Don't want you to be a bachelor forever."

His father's jovial manner was heartbreaking but Freddy couldn't take the time to worry about that now. He stood and shook his father's hand once more, smiled at Janice, thanked her for the tea, and complimented her on his father's good looks before heading to the door. He stood for a moment to watch his father sit back down on the damask sofa and pick up the plate of remaining sandwiches.

"Roast beef and horseradish?" he asked Janice, who smiled and poured him more tea as he tucked into the remaining food.

Heading down the stairs, taking them two at a time in his hurry to get away, Freddy went over the conversation in his head. He was pretty sure that his father had said he didn't know which one was which. Had he meant he didn't know which of his sons was born first? All this time, *all this time,* he had accepted his place as the second son, the one who had to find his own place in the world. The one who a few centuries ago would have been bought a place in the military where he could distinguish himself, or go into the church to live a life of solitude, with only the admiring glances of the local bonneted parishioners to console him.

But now it seemed that it could have been he who was destined to inherit the Donaldson empire. As Freddy crunched over the gravel towards his car, it was easy to make the small leap from could have been to should have been. And if there was a 50/50 chance then it was only fair that he and his brother get a 50/50 split of the company. It wasn't that he needed the money; he had a very good private income and a free home in a smaller lodge on the estate. And as a single man, there were no demands upon his wallet beyond his own fancy. But the role, the recognition, and the title; all were suddenly within his grasp.

Freddy knew he was not respected by the staff at *Compagne,* not as his brother was. He knew the subs desk called him Fredo, after the unfortunate elder son in *The Godfather*. For the first time, the weight of the failure fell on his shoulders. He realised they were more right than they could ever have guessed; he could be the elder son cheated out of his birthright and doomed to die an undistinguished death.

He shook his head and pressed the ignition button that started the car. It was important not to get carried away. He needed some kind of confirmation. His father may never mention it again. His mother was long dead and so beyond the realms of interrogation. What kind of parents didn't know which son was born first? He and Jesper weren't identical; a look through the family photo album showed that they had always looked sufficiently different to be told apart – and that was one of the reasons few people knew they were twins. But he knew his mother had struggled to give birth and had needed a long stay in hospital to recover. It was one of the reasons there were only two children. His mother had wanted a daughter, someone to pass the family jewellery on to, someone to take an interest in the history of the home, but she had been stalwart about not being able to have further children and had instead spoiled her sons and turned her attention to The Glades stables, which she had filled with world class thoroughbreds. Their father had been happy enough with two strapping sons. Perhaps at the time of birth those around her had been more concerned with the wellbeing of the mother than which of her twin sons was first-born.

Freddy drove on automatic pilot, trying to come up with a plan, returning to The Lodge and heading for his office, despite it now being almost six. The Flowers of Medieval were no longer in their chamber and only a few lights were on along the editorial floor so he headed to the boardroom where welcome drinks were in full swing for the new Managing Editor. He had yet to introduce himself to her. Perhaps he should announce himself as Joint Chairman of the Donaldson Publishing Group and watch his brother choke on his brandy.

# CHAPTER 7

Tory's headache from the lunchtime drinks had subsided in time for her to head down to the boardroom and gingerly accept a glass of chilled champagne from Sir Jesper, who had appeared at her elbow as she entered the room. She looked suspiciously at the bubbles dancing to the top like synchronised swimmers in the chilled crystal; usually a fan of champagne, looking at it now she decided it resembled a headache in a glass.

"Sorry not to have been here to welcome you this morning, but I understand you have settled in very well," Sir Jesper nodded towards Harry Hampton, who was filling up his glass from one of the bottles lining the side table, having first examined each label in detail. The boardroom's South wall was made almost entirely of glass and looked out onto thick woodlands. Bright sunlight still flooded the room, showing up the red veins in Harry's cheeks and the wrinkles around Sir Jesper's eyes.

"Yes, Harry was kind enough to take me out to test some of the local produce. And one of the editorial staff took me on a tour this morning, but I've spent quite a bit of time on the magazine and I've identified a few concerns about the August issue. Also, I couldn't find any planning documents for future issues on the editorial server, do you know where I might find them?"

Sir Jesper shook his head. "I'm afraid your predecessor became seriously, suddenly ill and so there was no possibility of any handover. But I'm sure you can get us all shipshape. Now enough work, let's introduce you to everyone." He put his hand into the small of her back, enjoying the feel of the cool silk of her blouse on his fingertips. Spreading his hand he felt the thin strap of her bra with the tip of his thumb as he steered her towards the groups congregating around a table loaded with plates of canapés.

At his light touch, Tory was instantly reminded of her first impression of him: trousers around his ankles, excitedly bending her over his ancient desk. She was a better judge of character than she gave herself credit for. Sir Jesper had already thought the same thing, but in rather more detail. He liked to think of himself as somewhat of an equal opportunities philanderer. Whatever age, culture, or class, he was always willing to flirt and, when reciprocated, nip off for a spot of sexual intercourse in his private bathroom, which, alongside a shower, toilet and sink, curiously included a bed. And he had several times made use of his large desk, kept clear for the purpose; it gave him a tremendous sense of power.

The summer was a great time of year; women walking around with bare, perfectly depilated and tanned legs, always suggestive of the possibilities of a quickie. His thoughts were never far from the vision of his hands disappearing up short skirts, ripping off knickers and entering the woman in question without ceremony.


Tory moved away from Sir Jesper's hand, faking enthusiasm to meet everyone. Without her notepad she would have no chance of remembering names but there were a couple of people she was keen to meet properly, among them the editors who had been missing in action all day.

A petite redhead who was eyeing up the canapés suspiciously turned willingly away from the miniature stacks of blinis and caviar and smiled, hand outstretched. "Hi, I'm Janey, Art Director. Nice to meet you."

Tory grasped her hand. "What are the snacks like?"

"Look good, but a little bit lardy," Janey wrinkled her freckled nose in faux disgust.

Tory eyed her slender frame. "Not something you need to worry about, surely."

Janey patted her stomach. "Problem with spending too much time on fashion shoots; models, models everywhere and not allowed to eat."

"So you do fashion?"

"Yes, I sort the shoots and spreads and then help to lay out the pages. So who haven't you met yet?"

"Pretty much everyone. I had lunch with Harry," Tory looked over at him, acknowledging his friendly wink. "And I've met Sophie, I think."

She looked around for the Society Editor, before remembering she'd had a much more exclusive soirée to attend. Tory followed Janey over to a group of mostly women, dressed down in black trousers and casual tops, determinedly working their way through large glasses of red wine. She felt over-dressed, and slightly envious of their comfortable-looking flat ballet pumps.

Janey tapped the shoulder of a blonde whose shorn head showed off a multitude of piercings in her ears. As she turned, Tory spotted a small hole in her nose, indicating where a diamond stud usually sat.

"Victoria, this is Marcia." The two women nodded at each other. "Marcia is our page planner. Her job is to mix up editorial and advertising pages with all the skills of a cocktailier at Claridge's."

"A very important person, then," Tory surmised.

Marcia grimaced. "More of a thankless task. You send me your editorial running order, what you want to appear where in the magazine, and then the advertising team assign advertising to sit around it." She finished the sentence by rotating her wrist several times.

"We should meet up properly and you can talk me through it fully." Tory had jotted down some dates into her iPhone ahead of the party so that she could set up some meetings.

"I just did." Marcia, like many busy people, was averse to meetings unless absolutely necessary. Tory's predecessor had let her get on with her job, unmolested. She hoped the new replacement would do the same, although she was hopeful of earlier input from the editorial team so she could more easily do what she was employed for – planning.

Tory, wrong-footed, nodded and put her phone back into her pocket. "Well, okay. Maybe I can just email you if there's anything I don't understand." At Marcia's slight nod she smiled, determined to be professional in the face of provocation. "I look forward to working with you."

Marcia turned back to her group, and Tory turned away.

"She's quite defensive of her team," Janey explained. "They get a lot of shit from the advertising team demanding the best pages."

"Maybe I can help."

"They've already sorted it – Marcia sends out the plan, waits for the commercial team to complain, goes for a coffee, and sends the same plan out an hour later. Sometimes this goes on for days, but eventually the plan gets signed off." She turned to look around the room. "Right, who else do you want to meet?"

"Who do you recommend?" Tory felt some of the tension release from her shoulders. Janey was exactly what she needed.

Sir Jesper spotted his brother arrive. He saw Freddy smooth his blond hair back from his high forehead; a nervous habit that he'd had since he was a child, usually employed before he had something to say that would upset the listener: *'Dad, I've been fired'*, *'She's pregnant'*, that kind of thing.

Freddy saw him watching and walked towards his brother, hand outstretched. "Sorry I'm late, Jesper."

Jesper smiled widely. "Freddy, darling," his arm was again under the elbow of the new editor. "This is Victoria, who has come to save us all."

Freddy smiled. The new editor had hair the colour of hay and strands had freed themselves from the rather severe pleat she had fashioned it into. She was well-dressed in a slightly see-through silk blouse with a flirtatious bow that was longing to be slowly pulled undone. Her skirt sat on her knee, where a tiny pull had appeared in her stockings. By the end of the evening, with enough bending and stretching it would develop into a ladder, creeping its way up her thigh. The high heels of her shoes were obviously unfamiliar and beginning to hurt; she subtly dropped hips every few minutes as she took the weight off one foot and then the other. His gaze returned to her face and he grasped her outstretched hand.

"So are you going to drag *Compagne* kicking and screaming into the 21st century? Somebody had to do it!" He forced levity into his voice.

Tory smiled widely, ignoring the rather lengthy and uncomfortable scrutiny of her body that had reminded her subconsciously of his older brother who was still grasping her elbow, his knuckles a hair's breadth from the underside of her right breast. "Hello, we saw each other in passing this morning."

Freddy nodded. His mind wandered from the forced pleasantries that the occasion demanded as he looked over at Jesper. He needed to discuss their father's revelations but first he would need to work out what it was he wanted. It was, after all, a negotiation and the success of any negotiation lay in whoever held the whip hand.

"Freddy here is our Director of Advertising, he keeps us afloat," Sir Jesper smiled at his brother. "I had to poach him from one of the big London advertising firms, tempt him back to the family business."

It was a story Sir Jesper told so smoothly that he almost believed it. In Sir Jesper's head it had merged with the truth, which was that after almost endless botched businesses and bad investments, Freddy had come to his older brother and asked for a place on the board of the family business. Sir Jesper had agreed and Freddy had been given an office and a very able secretary picked out of the typing pool, and placed within the hands of the very able Advertising Director, Jasper Lott. Grasper Lott, as he was better known, had been given a pay rise and had his company car upgraded to a Lexus in order to remain in charge of the advertising team while theoretically reporting to Freddy as his department's head. Like a constitutional monarch's, Freddy's was a position of relative powerlessness. *Until now*, he thought.

Matt arrived after seven, nodded to his father, and stood in the corner, working on his tablet and ignoring everyone around him. Sir Jesper had stopped by his son's new office to ask him to attend, and he was insistent enough that his second-to-newest employee felt unable to refuse.

The cut above Matt's eyebrow had begun to heal and the bruise around it had faded to an alarming shade of parsnip yellow. Sir Jesper watched him hunched over the screen in his hands and sighed. At least he had turned up. There would be no point browbeating him to fall in love with the world of publishing. It was like an arranged marriage; you had to introduce the prospective bride and groom slowly, hide any parental hopes for a deeper relationship, and let it develop as they got to know each other. Either love would blossom, or they would get comfortable enough with each other to consider a lifetime together. That was how it had been for him.

Matt had been busy since his *tête-à-tête* with the new Managing Editor earlier that morning. He had sat in the hastily created office and spent his first few hours going through *Compagne's* outdated website. Not only was it basic but also brutish and verging on the ugly. It had been one of Uncle Freddy's projects, set up two years ago, and after going live it had been left to fester. Staff at the magazine weren't encouraged to add content and it wasn't seen as a core responsibility of anyone within the editorial team.

Instead, Laura was left to manually upload every story from the previous month's issue on or around the print date of the new one. This meant the site went untouched for up to a month at a time.

There was no active social media campaign to attract readers, and his basic first-day breakdown of the past six months' viewing figures showed few people visited it with any regularity. At the same time, the advertising team were being asked about online advertising. This was done ad hoc, and he'd gleaned from his brief conversation with the Flowers of Medieval at lunchtime that there was definitely scope for massive improvement. Now Matt had to make a decision; did he want to do the job properly, which would take more time, or did he just want the website to look nice?

During a chat with the IT Manager, Don Lucas, over a quick coffee that afternoon it was willingly revealed that there was little appetite for the website amongst his staff, who were kept busy keeping the outdated servers healthy, and managing the fast-diminishing memory with an iron hand. The enemy, Don said, was editorial emails. Staff kept their inboxes loaded with images and video-clips, a defence against any system meltdown that would wipe their folders and leave them with no content.

"Ironically," Don said humourlessly, "this is the most likely way to bring the system crashing down around our ears."

As a result, Matt's shopping list now featured a new server and a content management system that would allow automatic uploads of content on a certain date, directly from the digital archive of the magazine when that issue expired. It would also create a back office on the website to make it easier to upload exclusive web content, without going through the already struggling magazine publishing software.

The list, alongside his report on the state of the website and a request for an assistant to help him deliver the changes within twelve months, was now sitting on Sir Jesper's usually unmarred office desk. After all, the quicker he did the job he was being paid for, the quicker he could get out of there. That remained his aim, regardless of what his father thought.

Matt pushed himself away from the wall and headed over to the food. He was keeping his distance from his dad, but also from the new Managing Editor. Tory was circulating the room, trying to meet people and make a good impression. He recognised that his presence wouldn't help her assimilation. He still felt vaguely bad for the rude way he had spoken to her that morning.

Heading back to his spot with a plateful of food, he worked his way through it, nodded to a few people, then headed out. He needed to speak to his mother about moving back home and he would get a better deal with his dad safely out of the way.

By nine o'clock the wine bottles were empty, the serving platters scattered with crumbs. A quick calculation by Janey, who had stuck to mineral water all night – "Have you any idea of the calories per unit of alcohol?" was her reply to any offer of getting her a 'proper drink' – showed that each person had consumed a bottle and a half within three hours. Harry Hampton had paired up with Jo, while Tory's headache had paired up with nausea.

Whatever the cause, Tory had only one question by the end of the night. "Do you have any taxi phone numbers?" she interrupted Jo's and Harry's gossiping. "I think it would be better if I didn't drive."

# CHAPTER 8

Matt arrived at The Glades shortly before nine. Lady Rose opened the door with a bright smile; her son was always a welcome distraction from the mammoth task of keeping the ancient seat she had married into from crumbling.

"Hello darling. What a wonderful surprise!"

Matt moved forward for the obligatory kiss from his mum, letting his hair fall over his injured eye, gathering from her welcome that his father had yet to share the news of his new job. He followed her through to the small sitting room she always sat in when alone; his father liked the larger drawing room next door, with its high ceilings and grand furniture, but his mother had once admitted, "I feel like a bit of a waxwork in there, forever waiting for a coach party from Bristol to come through and take my picture: *Lady Rose at leisure in The Glades.*"

His mum was definitely his favourite – she managed to combine perfect breeding with a sense of humour. Matt often wondered how she had ended up with his dad; although impeccably polite with each other, there was little evidence of lasting passion between them. Her well-known love of antiques had often led Matt to wonder if she had married his father for his attic.

In contrast to the ostentatious drawing room, her sitting room was simply furnished, bookshelves filled with books she had bought during her years at the helm of The Glades. A slender laptop sat closed on the 18$^{th}$ century writing table, while a small flat screen television hung discreetly on the wall by the fireplace. Matt dropped down onto the navy blue sofa facing it, the familiar surroundings immediately relaxing him.

Although she loved antiques, Lady Rose seemed not to feel the need to surround herself with them; instead she had chosen only a handful of pieces.

"Can I come home?"

Lady Rose looked at him in surprise. "Of course."

Matt smiled. "Dad has given me a job at the magazine, I'm helping to sort out the website, and I want to save some money."

"He's not paying you very well?" Lady Rose took in her son's appearance. He looked skinny and his hair was too long – and was that a bruise over his eye? Having her only son back home meant she could make sure he was looking after himself. While she often joked about her housekeeping job, motherhood was a job she took very, very seriously. She had learned that from her own mother.

Matt laughed. "Nope, he's paying me fine. I'd just like to come home for a while. I miss you."

Lady Rose let out a loud and genuine laugh. Her son had all the charm of her husband but none of the finesse. "You make an old lady very happy, but also a tad suspicious. Let's hear the full story. Starting with that bruise on your face."

Matt sighed. "It's nothing, I just got in the middle of a fight in a pub." It sounded more realistic than the 'walking into a door' story.

Lady Rose moved towards him and lifted up his hair. "Okay. I'll get Celia to get your room ready for you. Are you going to pop in and say hello? She'll be delighted to have you home where she can spoil you again."

Matt nodded and followed her into the kitchen. Celia, The Glades' housekeeper had started life as Matt's nanny, but Lady Rose had been such a hands-on mum that Celia had found herself out of a job. Instead, she had taken over from the ancient housekeeper who was retired off to a cottage on the grounds for the remaining years of her life. Despite being demoted – as she insisted on referring to the actual promotion and pay rise that had come with her new role – Celia still took an active role in Matt's upbringing, not only babysitting when Lady Rose was away but comforting him with her world-famous rice pudding when he was upset or ill. A visit by him, however brief, would not be complete without him racing into the kitchen and requesting something to eat – even when he wasn't hungry, like tonight. He recognised it was an important tradition, and it made Celia happy. Lady Rose joined him only to give directions for his rooms to be readied for his return before heading up to her own. It had been a long day.

Once there, she surveyed her appearance in the dusty 18th century full-length mirror in the corner of her room. Her hair was ash blonde and softly curled to her shoulders. Her make-up made the most of her rose complexion, black mascara widening her violet eyes, which only truly warmed up when she was looking at her son or the growing balance of her offshore bank accounts. While most thought her marriage was her life's work, Lady Rose had found her lesser-known career as a fencer of priceless antiquities far more fulfilling.

Her love affair with antiques had begun as a child. Her suddenly impoverished mother became separated from Lord Sheward when his love of slow racehorses and fast women depleted the family fortune. Rosie and her mother had moved out into a little flat in Kensington which Lady Margaret had bought several years previously - with the foresight to put it in her daughter's name - from money secreted from her husband's occasional winners, before the bailiffs arrived.

"We are leaving," her mother had called loudly, coming into her then eight-year-old daughter's room at 6.30am one spring morning and pulling back the heavy pink damask curtains that shielded her from the bright sunshine. Rosie had rubbed her eyes, immediately awake, recognising something important was happening. She rarely saw her mother before cocktail hour and her own bedtime, when she was summoned from the arms of her nanny to be presented bathed and swathed in pink silk to her parents and often an array of dinner guests who would coo at the beautiful blue-eyed, blonde-haired girl that her parents, particularly her mother, were so proud of. Lady Margaret would then take Rosie upstairs and put her into bed, stroking her hair, telling her of the wonderful day she had planned for her tomorrow.

"Mummy?" was all Rosie had managed to get out.

Her mother, fully dressed, had pulled two large cases and thrown them onto the bed at her feet. "Put on your clothes and meet me in my room in 20 minutes."

Intrigued, Rosie made it in ten. Her mother had trunks laid out, two filled with evening clothes and furs, and a third with velvet jewellery boxes. Pausing, she sat down on the chaise at the end of her bed, a book in her lap, patting the space next to her for Rosie to sit down.

"Rosie, this is a pictorial record of all the treasures of the Shewards. I've been collating it for the past few years." She flicked open a few pages. "You see here where I have put a red star? These are the ones we want to take with us. I want you to take this book and find the items with the stars. I've written down which rooms they are in. Everything needs to come with us. The transport will be here at twelve noon and if we haven't got it, it will stay behind and be lost to us forever. Begin in the drawing room with the Sèvres and don't forget the silver flatware in the kitchen."

"But I don't understand. Where are we going, why will we lose them?"

"Any questions will have to wait until we begin our journey," Lady Margaret stroked her daughter's cheek. "We only have a few hours to get this done." She rose abruptly and was already halfway down the corridor with her own list when Rosie nodded her assent towards her mother's departing back.

They had spent the next three hours packing up silverware, crystal and dinnerware, pictures, books, and had even taken twenty minutes to tightly roll up a grubby tapestry of a hunting scene and two ancient threadbare Persian rugs.

"Why not take the new ones?" Rosie had asked her mother. "They look nicer."

"Darling, antiques are not about things that look nice. The most valuable things in this house are things you wouldn't look twice at." Her mother pointed to a rickety-looking chair, with a faded seat, which had been removed from its usual place in the upstairs hall to join several other pieces of furniture by the front door. "That's more than 600 years old. It was here when the house was first built, it witnessed England's civil war when the Roundheads trampled through the county – and may have encased at least one Royal bottom. That makes it priceless."

Sitting in the hallway, surrounded by trunks and boxes, Rosie was still not sure what was happening, but as this was the longest time she had spent in company with her mother since she could remember, she was happy. Years later, she would remember that day as a turning point in their relationship. After that there were no more short after-dinner appearances, her mother rarely missed a meal with her daughter.

"There's one thing you have forgotten, Rosie."

Rosie frowned and tried to think, going towards the breakfront where the brochure had been left. Her mother stopped her.

"No dear, what about Muppy?" Rosie's eyes and mouth formed a triple 'O' before she ran back up the staircase to her room for the last time to collect her favourite bedtime toy: a blue rabbit, bought for her by an ancient grandmother.


It was only days later, when news broke of her father's bankruptcy that her mother fully explained the purpose of that morning.

"This is all that's left of your inheritance, darling." They surveyed the collections, most still packed away. The flat in Kensington was one of the nicest properties in the family portfolio, but there was no room for ancient hunting tapestries and Sèvres tea sets. "Really this belongs to the banks, but they wouldn't know what to do with it. We must get it all sold, quietly of course."

"How?" Rosie wanted to know. Her mother had just smiled.

Over the course of the next three years, the work of many generations was dispersed to London's best auction houses. The banks had long been satisfied by the sale of Sheward Castle to a luxury hotel chain. It fast became one of Wiltshire's most popular wedding venues and its executive hunting days were highly sought after by mid-ranking businessmen. Sometimes Lady Rose dreamed of going back there, but the idea of staying as a guest in a place that she had once called home made her incalculably sad.

The two women spent the next seventeen years in the flat in Kensington. For Rosie they were the happiest of her life.

Lady Margaret was a fast learner. She engineered a meeting with Barnaby Rillington, an auctioneer at one of London's top auction houses. He was short and bald but always well dressed, slightly younger than Lady Margaret and fiercely ambitious. While his peers developed expertise in certain collectibles and moved on to specialise in those areas, Rillington specialised in newly-made widows, using his charm to convince them to part with family heirlooms, putting them up for auction and enabling him to amass quite a fortune through his sizeable percentage.

The affair between Lady Margaret and Rillington quickly cooled but the relationship had continued for more than a decade, founded on a mutual love of making money. Rosie's education was funded by it and her lifestyle, and that of her mother, remained mostly unaltered because of it. Her father had hotfooted it to America, where he made a living out of his title; it was the only inheritance he had left – and the only one he couldn't sell. He toured the country, attending dinners, earning pocket money by after-dinner speaking and becoming something of a genealogy celebrity. He had even fronted a series of programmes on US television and there was now talk of him doing something in the UK. Lady Rose hoped not. She hadn't seen him since her marriage, when he had tapped her up to pay his hotel bill at the Ritz. Although she felt overall she had benefited from the childhood his change in circumstances had brought, she had never really forgiven him for what he had done to her mother.

Rosie had become quickly acquainted with her mother's system and, using the brochure created by Lady Margaret, she began to write detailed provenance of pieces that was always so important in getting a top price at auctions. She learned that people loved the idea of owning a piece of furniture with a history, especially if a royal bottom may have sat in the chair, or a royal head rested on a pillow. She became expert at suggesting a royal connection to items, without being able to say with absolute certainty that the item had ever been in the presence of royalty.

She had met Sir Jesper at 22 and married him at 24, but only after she'd had ample opportunity to riffle the ancient attics at The Glades and discovered the untold riches created over the generations, much of it happily forgotten.

"I want to make the place a fitting home for an ancient peerage," she had told Sir Jesper to explain her interest in his dusty treasures. Massaging his ego had got her the wedding spread in *Compagne* and convinced him to hand over his mother's extensive collection of jewellery, largely diamonds and other precious stones, set in the art nouveau style which was just coming back into fashion.

His mother had also been a lover of Lalique; many items had been on display when Rosie first visited his home but when Matt was born, she put most of it into storage, arguing the incompatibility of priceless glassware and a toddler. Despite their son's advancing age – and his absence from home since turning eighteen - the Lalique remained absent, having been sold off to the wife of a newly rich oil baron in America more than a decade before.

Despite her experience in auctioning off her own family's antiquities, Lady Rose had been nervous the first time one of the great Donaldson collection went up for sale: a small item, a set of art nouveau hair combs. Barnaby Rillington had become Sir Barnaby and retired from the antiques trade so she'd had to find someone new to work with.

Having spent the first years of her marriage cataloguing the Donaldson hoard, Lady Rose eventually felt ready to invite someone along to view it. Sitting down to breakfast with Sir Jesper, she broached the subject as a done deal.

"I can't stay long," she had said, pouring out his coffee before reaching for her own cup. Throughout their marriage they had always tried to have breakfast together. Despite everything, she was rather fond of him. "I've got quite a few visitors coming today."

Sir Jesper had raised an eyebrow in question.

"The Donaldson catalogues are almost complete and now we need to ensure it is all appropriately insured. That means getting valuations."

Sir Jesper had nodded and smiled. "What would I do without you? All these years, all that stuff has been sitting gathering dust. No one knowing anything about what was entombed up there." He squeezed her hand as he rose to go to work. "Hardly a day goes by when I don't look around this place and thank god for you."

Lady Rose had smiled, feeling vindicated by his comments; she had earned a little security. She had worked full-time for six years without pay. It was a severe way to look at it, but she felt she had earned more than a bad portrait by a mediocre artist hanging in the hall for future generations to ignore.

Getting involved with people was always the risky part of any shady endeavour but Lady Rose had inherited her mother's ability to read people and spot any weakness that she could turn to her advantage. She had gone through school on reduced fees, because the widowed headmaster never quite gave up on the idea he might get lucky with her mother.

She struck out with the first dealer; the second turned up late and was shown the door minutes later. But the third one, Godfrey Cleaver, had been more promising.

"Good morning Lady Rose," he had clasped her hand firmly, looking her directly in the eye on the threshold as the hall clock chimed the hour.

"You understand that we are looking to value our collection for insurance purposes," she had said when they were sitting in the drawing room, a Sèvres tea service on the low mahogany table between them. She pointed to the hallway chandelier, an early piece by Lalique. "How do you put a price on such a piece of work?"

"Indeed," he replied.

It was only when they moved on to a set of perfume bottles by the same glassmaker that she repeated the sentence with a raised eyebrow. This time Cleaver's response was more assured.

"It will take our team about five weeks to price everything up," he said when they had returned to the drawing room, following a tour of some of the highlights of the Donaldson collection. He paused before adding, "Just a turn of phrase, of course. Pricing up, I mean."

Lady Rose decided to get to the point. "There may be the occasional item we want to sell, but quietly."

Cleaver nodded his understanding.

"Anything we want to dispose of is best progressed as private sales, quietly and without public mention of where the items have come from," Lady Rose continued. "However, I do have some written histories on many of the pieces."

"Authenticated?"

"In some cases yes, in others it's a mix of fact and fiction – impossible to prove."

Fastidious by nature, Godfrey wrote precise notes in a small moleskin notebook with a sharp pencil he kept in his jacket pocket.

"Of course, we can offer the items as from the private collection of one of the country's most noble and ancient homes. The best items will be those that carry names like your Lalique bottle collection. The fact that it comes from a stately home with full provenance will add to its price, but they will sell well on the basis of the designers' names, so there is little reason to add the owner's," he paused, afraid of insulting her. "Even one as illustrious as yours."

"I find greed is one of man's most reliable character traits," said Lady Rose as they parted. "And this could make you a very rich man, but only if we can continue to keep our relationship private."

"Discretion is the better part of valour." Godfrey had said, "And apparently of success too."

Twenty years on and he had been as good as his word. Lady Rose had steadily amassed a very private fortune but just as importantly, she had never got caught.

She turned away from the mirror and headed to the bathroom that adjoined it to draw a long, leisurely bath.

# CHAPTER 9

Malachy Drummond rubbed the heel of his right hand across his nose, hearing the satisfying sound of cartilage clicking in and out of place. It was the only thing that helped clear the sinuses blocked by those pesky microscopic particles of pollen at this time of year.

It was one of life's little ironies that he should suffer hay fever yet love his garden so much. A much bigger irony was that the allergy was caused by the plants' active reproductive cycles when his own should remain unceasingly dormant.

His was a sweet little cottage. 250 years old and, although sitting flush to a main road, the garden looked out onto a water meadow. It had taken three years to get the garden looking perfect. There was no sign of the Cornish semi-tropical plants that were all the rage in this part of the country. His was a pure slice of traditional English cottage garden.

Old stone used in the lean-to that had been leaning rather too far over the back door when he bought the property had been recycled to make a cottage-style patio which set off the weeping willows that provided maximum privacy but were a little more inspiring than the usual trees and shrubs. In front of it were foxgloves and an ancient apple tree had been added to create a small copse halfway down the garden, balanced out by magnolias in the centre of the lawn and providing magnificent colour at this time of year. The smell was also heavenly – if only his sinuses would clear so he could smell them.

The builder of his patio had been the inspiration behind his second book, *Love's Labourer's Lust*, which had in turn helped to pay for the works and with which he had cemented his place in the literati of gay porn. It was evidence of that cycle of life again. His agent had been on the point of dropping him after she turned down his third book idea, and had suggested he draw more honestly from his imagination. It had just been at the right time; while women were feasting themselves on the soft glow of porn fiction, Dick Biggs hit the shelf, offering a good read with at least twelve lovingly described sexual acts helping him to get a good few inches in the critics' columns.

Malachy had risen at five to work on his latest story. Dick Biggs' books were an alliance of noir and gay porn. They were successful

– and his publisher was ever hopeful that he would generate a crossover novel that would find its way out of adult bookstores and onto the shelves of WHSmith; a kind of *50 Shades of Gay*.

One of the many downsides of his chosen genre was the Thesaurus's lack of synonyms for the male appendage. Instead he found himself reading a lot of Greek literature in search of new ways to describe the sacred – or profane, depending on your political stance – but everyday acts of gay men.

Today he had spent an hour sipping First Flush Darjeeling from his usual paper-thin china cup, as he typed the physical description of his latest hero. Don Bite was French and pared down. Men were so visually stimulated, Malachy recognised the importance of getting those few paragraphs of describing his look just right. Don, he decided, would be shaven-headed, dark-eyed and sallow-skinned. Of course he would be buff, but you couldn't just come out and write that. Each area of the body needed describing in intimate detail using all five senses.

However, there was little time to worry about the size of Don's appendage. It was time for the first monthly editorial meeting organised by the new Managing Editor, and Malachy didn't want to be late. He quite liked her. She was forthright and honest, and seemed to have the good sense to ignore her staff's worst excesses of personality. He closed down his laptop and sipped the remains of his tea, taking a last look around his garden and mentally adding the need to edge the lawn to his list for the gardener – a strapping Cornish lad who had a penchant for stripping to the waist at the first sign of sunshine.

Lelaina Douglas was busy working on her laptop just a few houses down. Choosing to work in bed, she had her Macbook propped precariously on a knee as she slurped coffee from a chunky red mug and chose her font for the day. Modern technology was a marvellous thing for the 21$^{st}$ century writer. Even if one took the sensible precaution of removing internet access from the machine, there was still endless entertainment to be had in creating a document and its layout.

This was the fourth draft of her book *Dead Men Talking*; a crime novel written entirely from the point of view of the serial killer. This was an idea she'd had many years ago; although crime novels often have a little section given over to the omniscient malefactor's words, there were none that she was aware of – great autobiographies of recent political leaders aside – that gave exclusive voice to the murderers themselves. The only problem was developing a satisfyingly complex plot.

Lelaina avoided looking at the little clock on the right-hand corner of her screen. In order to give her the space to immerse herself in her work, she relied on her phone alarm which was set to go off at 8.18am, giving her precisely three minutes for a shower and four minutes to dry her hair and dress. It used to be 8.15 but by putting on her make-up in the car she managed to give herself an extra three minutes – time to write an extra 60 words a day, or 420 words a week, or 1680 words a month - and potentially shaving two weeks from her deadline. All something she had spent the preceding ten minutes working out on her computer's handy calculator.

Calibri, she decided. That was the font for this lovely early summer morning. Her index fingers hovered over the F and J, ready to record her first line. As her little finger depressed the shift key and her index finger headed for the T, the opening bars of The Rolling Stones' *Wild Horses* trilled out. It was 8.18am and time to hit the shower and morph into *Compagne's* Fashion Editor. Today she would dress to impress the new Managing Editor, already in post for a week.


Tory wondered if it was possible to go blind looking at badly dressed women with too many precious stones and not enough hair and make-up skills. Where did they learn to dress themselves? Who over the age of seven wore a black velvet Alice band? And to a black-tie dinner?

She was learning quickly. Half the battle with Society spreads was to try and hide some of the fashion faux pas – ancient fat graying bra straps running away from the well-muscled shoulders of the less elegant ladies whose bodies were more built-up than toned by hours tramping the countryside in the saddle or pulling the lead on pure breeds. Equally muscled bare legs the colour of boiled pork poked out below ancient taffeta dresses, while whitening hair escaped antique tortoiseshell combs. Tory had even spotted a pair of rubber boots on one rather unfortunate-looking woman. It was as if they didn't care. And perhaps it wouldn't have mattered if they weren't standing next to the perfectly presented society climbers who so clearly did.

By contrast, their hair was perfectly styled, faces were made the most of, and the latest designer dresses exquisitely draped from their slender sunbed-kissed shoulders. Society Editor Sophie Dexter-Browning dismissively called them 'nous-nous', but at least they were easy to picture edit. Sophie should really be doing this, but she had a habit of removing anyone who didn't have a genuine double-barrelled name that she approved of, and Tory knew from the research that the nous-nous were the ones who bought the magazine and, if they appeared in it, they bought it by the bundle.

Spotting one woman wearing the same blue velvet dress as in an earlier spread for a different event, Tory blinked and turned away from the large screen long enough to pour herself a cup of coffee, wondering again whether, if she did go blind, would it be considered an industrial disease that she could claim on?

The coffee wasn't helping. Her heart rate was rising, but her eyes still felt gritty. She needed a proper screen break. Pushing the thoughts aside and rubbing her eyes to encourage the tear ducts to relieve the dryness, she wandered off to the nearest bathroom.

"Oh, sorry," she muttered involuntarily as the first bathroom cubicle resisted her push. She moved on to the next one and found the same thing. Leaning back against the sink, she folded her arms, puzzled. She had thought she was the only person in the office this early in the morning.

After a few minutes, it became clear that either the occupant had taken ownership for the foreseeable future, or the bathroom was out of order. With that thought in mind she headed back into the corridor and down to the reception area where another bathroom was housed.

In the course of the next hour, she discovered the situation hadn't changed and wondered if women in the office were somehow syncing their bladder movements – in the same way that girls who live together were supposed to sync periods. The answer turned out to be less biological and more bizarre.

Stopping off at Jo's desk to drop off some paperwork for Sir Jesper, Tory quietly asked if the bathroom on the executive editorial floor was going to be out of order for long. They hadn't become friends yet but Tory had exploited a slight thawing of Jo's professional demeanour with passing pleasantries at every opportunity. The question lifted the corners of Jo's lips and she pulled off the wireless Bluetooth that was stapled to her left ear.

"Have you met Pretty McPhail yet?" At Tory's headshake, Jo continued, "She is our Health and Beauty Editor. She has a little problem with sharing." Jo raised her eyebrows and a smile played on her lips as she readied herself for the telling of tales.

Tory frowned, wondering if she had unknowingly done something to upset the mysterious editor. "It's like some kind of OCD," continued Jo. "She has commandeered a cubicle for her own personal use."

"She's what?"

"She's a bit phobic about anyone else using the same toilet as she does, so she got a lock put on the cubicle. No one has ever really questioned it. After all, who does like to share?"

Tory shrugged, "But they are both locked."

"That's Posy, her assistant. She doesn't like to share either." Jo narrowed her eyes at Tory, slightly tilting her head as she considered her next action. She opened her drawer and pulled out a set of keys. "I had a few spare sets made. Consider this yours – but if you get caught, you never got it from me."

Tory took the proffered key, winked and dropped it down her top for safekeeping. It fell between her breasts and landed with a thunk on the floor.

"Thanks," she muttered, stooping down to scoop it up and heading back to her office. The spread of the Horses for Courses charity black-tie dinner, which she still hadn't approved, suddenly looking more enticing. Her postponed editorial meeting was due in an hour.

On her way back to her office, Tory noticed a new head bent over a desk. At the sound of her voice, the head turned around to reveal a face she recognised from the editorial page of *Compagne* – Lucy Ramsden, the Weddings Editor.

One of Tory's first actions after the drinks party had been to print out the editorial page, which featured soft-focus, glamorous images of all the editors, complete with names and job titles, so she could get to know the staff in name if not in person.

She herself had been summonsed to a photo shoot for her own picture the previous day. Expecting a quick snap in her office, she had headed down to the grand ballroom to discover a portable photographic studio in place with several coloured backgrounds, a rack of clothes, and a make-up and hair stylist called Keri flown in from London. The photographer had told her to stand a metre away from his white screen and had walked slowly around her, taking a few test shots designed to measure her skin tone against his chosen colour. "I'm thinking Rosalind Russell, *His Girl Friday*," the photographer told Janey, who had come along to style Tory and offer some moral support.

The photographer sat her on a desk, piled high with copies of *Compagne*, legs crossed, her right foot elegantly tucked behind the ankle of her left, which was angled downwards to lengthen her calves. The stylist had chosen a charcoal pencil skirt which tightly encased her thighs and a cream silk blouse that sat razor-sharp on her shoulders thanks to its padding, meeting her softly-curled 1940s war bride hair.

The make-up artist had created a new face: sharp, slender brows sat above strongly defined eyes and fire engine-red lips with an exaggerated cupid's bow. Her newly extended nails were painted to match and a sharpened pencil was artfully placed between her index and forefinger. Tory was pleased with the outcome in as much as it looked nothing like her – on the off chance that the Baltic Mafia went up in the world enough to read society magazines, they were unlikely to recognise her.

She still had nightmares about the man who mouthed 'gotcha' turning up on her doorstep.

*'Hide in the sunlight, not in the shadows,'* Lyle had advised her on the scribbled note that had accompanied a lavish bouquet of flowers that were still sitting in her kitchen sink, having no vase to go in.


Tory spotted a photograph on Lucy's desk, in a precision-distressed vintage frame. It sat by her computer screen, dominating the space where others kept piles of old magazines and post. Trying not to stare, Tory realised it was there to be noticed.

"What a gorgeous dress," she said.

"Oscar de la Renta," came the reply. Lucy was busy polishing the latest wedding feature on her screen, highlighting and deleting the word 'perfect' from the final sentence before turning to meet the new Managing Editor.

"Well, I would have expected the Weddings Editor to have an exquisite wedding dress – when did you get married?"

The room fell silent as the junior reporters in the neighbouring cubicles turned to look at Tory, sneaking a glance at Lucy's face and wondering what she would say next.

"That's not my wedding dress," Lucy stated shortly, continuing to look at her screen. Her tone didn't invite further discussion.

Tory looked away, catching the eye of Janey who indicated to the door with a slight tilt before returning her attention to her giant computer screen where she was laboriously Photoshopping-out the many physical imperfections of the peers of the realm from a recent charity auction that had raised tens of thousands of pounds for one of Lady Rose's pet charities. She was struggling with a particularly ruddy-complexioned duke, his purple nose clashing with the beaujolais in his raised glass.

"Well, it was nice to finally say hello," Tory offered. "I'll look forward to reading the copy when it's finished," she indicated towards the wedding spread on Lucy's screen and walked on.

"So what's the story with Lucy?" Back in the comfort of her office, Tory took off her high heels and leaned over to her mini fridge to pull two cans of Diet Coke from the top shelf as Janey walked into the office and headed for the sofa. The two had paired up, having had lunch together several times during her first week. It was fast becoming a friendship based on a shared love of the ridiculous so often displayed in the halls of *Compagne*.

Janey pulled her can open with a satisfying hiss. "Her wedding didn't match up to her expectations."

"Her wedding? I thought most people found that about their marriage."

"I think in this case it was literally the wedding. Have you met Jack?"

"Her husband? No."

"A chef. Won a Michelin star; owns Ramsden's – thinking of taking on some place in London, but doesn't want to abandon her. He's a really, really nice guy. Not too bad to look at either."

Tory remembered she had eaten in Ramsden's with Lyle after her interview. The former Methodist Church with the well-stocked wine list. "I'll keep an eye out next time I'm in there."

"Anyway, they married when he was a lowly sous chef and she was a trainee reporter and it was a small wedding at a register office and then back to their house for a barbecue with only a few guests."

"And she regrets it now?"

"Totally obsessed with the weddings she covers. She keeps a secret file on her computer with a bucket list for what she would do if she married again."

"Married again?"

"I know, very weird. But this place can do that to you. You should have met the last Fashion Editor. She had the most incredible clothes and shoes sent to her, swanned into work in a different outfit every day, boasted that she never wore the same clothes twice. Ended up donating them all to charity and went off to work in the PR department for George at Asda."

Tory laughed, not wanting to mention Janey's distorted body image fed by her proximity to models.

"So where did the designer dress come from in that picture on her desk?"

Janey shrugged. "A photoshoot."

"She tried on the dresses?"

"Not exactly. The previous editor wanted her picture byline to be a wedding photo – but she vetoed it when she saw the chainstore off-the-peg number Lucy had worn. I think that's when Lucy's obsession began. Mahri – the old editor – insisted they set up a photoshoot; designer dresses, make up – the lot. Even got a jeweller to upscale her wedding ring."

Tory noticed the proofs of her own photoshoot had arrived on her desk during her absence. She nodded towards them. "I kind of know how she feels. My wardrobe and make-up seem a bit lacklustre after doing that."

Janey smiled, taking an expert flick through the photos before choosing one. "This one – I'll get the digital version down to the designers."

Tory shrugged – they all looked the same to her. She threw her empty can in the bin.

"Right, time to meet the editors," she said, squaring her shoulders and heading for the editorial boardroom.

# CHAPTER 10

Tory looked around the conference room and decided everything looked just right. She had borrowed one of the Flowers of Medieval, a pretty redhead, who had helped her raid the stationery cupboard to set up for her mid-morning breakfast meeting with the senior staff.

The redhead had nipped off to take delivery of a pile of breakfast fruits and pastries that would sit on platters along the middle of the table and there were two steaming silver pots of coffee and hot water surrounded by china cups and saucers — a far cry from the ancient vending machine in the *Post*'s newsroom, which spat out cups of over-brewed stale tea no matter which option you requested. Tory leaned over and poured herself a cup, a tasty reminder of how far she had come.

A call to Donovan earlier that morning had revealed no more news, unless you counted the fact that an ear had now joined the hand still residing in the morgue. This part had been found at an undisclosed location, but Donovan had relented enough to assure her it wasn't anywhere she frequented.

While he had talked, explaining the leads they were following in capturing Cracker Smith's murderer, a sliver of conversation had come back to her. It wasn't in her notes, as it was something he had mentioned when he had first called to try and get a story in the *Post*.

"This might be nothing," she began, interrupting his platitudes and pulling a face at the cliché.

Donovan had immediately been on high alert. "What?"

"Cracker mentioned something to me when we first spoke, I wasn't taking much notice because I didn't really want to do a story. I thought he was bullshitting to get some column inches. But he said something about infiltrating a drug gang."

Donovan was silent over the phone. Tory felt stupid she hadn't remembered it before.

"That's the word he used, 'infiltrating'?"

Tory shrugged to herself. "I don't think so — I'm not sure he'd know what it meant. But I got the impression he was trying to set himself up as a kind of community vigilante. I did ask him about how he was doing it but he kind of changed tack; I thought it was because he was making it up."

Donovan was silent while he wrote notes. "Is it possible that he meant there was someone undercover?"

"Undercover?"

"He or someone else joining this drug gang to gather information?"

"I honestly don't know. But I think I would have remembered that – that would have been a story."

"Why didn't you note that down?"

Tory sighed. "He said a lot of stuff when we first spoke, but nothing about it when we met. He was vague, talking about immigration, rising crime rates, housing issues; well, you've got the notes."

"Okay – well this gives us a new lead."

"So will it all be over soon?"

Donovan had ignored her question. "I'll be in touch."


She dragged her mind back to the task in hand. Her email invitation had been sent out by Sir Jesper on her behalf to encourage everyone to turn up. She had asked him to deliver a three-line whip. The August issue was set to go to print in four days and so far it was a complete disaster.

She had already heard complaints about holding a meeting so close to deadline, but she was hopeful that her message could get through and make these last few days easier.

The room was slowly but reassuringly filling up. The section editors were in place, Harry Hampton holding court at one end of the room as he helped himself to a bagel heaped with Cornish cream cheese and Scottish smoked salmon, alongside a sticky cinnamon roll for pudding, keeping everyone amused while the stragglers arrived. In lieu of a PA, Tory had asked Laura to take some notes so she could follow up her comments with an email.

The clock had long struck 11am, the table was polished and the paper and pencils sat at perfect angles. She decided it was better to start on time, the better to get it over with. Surveying the faces around the oval table she saw expressions ranging from irritation and boredom to truculence and mild curiosity.

"It ended in divorce; now let's look at the marriage," she said.

It was a good opening line, thought Harry Hampton from the far end of the table, but it wasn't hers. He expertly flicked bagel crumbs from his silk tie and watched his new editor addressing his peers.

Dressed in a silk wraparound dress in a red and black print, she looked the part. Sophie must have set her up with her shopper already. Only a slight waver in her voice denoted her nervousness, but overall she managed to ensnare the staff from the off with the promise that better planning would mean less work, fewer late nights, less stress and a better magazine they could all be proud of, the latter less of a deal breaker than she might hope. She also had a diamond ace up her sleeve.

"I met with Sir Jesper to agree a number of changes, and alongside them is the introduction of a range of editorial staff bonuses. The company is agreeing to put a percentage of profits over a specific amount into a bonus fund, which will be released to editorial staff at the end of the financial year. This means your bonus is linked to magazine sales and the performance of the advertising team."

She paused, waiting for everyone to take it in. "This bonus is potentially worth into five figures," she paused. "All of them before the decimal point."

As she allowed the news to sink in, Tory noticed Lucy Ramsden scribbling energetically, no doubt working out how much she could add to her second wedding fund.

"At the moment, we would be lucky to get a single figure," Tory looked around the desk, seeing the pleasure drain from eyes as dreams of paying off hefty credit card bills or school fees and designer wedding dresses faded from their grasp. "Harry has come to the rescue of the August issue, with additional content," she paused and smiled at him, "And I know that Betsy," she looked around for the Homes and Interiors Editor Betsy Beaufort, before remembering she was out on a photoshoot, "was happy to increase her section at the last minute. But the rest of you were completely unprepared. It's totally unacceptable to begin every magazine with a blank sheet – it should be planned with precision; in some areas this can be done months in advance."

She looked down the table, ignoring some of the outraged expressions, picking out individuals, and beginning with the Social Editor. "Sophie, I know you have the social diary mapped out for the year, but the editorial coverage is down as TBC for most pages until it arrives on the designers' desk. Simply by sharing your diary with me, I can plan events properly, and give them the best possible space."

Pretty McPhail, the Health and Beauty Editor, was looking with disgust at the fruit platter in front of her, obsessively wiping her hands with disposable antibacterial wipes. Tory was momentarily mesmerised by the slow, thorough process that began with a clean wipe on the back of her hands before she moved on to her palms, working her way between each finger, before cleaning each nail. The used wipes joined the growing pile sitting by her plastic-enclosed Blackberry.

"The feedback we get from the Health and Beauty pages suggests we need to be more on-trend. Is our Health section about focusing on diseases? About inspiring stories of the afflicted? Or is it about keeping healthy and young and informing our readers of the latest diet and fitness fads?"

Pretty paused in her antibacterial ablutions to look up at the mention of her section, glaring at the editor as though she were a particularly stubborn germ.

"I think this is something we need to give serious thought to, perhaps in a separate meeting?" Tory stared her down. She knew she was right, and that helped her be more forthright. "The commercial teams are champing at the bit with spa companies desperate to advertise, but they don't want to go next to photos of enlarged prostates."

Tory noticed the beautifully coloured fruit plate remained untouched as the staff made their way through the equally beautiful but less healthy pastries, especially as they realised the meeting was becoming more pep talk, less bollocking. Restaurant critic Max Mullen was eyeing up the remaining food, adjectives to describe the meltingly good pastries flowing through his head. She must have got them from Rhubarbs, he thought. Attention to detail was vital in a good editor; perhaps she would make the grade after all.

Mullen continued to concentrate on his notepad where he was sketching out front cover ideas for his new book. Food had become Max Mullen's life. It was purely accidental, but then so were sandwiches. A whole culinary history created by a peer of the realm who had been too greedy to wait until dinnertime.

Max had started his working life in sports journalism, but quickly noticed that while he was sweating over his copy trying to find new adjectives to describe a less than Beckham bend, the food critic was heading off to yet another exclusive eatery desperate to fill him with good food and great wine in return for a collection of superlatives in the next colour supplement. Hanging around his desk had quickly transformed into a few freebie meals in return for filling in for the old soak and Max discovered he had a way with food and wine writing.

Over the years he had added a little TV presenting on the side, helped by his ability to describe food and - as importantly - he had managed to avoid the alcohol and weight problems usually associated with his profession. Only an occasional late night intestinal disturbance marred his otherwise perfect metabolism, and those sleepless nights huddled around the toilet bowl had helped him keep his enviable waistline. The only fly in his aioli was Harry Hampton. Impossible to dislike, Harry was still Food Editor, and while he tended to concentrate on recipes and his celebrity chef mates, Max, as the magazine's food reviewer, was most definitely his subordinate. Although happy in his work, he thought a more senior job title would help sell more of his books.

He was currently a third of the way through a recipe book based on the final meals of famous people. The idea had come from that legendary story – or was it an urban myth – that former French President François Mitterrand had eaten a last meal of an endangered songbird drowned in Armagnac – under cover of cloth to hide his shame. Apparently he'd had seconds. Said to taste of all the places the bird had travelled throughout its life, to Max the *ortolan cassoulet* just sounded like a waste of good brandy. The dish was currently proving the most promising denouement for his book – he'd yet to find anyone in recent centuries known for supping on roasted swan, but he lived in hope.

Max's agent, thinking of his ten per cent, wanted him to include a compendium of celebrities and their chosen final meals. But Max was still taking a high-brow approach, and wondered just how interested the public were in the desperate desire of soap opera stars and reality show-offs to once again sit down to their dearly-departed mother's Sunday roast.

Max finally gave in to the temptation before him and reached for a vanilla pastry, the apricot glaze glistening enticingly. He predicted it was now at room temperature and the filling would have lost that chill that inevitably came from refrigerating food in transit; a distasteful but necessary Health and Safety practice. Now at the room temperature of nineteen degrees, it would melt in the mouth and taste how the pâtissier had meant it to. He picked up his pen and scribbled down a few adjectives. Anticipation was, without a doubt, his favourite flavour.

As the meeting progressed, Max agreed with the rest of the editors to share his diary so issues could be planned ahead then he took his plate and untouched apricot pastry back to his office to enjoy in peace, nodding to a few of his colleagues who looked less thunderous coming out of the meeting than they had going in. The promise of big bonuses to match their successes had inevitably helped mollify the more unsavoury elements raised by Victoria Manders.

Back at his desk, Max clicked his wireless mouse to bring his computer back to life and turned his attention to an email in his inbox, which detailed the final menu for Lady Rose's summer garden party event the following weekend. Lady Rose had asked him to review it and he had earlier made a few suggestions, although being organised by an almost Michelin-starred chef meant it was already more than adequate. Perhaps the surfeit of landed gentry attending the event would furnish him with some more ideas for *Last Suppers: Famous Final Meals*.


Tory finally sat down at the head of the empty conference room table. The meeting had gone pretty much as planned. She had nodded to Harry Hampton, who had winked his approval as he had left the room last, closing the door to give her a few minutes' peace. She pulled the coffee pot over and dribbled the last drops into her cup, adding a splash of hot water from the thermos used for the First Flush Darjeeling that had also been served – she had asked Laura to research some of the likes and dislikes of her new staff before finalising the brunch menu. Cup in hand, Tory looked down at the lengthy list of things she wanted to cover in the meeting, satisfied that everything was ticked off. She only hoped the staff weren't.

Laura had agreed to get the minutes of the meeting to her by the end of the day. Tory made a note to speak to Sir Jesper about stealing Laura. A few snatches of conversation during the planning had revealed that she had been taken on believing she would be trained to become a writer. She had a degree in English Literature and was a native of Cornwall but she had spent three years opening post and ordering obscure foodstuffs for the lunch table of the senior editorial staff. With some support Laura would make a great assistant editor and, despite being offered her pick of the Flowers of Medieval for a secretary, Tory felt an assistant with an interest in journalism would be a better fit. Even if she left, she would have helped someone in their career, and that felt undeniably good.

Tory would use Laura's detailed minutes and send them out with a list of carefully worded instructions masquerading as polite requests.

Now she had a late lunch with Janey to look forward to. Tory was trying to keep any relationships quite casual – after all, she could be off back to London at any moment – but it had been difficult to maintain a distance from *Compagne's* genuinely friendly and often funny Art Director.

Entering Ramsden's, Tory and Janey smiled at the *maître d'* as he led them to a table near the window overlooking the dwindling River Fal, which was living up to its name. The brightness of the room was tempered by dark gold walls and the kind of ancient oiled oak floor which Tory always felt the need to tiptoe on if she was wearing stiletto heels, for fear of punching holes in it.

She pulled off her silk Hermès scarf – a welcome gift from Fashion Editor Lelaina – to hang on the back of the chair, before smiling up at the approaching waiter. "Hello. I'd like an enormous glass of wine, something really naff and unpretentious. Preferably out of a box."

He smiled. "Of course, may I suggest the Liebfraumilch? It's been left out of the fridge so it's nice and warm."

"Lovely." She turned to Janey. "What are you going to have?"

"I'll have still water; ice, but no lemon."

The waiter nodded. "Lime?"

"No lime."

"I've got orange or perhaps I can add a slice of kiwi?"

"No, nothing." Janey's voice rose slightly.

The waiter seemed undeterred. His drink-making skills were clearly under question and he wasn't going to fold without a fight. "What about a slice of mango or bruised passion fruit seeds?"

"No, just the water." Janey's voice rose to a slightly hysterical squeak.

He nodded his assent, hiding his surprise and, he admitted to himself on the way to the bar, disappointment. He returned with the glasses, placing the drinks down with a flourish. "Are you ready to order?"

Tory smiled to her companion, eyebrows slightly raised, waiting for her to order first. Janey shook her head slightly.

Tory nodded, taking it as a sign that she wasn't ready to order yet. "Oh okay, can you give us a couple more minutes?"

"No, no, you go ahead and order." Janey closed her menu.

"Are you not eating?'

"No."

"Oh." Wrong-footed, Tory requested a salad and grilled fish. Since moving to Cornwall her consumption of seafood had increased ten-fold.

The waiter walked away, scribbling in his pad.

"Why aren't you eating?" Tory asked as he disappeared into the kitchen. She was sure his shoulders were slightly slumped in defeat at Janey's lack of interest in the menu.

"I'm on a diet."

"Oh?"

"It's called the Naked Diet."

"Naked, what like a Jamie Oliver diet? Is he doing diets now?"

"No, nothing to do with him. Basically you can only eat when naked."

Tory snorted. "What?"

"It's brilliant. You can only eat when you are naked – so the opportunities for eating socially are pretty much reduced to nothing."

"That sounds awful."

"I admit I have been having fantasies about dragging someone from the office home to lick clotted cream and jam off their body. And I don't even like clotted cream. If I'm feeling particularly vicious, I eat naked in front of the mirror."

The waiter chose this moment to bring Tory's lunch.

"More water?" he asked Janey with an understanding smile. He had assumed the attitude of talking to one who is slightly deranged.

"No, thank you." Janey waited for him to move away, though he hovered at a nearby table, where a pair of tourists was busily photographing their beautifully laid-out food with camera phones.

"That's the other thing," she turned back to Tory. "I seem to spend half the day drinking water and the other half on the loo. I'm terrified of going out to a fashion shoot where there are no amenities."

Tory picked up her knife and fork, her appetite returning.

"So what do you think?' Janey asked.

Tory looked critically at her non-dining companion's size six frame. Privately she thought her Art Director was spending too much time surrounded by models. "I think good luck with it." Her fork paused halfway to her mouth as she had another thought. "Just don't expect me to come around your house for dinner any time soon."

# CHAPTER 11

This month was all about the farmhouse – not the type that welcomes you with clumps of cowshit in the yard and a high note of pig poo that never quite disappears, no matter how many preserves are bubbling on a grubby hand-me-down Aga. This was the kind of farmhouse whose front gate opens into a freshly scrubbed cobble-stoned yard dotted with early summer flowers housed in redundant feeding troughs artily aged with yoghurt. Homes and Interiors Editor Betsy Beaufort sighed as the day ahead unfolded before her.

She had emailed the new editor her apologies at being unable to attend the planning meeting due to this long-held appointment for an interview. Tory Manders had replied enthusiastically, since her meeting was concerned with planning, and Betsy's interview - set up to appear in the October issue – was evidence that the Homes and Interiors section was well-planned, more than exempting her.

Picking her way carefully across the glistening rust-coloured cobblestones, Betsy headed towards the expertly antiqued barn doors. The top half sat open, the better to share the delicious smell of 'home-baked' pies that would be artistically arranged on a scrubbed wooden table when she arrived. The likelihood of them being cooked by the new owner rather than ordered in from the nearest gourmet deli was matched only by Betsy's chances of actually getting to taste them.

Fortunately she had stopped off at the nearby deli to grab a quick espresso and *pain au raisin*. Its owner had bubbled over with excitement at serving her, filling her in without being asked about their recent opening, how they had picked up the thatched cottage-cum-butchers cheaply due to the generations-old business going into receivership and how they had spent three months unearthing its ancient architectural treasures to be put on show next to the pâté and gourmet cheeses. The new owners, who had retired from city life at 40, had chosen the spot because of all the converted barns in the area. Farmers had become smart enough to recognise that people would pay good money for their old cowsheds, especially if they could get planning permission. Sadly these same wily farmers had also become over-confident and over-stretched themselves by converting old outbuildings into office spaces for companies that were no longer in business due to an economic downturn. This had left them with big bills and no ready cash.

And so all those nous-nous who had been buying up all the spare barns for conversion could now get their hands on the prize – the farmhouse. After generations in the same family, these rural landmarks suddenly became available for quick sale.

But Betsy wasn't there to write about the rape and pillage of the country's farming heritage by cash-rich city burn-outs. Although sometimes she quite fancied suggesting it as an alternative spin on the usual 'living the country dream' feature.

Betsy had arranged to meet the photographer, Lyle Taylor, at Home Farm, which sat on the border of Devon and Somerset. She knew he lived in Cornwall as she did but was keen to avoid several hours of forced conversation during the car journey. Instead she chose to drive alone, giving her a few hours to decide the styling for each shoot. Despite having little in common with Lyle, she knew he took great photos and that was what Homes and Interiors was all about. Creating an idyllic lifestyle that was as unobtainable as it was fake. The man or woman who coined the term 'property porn' couldn't have been more right. She was creating the ultimate cock – or more often clitoris – tease. Turning people on with a glimpse of impossible lifestyles without any hope of finishing them off. How else could you get them to keep coming back for more?

Betsy pushed her thoughts aside and tapped on the open barn door, noting the so-naff-it-was-cool duck egg-blue painted house name on the top half. It would make a great headline shot.

"Welcome to Home Farm. Lovely to see you," the wide, professionally-whitened smile carried the right amount of surprise and pleasure at the arrival of her guest. Had Betsy not watched through the open window as her interviewee sat flicking through *Vogue* on the artfully shabby chaise longue before making her presence known she would have been totally convinced by the bare feet, vintage floral pinafore apron and slight dusting of freshly milled flour on the woman's right cheek.

They air kissed and the new owner of Home Farm turned away with a girlish yelp. "My pies!"

She padded over to the Aga as Betsy ostensibly admired a Welsh dresser filled with vintage china but was unable to resist watching from the corner of her eye as the alleged pie baker struggled with clearly unfamiliar oven gloves and opened two empty warming drawers before locating the pie dishes nestling in the main oven.

"My first batch – I hope you will have a taste."

Betsy smiled; the smell emanating from the golden-crusted pies filled the room with sweet apple and cinnamon. "We'd love to get pics of them first and of you in the apron, the smudge," she waved her hand around the room. "All of it."

Her subject looked pleased. Failing to ask what smudge Betsy was referring to confirmed its purposeful placement.

Lodd McPherson was a former WAG who was turning herself rather successfully into a homespun heroine following a vicious divorce from one of the country's top football managers. Her rather brittle performance in court was mirrored by her media trial, which was against her up until her perfectly timed and much-reported attempted suicide. The resulting headlines were big and seemed to agree that Lodd had scored the winning goal:

*'The pressure all got to be too much, I just wanted a way out,'* *admits frail and tearful Lodd to the crowd of reporters helpfully* *gathered outside the hospital when she was discharged.*

When she walked away with half her ex-husband's lifetime earnings, they felt she had earned it. "It's time for a change, I just want time to recover, and I need peace and quiet," she had told the many supermarket magazines during countless interviews in which she was anything but quiet.

Lodd's look had changed since her years as the Queen of WAG-shire. Mostly it was a colour change, a shift down a few gears. Her hair was no longer ramrod-straight to her shoulder blades, but softly curled, the soft auburn colour several notches down from the vibrant red it had been when she had married and the spread had appeared in one of *Compagne*'s rivals: *'He makes me complete, I couldn't imagine life without him'*.

Her skin was now paler and her make-up too had been toned down to a subtle barely-there look that had probably taken two hours to achieve. The overall effect was of looking at a media icon, whose features had become so familiar to everyone over the years, through a very soft-focus lens.

Betsy knew it was exactly the look that would work for her feature, deciding that of all the accessories in the house, Lodd was the most stylish.

She followed her hostess through to the hallway, her heels ringing out on the flagstones, which had undergone deep cleansing treatments to look old and washed-out. Betsy noted the photo opportunities as she went: a sludgy teal pottery jug filled with sweet-smelling lilac on an black and gold Chinese cabinet in the hall; an enormous fireplace large enough to stand in with apple logs awaiting a cool autumn night still some months away - a clever nod towards the October issue the article was planned for. She made a mental note to ask Lodd to light the fire later when the sun had swung round to the other side of the house, creating a pleasingly dusky-looking room.

"The kitchen is the heart of any farmhouse, but I think we need to give some sense of the space and light you have created elsewhere in the house, while retaining so much of its character," Betsy noted the William Morris wallpaper in the large family bathroom. It was an interesting interior twist and a luxurious one at £1000 a metre. An antique Edwardian bath suite was clearly the real thing and happily there was no matching shower stall or bidet.

Heading back downstairs, loose tea leaves were added to a solid-looking silver pot, hot water poured, and a tray brought to the table. Lodd collected mis-matched china from the stripped oak shelves of the Welsh dresser, and the pot was covered with a vibrantly striped tea cosy – 'home crocheted' of course - to keep it warm on this pretend autumnal day.

Betsy got out her notepad – the interview proper would start once Lyle had arrived, when more interesting and less rehearsed quotes would fall from her subject's lips as her attention was split between looking good and sounding good. But the chat beforehand would give Betsy an idea of how Lodd wanted to be viewed in the piece; after all, this wasn't an exposé on the realities of life as a media whore. Still, that didn't mean the interview shouldn't make an interesting read.

"I really needed a period of recovery – and this project has really helped that," began Lodd. "When I bought the farmhouse it was terribly run-down. It hadn't had any work done to it since it was built 250 years ago, other than adding the indoor plumbing and electricity – and both of those were pretty basic," Lodd paused to allow Betsy time to catch up on her notes.

"Do you have favourite things that you've done to the house?"

"Ripping things out and discovering original features was an incredible adventure, but I think the real discovery for me was finding myself. I really found myself in this project."

Betsy smiled. There was the central theme of the feature for Lodd. A journey; hidden treasures and the surprise at finding oneself amongst the other discoveries within this 250-year-old farmhouse. Lodd had clearly already worked this out with her publicist, along with several ways of saying the same thing to ensure it was sufficiently quoted.

"I get enormous pleasure from collecting beautiful things. But I'm not someone who wants to buy matching sets. These teacups are an expression of me, of who I am; frail, sometimes chaotic and mis-matched."

"And beautiful," Betsy added, knowing it was part of the script.

Lodd smiled at the compliment. "There was a time that I would have been afraid to express myself in this way. My old life was more about donning the latest labels and being seen in the right places. Making sure I always looked the part, even if inside I felt the opposite. It was tremendously important that I was never seen in sweaty gymwear walking the streets." She looked around her kitchen with genuine pleasure. "But here I feel much more free to express myself. I bake, I make preserves – I've even started my own little kitchen garden." Betsy looked up, intrigued; an image of Lodd with a trowel, bending over serried rows of perfectly grown veg.

"Although at the moment it's nothing but a pile of dirt," Lodd continued, cursing herself for not thinking of getting her agent to buy vegetable plants for the shoot. "I've never gardened so it feels like a huge project to me, but the idea of being able to pull potatoes out of the ground and putting them straight into the cooking pot and on the table within the hour is far more exciting to me than heading off to a champagne reception in London."

Betsy nodded; Lodd was much smarter than she had given her credit for. The interview was working out pretty well – and despite the clearly staged opening she was getting some good stuff. Maybe the tabloids were right and Lodd was a great actress destined for Hollywood. But from what she was saying, it wasn't what she wanted. Of course that could all change, all it takes is the right invitation.

Betsy heard horses neigh outside and Lodd nodded. "I've been having riding lessons since moving here – I have to say an hour in the saddle is an incredible form of exercise; better than those state-of-the-art gyms I lived in when I was married. And despite the vet and food bills, it's probably still cheaper!"

Lodd pulled the heavy teapot towards her and began to pour, releasing the fragrant bergamot from the Earl Grey. Betsy gratefully accepted a cup.

"I'd really like to find time now to help others too – nothing too big. As a football wife you get used to being dragged out for media events and to provide soundbites on the big three."

"The big three?"

"The big three charities: children, animals and cancer," Lodd paused, shaking her head. "Please don't put that in. It sounds awfully callous. But I suppose that's what that lifestyle does to you. You say something about how awful it is that children are starving in parts of the world, or that girls are being denied education or elephants are losing their tusks, and you don't really get time to think about it or work out what you want to do to help. You just turn up, get photographed or read from a script, and go off shopping."

"And do you now know?"

"I'm really intrigued by the rural/urban divide that has come up in recent years – perhaps it has always been there. But rural poverty and urban poverty are very different. Farmers are struggling and some have given up after generations of their families working their land." She paused, half smiling in acknowledgement that she was living in one of those lost farms. "Those who worked the land for them have no work, they live too far away from places where they can find work, and there are no transport links to get them there anyway. They are forced out of the housing market by rich city weekenders," again she paused with a smile. "At least I live here full-time."

Betsy put down her cup and scribbled her comments. Here was someone self-aware and reasonably genuine. Having written about so many washed-up celebrities trying their hand at raising rare sheep or making cheese, it was refreshing to meet someone who seemed to be so relaxed about life in the countryside. She remembered the drummer of a 1990s rock band, a drug addict and rumoured alcoholic, who had decided to move to the country, get clean and start a vineyard. She had struggled for days over whether to mention the obvious dichotomy. In the end she had turned it into a perky 'against all odds' type of piece. Kid-in-a-sweetshop references were avoided. As far as she was aware, the vineyard was still going, although the drummer had moved on to other things.

"What about marriage?"

"My marriage to John was exhausting. They say that a celebrity year of marriage is like seven for other people. If that's true then I was married for about 60 years. I guess that's better than most people can say. Although we saw each other so rarely, the time spent together probably only added up to a few weeks."

"So no looking for love?"

"No. I'm happy at the moment. There's a difference between being alone and lonely. I learned that being surrounded by people all the time in London."

Betsy nodded, adding a star in her notepad next to her neat, precise shorthand to indicate a useable quote. "You were lonely?"

"At times. Surrounded by people at an event, photographers waiting to get a shot of you stuffing your face, spilling your champagne down your couture or arguing with your husband for turning up two hours late. It was stressful and boring and lonely. But when you are in the middle of it, it's hard to know how to get out. I sometimes wish I could get that across to all those youngsters who pore over the tabloids, slavering over every new dress or change of hairstyle. Sorry, it sounds like I'm preaching."

They broke off the conversation as Lyle had arrived. He came in, greeting them both as he unpacked his kit, managing to set up the complex lighting system without rearranging the furniture. Despite her seeming honesty, there was no doubt that Lodd had prepared for her *Compagne* premiere, possibly hiring an art director to help set up the house for endless photo ops.

As she disappeared to bring in some outfits she had chosen, Lyle exchanged pleasantries with Betsy.

"How's your new editor settling in?" he phrased the question casually. He had texted and emailed Tory a few times since she had started her new job but the replies had always been short and his invitations to dinner, lunch and even breakfast politely refused.

Betsy smiled. "Okay, I've not seen much of her yet. Do you know her?"

Lyle laughed. *Not as well as I'd like to*, he thought. "We used to work together – I told her about the job at *Compagne*."

Betsy nodded, her mind switching back to Lodd as she returned with several outfits expertly pressed and on hangers.

Lyle got straight down to business. "I'd really like to do something outside – a nice sunset is expected tonight – I think some relaxed shots in your garden, skin warmed by the golden hour, hair softly escaping from its casual pinning, trowel at the ready, basket of veg… you get the idea."

Lodd clearly did – Lyle had expertly painted a pleasing picture of a woman at home on her land. Perhaps the headline could make a *Far From the Madding Crowd* reference. Or perhaps she could keep that as the title of her ghostwritten autobiography. She would suggest it to her publicist at lunch when she was next in town.

Betsy's prediction was right; the pies were never eaten, and the rest of the tea left undrunk. Instead, endless bottles of Evian were distributed as Lyle took shot after shot, gently flirting with his subject to gain more natural expressions, and even convincing Lodd to bathe in an artificially candle-lit bathroom, borrowing the outsized candelabra housed predictably on the dining table.

"Leave it there," Lodd had said, wrapping herself in a fluffy white bath sheet when they had finished. "I never liked it on the dining table either."

Dressed in surprisingly genuinely scuffed riding wear, Lodd headed outside with Lyle to introduce her horse, a dapple-grey mare named Tilly, and Tilly's stable mate, a giant orange cat known only as Fatty. Tilly neighed with pleasure at the sight of her mistress and left a smear of green slime on her shoulder as Lyle took some quick snaps before giving Lodd a leg up – his hand grasping the top of her thigh.

He photographed the pair in action, even waiting to capture Lodd in the saddle as the sun set.

"Looks like the cover of a romantic novel," Betsy said with a laugh as Lyle changed his lens.

Agreeing to send contact sheets to Betsy before the end of the next day, and swapping phone numbers with Lodd to discuss further photography work, Lyle packed up his equipment and left. Lodd and Betsy then said their goodbyes, both genuinely thankful for spending a nice day meeting someone interesting to talk to.

The usual platitudes of reassurance weren't required. The demand to see copy before it went to print or have final say on the shots used weren't forthcoming either. Perhaps that would follow from the buoyant PR who had set it all up. But of course that would be easy to bat back.

"Here's my mobile," Lodd said, scribbling on a corner of *Vogue* before tearing it off and handing it over. "Give me a call if you want any more info or want to check anything."

Betsy took the scribbled sheet. "Here's my card. I've put my mobile number on the back."

Before setting off, Betsy wrote a quick email to Tory. *'Didn't know you knew Lyle? He asked after you. Also wondered if you were in the market for a new columnist. Lodd McPherson - surprisingly warm, smart and funny.'*

# CHAPTER 12

Looking out of the window of the First Class train carriage on his way to Paddington Station as the beautiful coastline of the South West rolled past, Sir Jesper began to feel that, like the fields and towns they travelled through at high speed, the opportunity to make his mark was passing him by. The magazine was doing well, profits were healthy, readership was growing and the new editor seemed to be settling in. Thanks to his wife The Glades was the envy of the world, with endless requests to use it as a background to period dramas and a year-long waiting list for house tours. But Sir Jesper wanted to leave behind more than the obligatory paragraph in *Debrett's Peerage*.

He knew Freddy resented his singular hold on the magazine, but it was as it had always been: in families like theirs, the eldest son got everything, leaving the younger ones to find their own way. There was a cruelty to the fact the age gap could be counted in minutes rather than years, but Sir Jesper felt he had more than made up for it by taking Freddy under his wing when he had failed so spectacularly at everything else.

Of course, life had its compensations. With the sun shining and the warm spring giving way to a hot summer, what man didn't long to leave his desk and head outside to enjoy the ripening fruits? Jesper had spent most of his journey to London eyeing up a young redhead sitting across the aisle from him. By the time they had reached Dartmoor, he had poured two large gin and tonics into her and let her talk about the disappointment of her philandering soon-to-be-ex husband. Sir Jesper had convinced her she owed herself a little fun and perhaps a spot of revenge and arranged to meet her for a late supper at his London flat. But first he had to attend the launch party of a new men's magazine named *Rosebud*, apparently in homage to *Citizen Kane*. "The greatest film ever made," its new editor had clearly already tired of having to explain to his guest list.

Although not strictly invited, and although not strictly competition, Sir Jesper liked to attend magazine launches and meet the talent. He wasn't really interested in the writers, they were pretty replaceable, but he had poached quite a few talented advertising staff, who were seduced by the idea of life on the Cornish coast and working for his venerable title, especially as around half of all magazines fell at the first gate.

Among the invited guests was Albert Pitchfork, *l'enfant terrible* of the literary world. Albert – or Albie to his friends, but never, ever Bertie – had written his first novel at just 19 and it had become an overnight literary classic. His naïve characterisation of a politician who had risen to the top without ever expressing a political view had captured the liberal zeitgeist of the mid-1990s. The book, *The Man Who Wasn't There*, had also become a bizarre manifesto to wannabe politicians and pundits, almost a 'how to' guide to a successful life in public office. Within its pages, they found the secret to making it big in the world of politics. "Mostly that means avoiding any political view that could upset potential voters," Albie was fond of explaining in the interviews that generally followed each reprint.

Pitchfork had been living off his reputation and royalties ever since – as every new generation of angry young man/political hopeful discovered his work – and had freed himself up from the unrewarding slog of coming up with an equally typifying story for the current age, instead developing a reputation for wholesale savagery. No election night was complete without his snarling edifice to lay into the lack of meaning of each party's intentions or the general stupidity of the electorate; newspapers and men's magazines continued to fight over his column inches, which had allowed him to not only charge £10 per word for anything he wrote but maintain the copyright, which allowed his agent to do deals to publish collections of his columns on a biannual basis.

But Albie, turning 40 in less than a month, was feeling, like Sir Jesper, as though his chance to make his mark was slipping by. He had arrived fashionably late and draped over his primped and liposuctioned to perfection date for the evening: a reality TV star whose ghost-written biography would probably earn more than his ever would. Albie was more than aware that the book he had written 20 years ago, although about to be republished in its 19th edition with a new foreword from the author, was becoming an historical artefact. He had become a talking head, famous for being famous, no longer introduced as a prize-winning author. It was time for a change. He just hadn't yet worked out what it was going to be.

It was in this restless mood that he was introduced to Sir Jesper Donaldson, Chairman of Donaldson Publishing. It was a meeting of minds. Impressed despite himself by the gentlemanly Sir Jesper,

Albie quickly ditched Martine, a tortuously thick girl who he had dismissed as an easy shag within minutes of meeting. Instead he chatted up the publishing magnate whose talk was much sexier to his jaded ear.

For once, the talent impressed Sir Jesper. "How can I tempt you to come and write for *Compagne*?" he had asked within a few minutes of their meeting.

"*Compagne* remains the country's leading social magazine, but I'd like to create a section for men and the arts that's a little bit more biting," Sir Jesper continued, seduced by Albie's not inconsiderable charms. "Perhaps we could make you the section's editor?"

Albie nodded, taking another swig of wine, thinking about the possibilities if they joined forces: his talent and Sir Jesper's funds. But his ambitions ran to more than just a section in an already established magazine. The word 'editor' reverberated in his mind. It sounded like the opportunity he was looking for. A new magazine, with him at the helm; something totally different; where each issue was considered an instant classic. Perhaps even named after him, *Pitchfork*. No, it sounded like a 1970s Hammer Horror production.

"Why don't you launch your own magazine?" Albie asked innocently. He could work out the masthead once he had the job. Like most writers, he was a talented reader of people, and Sir Jesper was particularly transparent. 80 per cent ego, 20 per cent sex pest, Albie calculated. The latter was of little interest to him, although he had noticed the hot glances Sir Jesper kept giving Martine. Albie would be happy to introduce them when he had completed their business and got what he wanted: a fuck pro quo to seal the deal.

He chose his words carefully. "You've made a huge success out of *Compagne*, really made it your own. You can almost forget that it was your grandfather's magazine." He paused for a drink, allowing his comment to sink in. "Did you always want to work for the magazine?"

Sir Jesper paused. It was true; although he owned the magazine, in reality he did just work for it because it wasn't really his. He envied Albie the talent that had made him such a household face. Sir Jesper was so rarely recognised – on occasion even by his own staff. The desire to make his mark stirred as much as his libido had during his journey to London. The magazine launch was proving much more enjoyable than he had expected; his ego was being as expertly massaged as he expected his cock to be later in the evening.

"I'm surprised you've never added to *Compagne's* stables – turned it into a real publishing empire," Albie finally said, casually at first. "*Compagne* must be running itself by now – didn't you just get yourself a new Managing Editor?" At Sir Jesper's nod he continued. "What you need is your own magazine, maybe something for men; men like you. A completely different magazine from *Compagne;* something with balls."

Sir Jesper felt a sudden leap in his groin; Albie was saying just want he wanted to hear at the precise moment he needed to hear it. A magazine of his own, not just extending the reach of the Donaldson Publishing Company online but making it a truly global company. A men's magazine could be just the start; launch one magazine, another could follow, and then there were all those special interest magazines he regularly perused during his wait for his car to collect him at Paddington Station. He could be the new Rupert Murdoch, without the court cases and controversy, of course.

"With your skills and contacts, it could be just the start," Albie said, echoing Sir Jesper's own thoughts. He noticed a hovering waiter with a tray of garish coloured cocktails was about to interrupt to replenish their empty glasses and told him to fuck off so he could continue with his seduction unheard.

Albie paused and waited for the obvious question.

"And who would edit it?" asked Sir Jesper.

"You need a dynamic and well-known talented writer to edit the magazine, someone to bring a touch of instant celebrity. You also need someone with great contacts, who will bring you the kind of names you need to see on the cover. You want artists lining up to create something specific for the title, the greatest directors and sportsmen in the world desperate for a cover story." Albie paused again before adding, he felt somewhat redundantly, "Basically you need me."

Sir Jesper found himself nodding in agreement. It was just the thing to revive his jaded publishing palate. A magazine for men; smart, intelligent, rich men with Pulitzer Prize-level writing and photography that wouldn't look out of place in the National

Portrait Gallery. It would be huge. He would need a shit-hot advertising director and fortunately he had just the man in mind. He looked over towards the gaggle of *Rosebud* staff and picked out Mike Bell, the ad director he had already introduced himself to. With a shake and sleight of hand, he had dropped his business card into Mike's palm with a discreet "Call me, we'll talk," which had been honed over years of both marital and business infidelity.

By the end of the evening, a deal was struck. For a ludicrously high fee, Albie would head up a new literary men's magazine. It would have a small regular staff but its pages would be penned by some of the country's leading writers, illustrated by great artists and the best photographers of the age. It would combine film, art and fashion, all beautifully laid out and under the direction of a world-famous writer who would also pen a column each month. How could it fail?

Business over, Albie decided it was time to seal the deal. "Now let me introduce you to a lovely lady," he turned to his bored-looking date who had returned to his side after a long absence powdering her nose, judging by the dusting of white powder attached to her diminishing septum. "Martine, meet Sir Jesper, one of the most powerful men in the media today. And he's about to launch a new men's magazine – perhaps you could be its first cover girl?"

Martine's artificially enhanced lips curved upwards, boredom replaced by a sudden rapaciousness. Sir Jesper licked his lips as he turned on the charm. His redhead would be waiting. But as he held her hand, stroking her wrist suggestively with his thumb, he wondered if Martine would like to join them for a nightcap.

# CHAPTER 13

"Shit," Tory threw down the folder of pages for the September issue onto the coffee table and, pulling her legs from under her, pushed her feet back into her heels. She had organised a meeting with the advertising team. Recognising their more richly acquired tastes, she had taken up a table at Clancy's for lunch. This well-known den of celebrities had taken several efforts to book, but there would be no bagels and coffee in the boardroom for this group of vipers. The alarm going off on her iPhone indicated she had to be there in 25 minutes.

Arriving first, she sat and ordered water for the table. Looking at the cocktail menu above the bar, she fought an urge to order the vodka and tonic she so desperately needed. Among those invited were the Commercial Director, Advertising Director and account managers of the various sections of the magazine.

This was the second meeting she had set up. The first had been cancelled when it became clear no one would turn up. It was nothing personal, she had been assured by Grasper Lott's PA, whom she had sought out from within the Flowers of Medieval after she got her sixth refusal. "It's not personal. They just know that there's no money to be made in a meeting with you, and time is commission."

And so Tory had decided to arrange a lunch worth attending. Her email invitation had been printed out in hard copy and posted to each attendee, to their office and their home addresses. In it was the implicit promise of creating a working relationship that would increase their revenues by at least five per cent, and with it their already distended bank accounts. She had included Freddy Donaldson in the invitation; his nominal job title included a nod towards the commercial side of the business. Tory had been relieved when he had replied via his secretary to say he had a previous engagement. She had only been at *Compagne* for a few weeks but already recognised that his directorship was more constitutional than absolute. Involving him in a meeting designed to bring advertising and editorial together for the benefit of all could have been embarrassing for a man who seemed to have only a rudimentary understanding of the magazine business. But she was pleased that everyone else had finally responded enthusiastically.

The first to arrive was Johnston B Anthony – as splendid as his name, he was just as dishonest: Johnston was a creation of a man born from simpler beginnings by simply reversing the more mundane Tony Johnston. He approached the table majestically, pausing dramatically in front of the table to allow his large frame to cast a big shadow over its only occupant.

He considered himself a powerful-looking man; he liked to think his extra girth added to his gravitas rather than simply adding to his body mass index. For those around him, it meant fear that, while screaming his legendary invectives at his staff, they were in danger of being squashed like bugs. His clients also feared picking up the bill after lunch. Having assured himself that the menu at Clancy's was resplendent enough to meet his approval, he had accepted the invitation and sent out a 'recommendation' to his underlings to reply likewise.

As Commercial Director of *Compagne*, his job was simple. Make money, and lots of it. He lined the pockets of the agencies looking for cheap advertising for their clients, also those of the company, but most importantly his own. He owned a splendid Georgian mansion in London, beautifully restored by his equally beautiful wife Monique, and a gorgeous flat in the same city, adorned by an equally gorgeous mistress. But his one true love was money. And one could never have enough of one's true love.

Fortunately for Monique, the restoration of their Georgian home had kept her too busy to notice his many absences. Although twelve years younger than Johnston, she was far from being a trophy wife. Born in Portugal, she had lived in America and studied Law at Harvard before crossing the Atlantic for a year-long sabbatical at chambers in London to learn about the fathers of modern law. It was there, at the age of 24, she had met and – to the surprise of those who knew him – fallen in love with Johnston. Now four years later, her passion for him was being tested by her growing desire for children.

"But darling, we have such a wonderful life," Johnston had said to her only that morning, when she had tried to raise the subject yet again as she straddled him naked. Secretly Johnston thought she had such a wonderful body, he really didn't want to see it taken over; infected, even, by a foreign body, even if half of it was essentially him. To imagine those beautiful pert breasts, saggy and bloated with milk, the wonderful vagina that clasped him so tightly become slack and vacuous. No, he had long ago recognised that he must do all in his power to prevent it. As an only child, Johnston had never learned to share, and he certainly didn't want to start now.

"Wonderful to finally meet you," he said, leaning over to the new Managing Editor with a well-practised air kiss. He made it sound as though he had been waiting desperately for the opportunity, that seeing her had made his month. Tory grinned, totally hooked by his charm before reminding herself he was a salesman; and a good salesman recognised he was selling himself as much as any product.

"And you," she said, taking her smile down a notch. "I'm sorry to have not seen you arrive – I've just been reading about Sir Jesper's plans to launch a new men's magazine."

Johnston had no intention of leaning over her shoulder to read the email that had been sent out by their chairman that morning. He was no more than slightly curious – although he did wonder who would head up the sales team.

"What kind of men's magazine?" he asked politely.

"A sort of arts, sports, literary one. Albie Pitchfork – you know that TV pundit who wrote that book about politics in the 90s? He's going to be the editor."

"Does it have a name?"

Tory speed-read to the end of the email. "*The MacGuffin*." She pondered the bizarre name.

Johnston nodded, as though the name made perfect sense to him. He would find out more after lunch.

Next to arrive was the Advertising Director. Jasper – Grasper – Lott was on a par with Johnston within the company but as highly competitive men, one was always trying to outdo the other. Grasper had less polish but was currently earning slightly more. Like Johnston, he tended to spend most of his time in London, working with the big advertising agencies. Few companies these days handled their own marketing accounts – instead they handed them over to the greedy expertise of agencies, who created and developed their brand and supported it with the right kind of advertising in the right places. Fortunately *Compagne,* with its readership among the echelons of the rich, old and new, was a must for most of these agencies, and Grasper found there was no shortage of willing advertisers. It made his job easy and meant he could spend plenty of time enriching his favourite bookmaker.

This time Tory was ready. She stood and clashed cheeks with him as he held her hand in both of his, his face expressing abject delight at their meeting. Tory reminded herself again that she was witnessing salesmen at the top of their game. She was thankful she had resisted the vodka and tonic. She would need her wits about her.

As the table began to fill up, she nodded to the waiter to bring over the wine she had pre-ordered and to fill everyone's glasses. She had picked the resident sommelier's brains to find a suitable bottle: knowing both Johnston and Grasper's drinking habits intimately, he had plumped for a vintage burgundy, rich in body and full of fruit. There was silence as the first sip was taken and her guests rolled it around in their mouths, their pleasure writ large on their greedy faces. Tory beamed back at them. It was a great start.

The wine replenished, canapés were handed around with the menus; tiny mouthful-sized morsels of salmon and dill encased in a light pastry with a sliver of Sicilian lemon which melted in the mouth were arranged alongside delicate crostinis topped with free-range chicken liver pâté and decorated with a spot of caviar. Tory was hungry, but allowed her guests to fill their side plates first.

"I wanted to thank you for coming," she took advantage of her empty plate and their full mouths to get her opening gambit in first. "I know that time is money for you advertising guys, while editorial simply saps it. But I think if we can work more closely together and improve our relationship, we can ensure that you get what you need from editorial to maximise profits, which of course is what we are all here for."

Johnston spoke first, by dent of being the first to finish his plate. "Delighted to hear you say it. We often find that Editorial can be rather brittle in helping us out," he paused to drain his glass, simultaneously nodding at the waiter, who had been reserved especially to serve their table, to refill it. "And while many advertisers, like a wife holding her first dinner party, are most concerned with placement, some do still want to pursue editorial opportunities."

Tory nodded. "What I want to suggest is that any request for editorial is directed to me," she placed specially created business cards in front of her guests. "By offering them direct access to the editor of the magazine, your advertisers will feel their request is taken seriously, and they can be sure of a cast-iron decision on whether we can run any editorial." She paused to allow the waiter to remove the empty serving plates and replace the soiled flatware. "This system will ensure only those advertisers who are serious about editorial will contact me, but also that I can ensure our advertisers are treated as you would wish them to be. If you prefer, you can provide an email introduction to me; that way I will know which of you requires an update."

She didn't add that the cards she now handed out had been made up featuring a different email address to her own, that she had already assigned to Laura, who had an agreed process to deal with any requests in her name. She also didn't mention that the impetus had come about more to protect her editorial staff from the endless requests to add advertiser content to their Fashion features or Social pages at the last minute.

Taking a sip of her water, Tory allowed her guests to ruminate over her comments while they dissected the menu with expert eyes. The time was well spent as the waiter returned to refill glasses and take orders. Harry had recommended the fish pie, which Tory preceded with the restaurant's signature platter of exquisitely prepared crudités alongside a selection of cold sauces. Her guests were less restrained and soon the table was filled with starter dishes of *filet mignon*, grilled oysters, and langoustines, to match a new wine ordered by Grasper and approved by the rest, based on its price at £135 a bottle. Conversation became more socially oriented while Johnston and Tory shared the news with the table about *The MacGuffin*.

While Tory was more interested in the editorial content, her guests discussed the advertising revenues with glee. There was no way, they reassured themselves, that a magazine for men could even come close to the kind of numbers they were achieving with *Compagne*.

"Penis project," Grasper said dismissively, speaking for them all.

Tory thought she had misheard. "Pet project?" she asked uncertainly.

"Pe-nis project," Grasper enunciated, dragging out the two syllables. He allowed her to look confused for a moment before relenting.

"Jesper is at that age – needs to prove himself. It's the sort of random idea his brother Fredo would have had at some time or other."

Johnston agreed. "He's trying to prove his dick is bigger than his forebears'."

Tory nodded, not wanting to think about Sir Jesper's dick, and accepted with thanks her main course. A creamy potato topping sat on top of generous pieces of scallop, lobster and other fish in a lightly whipped cream sauce.

Despite working together, the advertising team mixed rarely; unlike the editorial team they had no time for gossiping over a microwaved ready meal in The Lodge's staff kitchen. All saw this as a welcome chance to catch up and show off to their peers about the latest account landed, or staff chastised for failing to reach targets. This allowed Tory to give her lunch the attention it deserved, before adding to the conversation with some made up compliments from her staff designed to ensnare the account managers into feeling appreciated by their editorial colleagues.

Johnston had relaxed enough to discuss his Georgian house restoration with her, while Grasper had the table in stitches about a former colleague given to self-administered advertising.

Tory had interrupted. "How do you self-administer advertising?"

He was only too happy to explain. "The guy was a total Walter Mitty. He would drive up and down the M4 in his company car, carefully working out what his mileage should be, while booking adverts against companies that didn't exist. It was the worst pyramid scheme you could imagine. Through a shell company he was paying all these invoices for non-existent companies advertising in the magazine, pocketing his generous mileage expenses and claiming for practically every meal he ate."

"But surely he was losing money?"

"Yes, but that's not how he was caught out. We had a number of complaints from readers saying they had tried to visit shops or websites, companies advertised in the magazine, only to find they didn't exist. When we asked him why he was doing it, he said he was too shy to call on real customers. He would sit in motorway service stations, nursing endless cups of coffee and making up ads."

"So what happened?"

"We promoted him, made him Head of Telesales."

Slowly, Tory's guests headed out of the restaurant, each one sated on three courses and, at a quick calculation, a bottle of wine each. The aim of the meeting had been achieved. Tory sat nursing her glass of dessert wine for a few minutes before throwing down her company credit card, hoping the credit limit really was £25,000.

She had met them, showed her appreciation for their hard work, and promised to maximise their commission by making it easier for advertisers to get what they wanted. It was past four, and she gave herself a little shake then asked the waiter to call for a taxi. She would go home for a short nap and back to The Lodge later to go through the pile of proofs for the September issue; thankfully the earlier pages seemed to need less work. Getting up, she handed two £20 notes to the waiter with a smile of thanks and headed outside.

Standing on the steps of the restaurant, breathing in some welcome fresh air, she felt her pay-as-you-go phone vibrate in her bag. There was only one man who had the number.

She dropped her bag in her haste to find the phone.

"Sergeant Donovan?" she said, her heart pounding.

"Miss Manders, how are you?"

"I'm well. What news do you have?"

"I know we were due to speak today so I wanted to give you a call and update you."

"Yes?" Tory wished he would skip the carefully paced build-up.

"We've found some more of him."

"Some more?"

"Of Smith."

"Where?"

"I can't say, but we now have a torso."

"But what about who's doing this? What about the men you arrested?"

"Under surveillance, but so far no leads. They are due to appear in court for breaking and entering your flat. We are trying to delay it so we can find out who they work for."

"How is my flat?"

"Empty."

"And what about the new information I gave you. Is there an infiltrator?"

"Working on it."

"How?"

"Questioning Smith's known associates — we have to go

carefully because if they did put someone undercover, they could be in real danger."

"Okay."

Donovan sighed. "I realise things are going more slowly than we had hoped, and that you are stuck down there until we can clear this up, but I'm hopeful that this new lead will give us a break."

Tory felt herself shrug. "I have to go. I'll speak to you again next week?"

"Yes." Donovan ended the connection and Tory dropped the phone back into her bag. So far they had found several body parts throughout London, but there was still no indication of whether the men behind it had any interest in her. If Smith and his gang had tried to place someone in one of these drug gangs, they may think she knew who it was. And if that was the case, she had made the right decision to move out of London for a while.

She watched the taxi pull up at the front of the restaurant, the driver getting out of the black Mercedes to open the door for her. Life in London seemed a long way away. She gave him her address and leaned back to close her eyes.

# CHAPTER 14

Beneath the tight clothes and Wonderbra'd breasts, Janice the lap-dancing nurse was surprisingly kind-hearted. She made enough money from her night job at GaGa's and online; the nursing was just a bit of extra pin money and was something she genuinely enjoyed doing. Despite her boss's assumptions, and his occasional come-ons – which she professionally repudiated without offence – she wasn't a tart, and never slept with the clients, who were usually indifferently married rowdy salesmen who enjoyed stuffing their expenses down her g-string, or lads out for a stag do.

Janice had her heavily made-up but warm brown eyes on a bigger prize.

She had become fond of Sir Jesper Senile but then his staff generally were. He combined an old world charm with the lost little boy brought on by his descent into dementia. Never violent like dementia patients could sometimes unintentionally be, he was a real sweetie – and surprisingly fit, as his own regular strip shows demonstrated. Sinewy from many years riding horses and perma-tanned from countless summers sailing, Sir J could put many of the beer-bellied, tattooed twenty-somethings she had bedded in her time to shame.

Working the late shift meant cleaning up the tea things, serving supper and getting Sir J to bed without mishap. There was a bedroom suite further down the corridor for the hired help to sleep in. Lady Rose had installed a pressure sensor in Sir Jesper Senior's bed that set off an alarm in the staff bedroom if he got up for any reason.

It was Janice's favourite shift. There were no visitors, and she loved drawing his bath; the wonderful smell of his lemony cologne discordant with the ripe stench of over-sprayed Lynx she was used to at GaGa's. She would set out his freshly laundered silk pyjamas on his bed, straighten and sometimes clean the ivory-backed brushes which sat on a polished silver tray on the tallboy, and pull up a chair outside the bathroom so she could listen in and ensure he was safe. Sometimes they would talk and sometimes he would let her shave him, carefully using the ivory-handled open cut razor he handled with amazing dexterity.

Janice quietly cleared the remnants of tea, which included several smashed china side plates, from the floor. She had learned it was easier to ignore any breakages until Sir J was safely in the tub and she could clean without him becoming distressed at his clumsiness, but today she wanted a clean floor. Lady Rose had insisted that despite these mishaps, Sir Jesper Senior should continue to be served his meals on fine china befitting his social standing. Lady Rose generally chose the least precious of the Donaldson collection, although Janice had heard the housekeeper mention that some of the more precious pieces had disappeared recently. Everyone assumed Sir J had become more clumsy and learned to hide it.

Many people saw looking after people with dementia as a thankless task, but Janice genuinely enjoyed it. Unlike relatives, she didn't take the memory lapses personally, and was able to talk to her patients normally during their lucid moments and switch to the non-confrontational neutral tones and subjects when confusion appeared. She had taken on the job at The Glades after working in a state-run home, which had also been her mother's home for the last year of her life. It had sometimes been distressing, but more often inspiring. When her mum died, she had wanted to move on and had seen an intriguing advert in the *Nursing Times* for a private nurse, discretion vital.

During her three months in the job, she had come to know Sir J well. She never referred to her patients by their Christian names unless specifically asked to, and would never use the nickname he was given below stairs, no matter how benignly it was meant. Instead she spent hours talking to him, and listening, learning a lot about the world of publishing, his experiences of life, his fascinating insight into the landed gentry that had ruled England for many centuries. He had even helped her to invest some of her considerable lap dancing funds in the stock market, netting her a tidy profit. Janice was house-hunting and they spent many hours sitting on his sofa, her iPad propped on her lap as they looked at potential homes together. It was very intimate.

Today though, she had a special treat in mind. It was a bit risky, and she wasn't really sure if it was legal, but a man had needs, regardless of his state of mind.

"Good evening Sir Jesper," she trilled, waiting for him to turn and see whether there was any recognition in his face. She smiled widely when she saw his eyes light up. "I had a great idea for us to do tonight. I thought I could teach you how to take your clothes off!"

Sir Jesper Senior looked confused, "I know how to bloody undress myself, woman," he told her in his gruff tone. "I'm not an invalid."

In his moments of lucidity, he fought to regain independence, something Janice understood only too well.

Janice pulled out her iPad, flicking to the music she had already lined up. "Not that kind of undressing," she told him.

She pressed 'play' and the irresistible first notes of Ravel's *Boléro* blasted out. Taking Sir J's hand, she pulled him to his feet. "Now first we begin with the tease. No point taking your clothes off if no one is looking." She swung her hips enticingly and looked over at him. "Now it's your turn."

Sir J swung with surprising fluidity.

"Very good," Janice said, "now eye contact is very important." She moved to stand opposite him. "Looks can be everything."

Looking him square in his faded blue eyes, she continued to move her hips.

Sir Jesper swayed his hips with her. "You know, in my day, we were encouraged to go elsewhere for our pleasures. The wife was for breeding purposes only. I rather liked her, but separate rooms were the norm, and you almost had to book an appointment, no chance for any spontaneity. One of my greatest regrets."

Janice, keen to dispel any unhappy memories, continued her lesson. "Right, now we move on to the de-robing. Always start at the top."

She continued to swing her hips, turning to wiggle her bottom at Sir J, and beginning to undo the buttons on her prim uniform shirt as she turned back to him. He watched her, fascinated, as the shirt was pulled from her skirt and discarded onto the sofa.

"Your turn."

Sir J turned and wriggled his bottom before turning to face her and flamboyantly attacking the buttons on his own shirt.

Finally they were both down to their underwear, and now Janice was outside her level of experience. She could see Sir J was excited and, if she was honest, she could feel her own juices flowing. If she could keep him with her long enough, she would be in luck.

Ravel had hit his crescendo long before Sir Jesper reached his own climax. Janice sat straddling him on the damask sofa. Her fingers continued to work at her clitoris and she arched herself onto him as she came.

She opened her eyes to look into his, but they were dulled over; she had lost him again. He seemed oblivious to his now shrinking cock inside her.

"So," he said brightly, no sign of recognition in his eyes. "What are we having for supper?"

Janice gently uncorked herself from him and reached for her shirt. "We have some lovely smoked salmon," she replied, her voice neutral.

After supper, Sir Jesper rose from his seat. "Bed, I think," he said, heading towards his room, stopping briefly in front of her to pull her to her feet and lead her into his room. She must remember to request nights next week, she thought, suppressing a giggle.

# CHAPTER 15

In the converted stables of The Lodge, the sub-editors and designers were creating the fifth set of mock-up covers for *The MacGuffin*.

Albie Pitchfork was currently directing operations from his bachelor pad in London's South Bank, until his Newquay penthouse overlooking Fistral Beach was ready for him and his collection of classic Danish-designed furniture. His emails and phone calls were testing their patience to the limit. He had asked for a masthead and dummy cover that could be used for the magazine while it was being created. The dummy would be featured in press releases, in advertising packs and online, so it was vital to get it right even though no one would ever see it on the newsstand. Albie had managed to negotiate a very early print date and, assuming a blank cheque, had begun buying up talent the minute Sir Jesper had left the *Rosebud* launch, clutching Martine the reality star tightly by the waist.

Matt had been commandeered from his *Compagne* online rescue mission to design a new cutting edge website for *The MacGuffin*. This was far more up his street and he was able to test out – and buy - a few pieces of interactive and expensive software that he wanted to use for Horseface. He had even managed to work in a reference to Alfred Hitchcock's *The 39 Steps*, which had used his plot device the MacGuffin so successfully, into the home page. Of course Matt shared the view of the donkeys – it was still a stupid name. But who was he to talk? He had yet to think of a more appropriate name for his own site.

Donkeys were widely regarded as those who did the most work and got the least reward, and the subs were responsible for turning the content generated by the writers and photographers into glamorous word-perfect spreads within an unputdownable publication. Chief sub Daniella Davidson was known as Double D, despite her athletic body and boyishly flat chest, and was the only one who spoke directly to the editorial team. This was less power trip, more selfless sacrifice, as she shielded her staff from the histrionics of the various senior editors and their outlandish requests.

Social Editor Sophie Dexter-Browning regularly screamed for heavy Photoshopping of the jowls, red veins and fleshy upper arms of the ruling classes featured in her spreads, while Royal Editor Timothy Cornell-Johnes was equally vicious about any minor alteration to his prose. Often all that was required was a bland agreement to his requests and a suitable period of waiting, followed by the same proof being sent back upstairs. So it was a surprise to Double D to find the new Managing Editor sitting at her desk when she arrived back from her daily 15-minute lunch break run around the grounds of The Lodge. Grabbing a towel she kept in her desk drawer and cleaning the sweat that had accumulated on her brow and at the base of her spine, she nodded an hello and awaited the inevitable criticism of the latest pages sent up that morning.

Tory stood up from behind the giant screen that dominated Double D's desk and held out her hand, recognising Daniella from the brief introduction at her drinks reception on her first day.

"I just wanted to say hello, properly," she said, smiling. "I'm sorry I've not been to see you properly before now, but there's been a lot to do."

Daniella took the proffered hand and smiled back. "Welcome to *Compagne*. Settling in okay?"

Tory's smile widened. "Kind of. I was hoping for a quick run-through of what you guys do down here. I'm from newspapers so I am familiar with the subs, but your designers have a mammoth task each month, I'm guessing. Especially keeping that lot happy," her eyes moved left to indicate where the editorial team was housed.

"All part of the service," Daniella offered. Her eyes turned back to her enormous screen, which was now filled with a new image behind the masthead of *The MacGuffin*, that of Albie Pitchfork at his most smouldering.

"Are you going to be putting that together as well?" Tory asked.

Daniella shook her head. "We're not good enough – apparently he's got a whole team together who will be setting up their own enclave on the grounds."

Tory nodded, relieved. Used to newspapers' ability to see how far a sub-editor could stretch, she was concerned that the celeb would seduce away the best designers and leave *Compagne* with a few interns.

"I guess you have enough on your hands anyway," Tory gestured to the print-out of A3 proofs that had been returned to her already covered in red pen. Many of the editors seemed to proof on paper and return them to the subs to input the changes. Tory wondered if she could get them some training to make amendments themselves. Anything that would improve relations. She changed tack. "I understand from our planning meeting that you are not usually invited to attend."

Daniella nodded her agreement.

"So how do you usually find out about the next issue's content?"

"I get a list emailed down to me after the previous one goes to print. It usually has a features list and pagination, so we can start work on designing the pages and wait for content to drop into our system."

"And do you generally have any problems with that list? Who do you talk to?"

"I email the editor in question. Sometimes they answer, sometimes we have to wait until the content arrives to find out the answer. For example, we may need to confirm if it's a right-hand start feature so we can build the pages."

Tory frowned, and jotted the information down. "You're the expert here, but it sounds like we could arrange things a little better. What about the planners?"

Daniella shrugged. "They are kept busy by advertising demands, editorial is assigned to pages in the last few days before we go to print."

"The design and look of the magazine is as important as the content, and by involving you from the off, it may help your team and mine. I wonder if you would agree to come along to our planning meetings? I've sent you an email invite." Tory paused. When no answer was forthcoming she added, "Breakfast is included."

Daniella nodded again. "Okay. I may even have some suggestions on how to lay out some of the features if I know earlier on what's coming in."

"Great." Tory nodded in satisfaction. "I think that the reader would benefit from having an idea of where to find their favourite sections each month. Perhaps if I put together a master running order of features, we could create a dummy plan that we work from each month. I'll have a word with the planning team."

Daniella looked at her computer screen, Albie Pitchfork's face still smouldering at her. She fought an urge to type dummy text all over it: the graphic design equivalent of drawing fangs and devil horns.

Tory smiled. "Well, I'll see you at the next meeting. Thanks again."

Daniella stared after her for a moment, ignoring the ringing of her phone. The Royal Editor had been sent a new proof of the Prince's recent visit to the West Country and was no doubt champing at the bit because his words had been cut again. She sighed and waited until it started again before picking up. "Hello Timothy, what do you need?"

Daniella dropped the phone onto her desk, returning instead to *The MacGuffin* cover. She copied over the latest cover lines Albie Pitchfork had written, mostly a promise of what the magazine was going to offer up: everything, it would seem. Attaching the image to an email, she forwarded it on to Pitchfork with a brief message. *'I think this is the image to go for: strong, decisive and indicative of what your readers can expect.'*

She pressed 'send' and picked the phone back up. Gusher had finished his rant and slammed down the phone, so she replaced her receiver.

"Double D, you're wasted here," her nearest neighbour had been watching her deal with the varying demands. "You should be in the Foreign Office."

"Foreign Legion," Daniella joked back. "Now get back to work."

"Yes boss."

# CHAPTER 16

The house always looked at its best when filled with guests, thought Lady Rose as she swept down the stairs, resplendent in a simple but superbly-cut cream silk suit set off by a single string of pearls around her neck. She walked through the hall, pausing to clash cheeks with the surgically enhanced cheekbones of several of her guests. Her eyes took in everything as she walked through the downstairs rooms, noting a drooping oriental lily in one corner ruining a display and a wallflower in a cheap dress and clashing lipstick looking uncomfortable as she clutched an empty champagne flute by the front door. Deciding the lily was more important, Lady Rose headed for the Sèvres vase first.

The housekeeping assistant, Lydia Pootle, had noticed the lily too but the wallflower was below her notice; someone of no importance. Lydia was an avid reader of the magazines usually found on supermarket checkout stands, making her an invaluable source to her employer by providing information about the B, C and DD-list celebrities who were occasionally invited to parties at The Glades.

Today she had already helped to identify a couple of actors and a supermodel who had turned up at the garden party that was always held at The Glades at midsummer. Sir Jesper liked to enliven these events with a few glamorous types, which helped ensure they got a mention in the diaries of the national newspapers. In turn, celebrities were always desperate to get added to the Donaldsons' guest list.

"Lovely party darling, as always," Lady Bowe, an old neighbour, stopped Rose with a slight touch to her forearm en route to the orangery.

"Thank you. You look divine, as always." The last said because Lady Bowe had worn the same outfit to her garden party as last year. Lady Rose wondered if she was having trouble paying her dressmaker's bills. If so, she might be able to introduce Godfrey to Lady Bowe's attic this year. It was a natural progression of any business to want to expand, and hers was no different. She often thought she could help out neighbours, in return for a small cut of course.

Lydia wandered through the house checking guests and mentally noting who was talking to whom.

"The best thing about my job," she was fond of telling people in her local pub, where she liked to go after work, "is the grade-A gossip."

What she didn't add was that top of that list was the extra income she generated by calling her sister-in-law who worked for *Wow!* magazine to share the gossip with their loyal readers. *Wow!* was one of the most successful of the so-called checkout-stand magazines. Brenda was the receptionist, but a quick call to her usually meant £100 finding its way into Lydia's bank account, coinciding with print day. Of course Lady Rose knew she did it, but as long as Lydia didn't spread anything about the family, it wasn't an issue. Lady Rose knew better than most that a woman needed a little extra-curricular cash and, like Sir Jesper, she recognised the worth of a high national media profile, even if it was in the kind of magazine that would never grace the antique occasional table in The Glades library.

That particular day Lydia had already spotted Yarriah, the high profile supermodel, purging in the downstairs loo. Probably not big news in itself, but with the added ingredient (no pun intended but she was sure the headline writers at *Wow!* could use it) that she had been named as spokeswoman for the Campaign for Real Women's Bodies (better known as 'real bods') launched by some of the worst offenders of using size zero bodies in the industry, and in which she was quoted as saying she was naturally slim and ate like a horse. *'Size zero supermodel admits: I can't get enough of chips and brown sauce'* ran the headline in a broadsheet only the previous week, prompting a million sarcastic tweets. Allegedly one salubrious website had pledged £10,000 to the campaign if they uploaded a video of the model eating an entire bag of chips. Perhaps not unsurprisingly, the campaign's online channel remained unpopulated.

There were several photographers stalking the rooms, looking for photo opportunities that would grace *Compagne's* society pages and Lydia could ask one to take a photo that they could sell on and split the profits. But that would all have to wait, as Lydia spotted one of the servers taking a not-sneaky-enough nip of the champagne she was meant to be serving. It was the one who had turned up for work that morning complete with knee-high boots, ripped tights and too much black eye make-up. Lydia knew how Lady Rose liked things to be run. She would be calling the agency in the morning to complain.

"I can see what you are doing," she spoke quietly but firmly three inches from the young woman's overly pierced ear. "But worse still, so can the guests."

The waitress kept her eyes on the floor. "I didn't," she faltered, hardly bothering to lie.

Lydia ignored it. "I suggest you go into the kitchen and help dish out the nibbles, if you can do it without eating them of course."

The waitress nodded and handed over the silver salver of champagne flutes before turning around and picking her way through the chiffoned guests. To all outward appearances she appeared suitably chastised, while those guests who cared to look more closely, of which there were none, would see a rather different view.

"I'm just heading for the kitchen, over." The young girl spoke in a low tone, apparently to no one. She listened to a voice in her ear. "Yes, confirmed." She disappeared into the kitchen.

The midsummer garden party was a long-standing tradition with a guest list which had grown and changed through the ages. The Donaldsons' home and extensive gardens were opened to anyone who bought their tickets with a sizeable donation to a local charity – this year it was the local hospice. For most of the guests, it wouldn't matter if it went to a Save the Grey Squirrel fund: the £150 ticket gave almost unlimited access to one of the finest homes in the country and almost guaranteed inclusion in the eight pages of coverage which invariably appeared in the next issue of *Compagne*. Of course, these days money had no social filter so to keep the chavs, WAGs and nous-nous to a minimum, Sir Jesper and Lady Rose had final say on entrants, through an automatic 'sold out until checked out' policy for all but the most select names.

Having dealt with the drooping lily, Lady Rose headed for the wallowing wallflower, introducing herself and asking a few questions which revealed she had been stood up. Rose kindly offered to show her around the house; only the downstairs rooms, of course. Her kindness didn't extend to ignoring her other guests and she invited a few additional people, including the new Managing Editor of *Compagne,* to join the impromptu tour. Tory smiled her acceptance. Anything that would take her away from the throng and the forced conversation was welcome.

Neither Lady Rose nor Tory noticed the waitress re-enter the room, her hair now brushed to her shoulders and uniform covered by a black silk dress coat.

Sir Jesper had gathered a group together in the drawing room, holding forth as he told some favourite stories about the house and its many predecessors. He had managed to collect around him the party's most beautiful women, and was already planning which ones he would invite to a more private tour of The Glades when his wife left for one of her regular trips to Gibraltar.

"The duke absolutely loathed the king, apparently," he was saying, roaring with laughter. "Miss Drake, can I get you a refill?" he paused to catch the eye of the nearest server and with a small nod got the glass of the young star of TV's *Reality Bites* refilled. Several others in his audience took advantage and raised their near-empty glasses, determined to get their money's worth. "So the king arrived with all his pomp and ceremony and the third duke instructed the maids to blow out all the candles and ignore the door.

"Somehow he got away with it and the king and his entourage got back on their horses and headed off to stay at the hunting lodge on the estate instead. The next morning he returned, and was met with a similar response. The third duke," Sir Jesper raised his glass to a portrait of his anti-royal ancestor sitting on the wall among his relatives on the walls of the hall, "treated the head of the free world like a double glazing salesman and got away with it."

"But why wouldn't he want the king to stay?" Miss Drake was eager to hear more. Her rise to fame had been sudden as she emerged as the unlikely winner of *Reality Bites* – a TV show in which celebrity wannabes were given charge of a range of ever bigger and more frightening mammals. Suzie Drake had won after sharing her bedsit in Crawley with a man-eating lion.

"Rumour had it, it was over a young lady. What else?"

Sir Jesper used the ensuing laughter to excuse himself. "I must go and find my wife," he said and headed off, nominally in search of Lady Rose.

"You look wonderful, always so relaxed, and at ease," Lady Bowe had appeared again. *Appearances can be deceptive*, Lady Rose thought to herself with the first genuine smile of the afternoon.

It was only later she remembered what had bothered her so during the afternoon. She had spotted something not quite right at the party. A few members of serving staff who clearly had no idea how to serve drinks or pour champagne. Too many sticky glasses which had been carelessly allowed to overflow, drenching the delicate manicured fingers of the guests. It wasn't the waste that bothered her - the champagne at these events was never served at the right temperature, so they could afford to go with an inferior year – but it wasn't in keeping with the environs; like running out of toilet paper in Buckingham Palace. She would speak to Lydia and ask her to have a word with the agency. Make sure they were not used again.

# CHAPTER 17

Jack Ramsden's heart sank as he entered the living room. The wedding photograph albums were lying open on the coffee table again. *Shit*, he said silently to himself.

Despite being exhausted by the time he finished for the day, Jack was beginning to dread coming home. It was always the same fucking thing lately. Home was meant to be a place of relaxation and respite; and so was marriage. But both were becoming a source of tension and, he hated to admit it, terror.

At least he had learned not to say anything; he only seemed to make it worse. Last weekend he had sat down with his wife, pulled open one of the albums and looked through them with her, remembering a nice day, spent with friends.

"I think you looked really pretty," he had said, tracing the laughing face of his bride with his index finger. The moment the words had left his mouth, he knew they were a mistake.

"Pretty? Fucking pretty? I wasn't a nine-year-old bridesmaid," Lucy slammed the photo album shut. "I was the fucking bride. I should have been beautiful."

He had learned that it was always best to let her wear herself out with these rants. But today he really had had enough. He didn't want to point out that he had managed to get his long-time deputy and friend, L'il, to cover for him at the restaurant all day so he could come home and cook his wife all her favourite things. Since she had taken on the Weddings Editor job at *Compagne*, she had become obsessed.

He would be lying if he said that there had never been an issue. There had always been a glimmer of disappointment. They were among the first of their friends to tie the knot and then over the years, as more of their friends joined the ranks of the happily married, they attended other weddings, and each one was compared to theirs with increasingly irrational envy on his wife's side, especially when many of those marriages had ended in divorce long before the loans taken out to pay for the wedding had even been paid off.

Jack sighed and returned to the kitchen. Over the years he had heard it all: his suit should have been Armani, her dress by Vera Wang, their wedding rings should have been bespoke creations in titanium.

About a year ago he had noticed that her engagement ring had been replaced with a platinum ring containing a giant pearl. It was an antique, she had said vaguely, left to her by an ancient aunt she hadn't seen since she was a child. But he knew the truth the instant he saw it on the fourth finger of her left hand. The diamond in her engagement ring was half a carat. At the time he had given it to her, it had cost three times his monthly wages and she had seemed pretty pleased with it when he had proposed while they were out celebrating their first anniversary. But it had become like so much about their life together, simply not good enough.

After almost ten years, the only thing that still stung was her constant assertion that the food served at their wedding had been naff. This despite the fact he had spent a great deal of time creating the dishes for their barbecue: marinades for the meats and vegetable kebabs; handmade breads and various salsas and accompaniments, all made by him in the days leading up to the big day, a labour of love for his soon-to-be wife. And their friends had loved it. Their wedding had been simple, unpretentious and fun.

He stirred the sauce. The shallots and garlic had all but dissolved and it was time for him to add the peas. It was a dish he had first made for Lucy when they met. Both were only a few days away from their respective paydays and had decided to pool the contents of their fridges to test his skills in coming up with a three-course dinner. It had been a memorable meal. Although the baked chocolate Shreddies surprise pudding hadn't featured on a menu since, the pasta puttanesca had been a great success. Leftover spring onions and garlic, a wizened chilli, a splash of yoghurt from one side of a Fruit Corner, frozen peas, slices of slightly out-of-date pepperoni and a hit of vodka had all gone into the pot.

For today's menu, Jack had swapped the onions for shallots, the pepperoni for pancetta, and there was freshly made rosemary bread instead of the stale loaf that he had sprinkled with a dribble of left over olive oil (his) and table salt (hers) and rubbed with garlic before baking in serried ranks of soldiers. The dried supermarket value brand spaghetti had been modified. Instead, the sauce would dress the fresh pasta he had made that morning and which was hanging from the hooks he had inserted into the ceiling until it was ready to add to the salted and seasoned water.

The meal mellowed her mood. She smiled at the menu he had written out on the linen-clothed table set out with the few wedding presents she hadn't replaced with better. But the real gift was still to come. He had decided to serve up the surprise with dessert.

"Lucy, I know you've always felt that our wedding was a disappointment to you," he began as she put her fork and spoon down on her empty plate. "We are both doing really well now and I thought, perhaps, we could have a big party to celebrate our tenth anniversary in a few months. You could get your hair done, buy a new dress – I could even get that Armani suit you're always saying would look so good on me. What do you think?"

Lucy's eyes lit up, her mind racing. "I think it's amazing. I even know the perfect venue."

Jack nodded. "I think the restaurant would be a great place to do it."

"I was thinking more of Tremere Castle. It's not actually available as a wedding venue, but I met the owners when their daughter married there last month – it's the cover story of our new issue in fact. They have this amazing hallway where you can greet guests with champagne and canapés - I know just the place to get those – there's that incredible little oyster farm in Rock, very exclusive. What's the budget?"

Jack blinked in the intensity of her gaze. Of course he knew Rock, the restaurant used their oysters. But a light had suddenly been switched on in her. "I'm not sure. I mean, we're doing okay. But I'm investing quite heavily in the London Ramsden's at the moment. What do you think?"

"To have anything even remotely decent, you need to budget at least £70,000. And a wedding like this has to be perfect."

"But we're already married. This is a party. I can do the food, and you can just sort out your hair and dress and stuff."

"But what if it was a wedding?"

"You mean like a renewal of vows type of thing?" Jack rubbed the back of his head, an unconscious gesture when he was under stress. He had been doing it a lot lately. It had always irritated Lucy, the way he rubbed his palm across his hair, leaving it sticking up at the back. She had always thought of it as fucking hair – when the hair at the back became mussed from lying down having sex. She knew Jack's reply would be that there wasn't much chance of fucking hair recently.

Lucy thought about it. "Okay."

But already she was wondering if maybe this could be her second chance: to finally have the wedding of her dreams, the wedding she deserved.

"I'm not sure about where we would get that kind of money."

Lucy wasn't listening. She was wondering if it was too late to nip back to the office for the wedding ideas list she kept there. She would need to contact Lord and Lady Marack in the morning to secure some dates with them. And there was that gorgeous Highland florist from that wedding in Scotland she had attended earlier in the year. They made one-off designs that had won countless awards. She would need to revisit them to discuss some of her ideas. Her last wedding had featured red roses. This time she wanted something a bit more original. She ignored Jack's frown and the dirty crockery and headed upstairs in search of a pad and pen. She had a wedding to arrange in six weeks. And it was going to be perfect.

She paused halfway up the stairs. She and Jack would need to be single for it to count as a real wedding. She looked down towards the dining room where Jack was probably still sitting. Should she ask?

# CHAPTER 18

Freddy Donaldson had made his decision. Since his father had revealed that the twins might be in the wrong order, every conversation he had with Jesper had taken on new meaning. Now he was reporting his progress on the acquisition of a small publishing company, specialising in farming titles, which he had practically had to beg Jesper to invest in. Jesper had insisted on looking over the figures before committing himself, despite Freddy being, among other things, responsible for all special projects.

Sir Jesper had announced the acquisition, congratulating himself and the company that had gone from strength to strength since his leadership. *It should have been me.* Freddy couldn't get the words out of his head. *It should have been me.* And now he was going to reveal all.

Seeing Jo nip off for an illicit cigarette, Freddy headed towards his brother's office, opening the door without ceremony. "We need to talk."

Sir Jesper looked up; irritation quickly masked by a welcoming smile that fooled nobody. "Freddy, dear boy, no time. Off to a meeting." He didn't add that he was celebrating with an illicit date with a brunette he had met at a recent charity luncheon. She was married to one of his old school chums, who Sir Jesper had never forgiven for disclosing a bedwetting incident during his first week at Prep while at a social event many years ago. Now his significantly younger wife would be spreading largesse and her legs within the next few hours.

"Jesper, this is important."

Sir Jesper sat down, surprised. His brother was usually mild-mannered, and his insistent tone had instant effect.

"Okay," he looked at the antique Rolex on his right wrist. Freddy noticed it had been his father's, no doubt something else that had been passed down to his 'eldest' son. "I can give you ten minutes."

Freddy stayed standing, fighting the urge to pace up and down in front of his brother's desk. His big brother, he had always thought of him. "Father told me something recently, and I have been thinking about what it means."

"Dad? Is he okay?"

"Fine, same as. But he told me you are not the elder twin."

Jesper mis-heard, his mind on his father and the visit he was overdue to make, and carried on with his train of thought. "He seems quite settled, the staff say. The new nurse has been a great success."

"Jesper! Did you hear what I said? You are not the eldest."

Jesper eyed his brother, wondering what he was talking about. What his latest fad was. "What do you mean?"

"Dad told me, I don't think he meant to say it, but maybe he felt the need to finally admit it."

"Dad told you what?"

"That you are not the eldest son, that you got The Glades, the estate and all the family money, when it should have gone to me."

Jesper paused, thoughts of his lunchtime assignation forgotten. "Dad said this?"

"Yes."

"He won't have known what he was saying – he must have thought he was talking to me."

"No. He said that they didn't know who came first," Sir Jesper started to interrupt, to ask how that was possible, but Freddy shouted him down. "I know, I know, I asked how it could happen when we looked so different, but Mum wasn't well and there was confusion, and he said they didn't know who came out first."

"Did anyone else hear him?"

"That new nurse was there, but I'm not sure she was listening."

Sir Jesper tapped his index fingers on his desk, a sign of nerves. "What do you expect me to do?"

"You got all this," Freddy gestured around the room, but it was clear that 'this' referred to beyond the four walls of Sir Jesper's splendid office.

"And you think it should be yours?"

Freddy shrugged. "It could be."

Jesper nodded. It was better to settle this quickly. Freddy had a tendency to let things fester. "Well, we'd better speak to Dad."

"Now? What about your meeting?"

"It can wait." He stood and led the way out into the car park.

At his car, Sir Jesper paused, keys in hand, eyeing his brother. Thinking, remembering. A night-time vigil at his mother's bed, her need to tell him something, her confusion about which one of her sons was before her. Confusion, expected and unexceptional given the morphine pump then attached to her arm, providing pain relief from the cancer which had invaded her organs. Jesper shook his head, letting the memory fade. It didn't prove anything. "Come on Freddy, let's see what Dad has to say."

They drove the few miles to The Glades in silence, each imagining their lives if they had been different. Freddy remembering a childhood summer holiday when he had read *The Man in the Iron Mask*, and fantasised about the removal of his brother from his elder son's throne into a dark prison room. Of course the mask would be unnecessary because they weren't identical, and that would prove a difficulty when it came to replacing him. But it had been an enjoyable summer romance. Now he wondered if it would prove to be prophetic.

Heading for the private entrance to their father's suite, the brothers knocked loudly and waited for admittance. Jesper wondered if Janice was on duty. He hadn't given up the idea of having a crack at her. She had the most splendid pair of tits he had ever seen. But other than the occasional heavy flirting during his visits to see his father – and a couple of visits to her lap dancing club incognito – he had left her alone.

He waited and knocked again, wondering if his father had been taken out for the day. Finally, a cleaner opened the door. Confusion and fear mingled in her face as she recognised her guests.

"Sir Jesper, Mr Donaldson, is he back already?"

"Who?" asked Freddy.

"Sir Jesper Senior," she said his name carefully, not wanting to accidentally use his nickname.

"Is our father not here?" It wasn't unusual for Sir Jesper Senior to go out for a walk with his nurse, but his lunch was generally being served at this time of day.

"No, we haven't seen him."

"Since when?"

"Last night, well tea-time."

"Tea-time?" Freddy's voice rose. "Why weren't we informed?"

"It was only noticed when the staff came on this morning, I think."

"And where is last night's nurse? Who was it?"

"Janice. She arrived and took over at six yesterday evening."

Freddy pushed his way into the flat, wondering if his brother had hidden their father away so he couldn't question him. But how would he have known?

"I want all the staff up here immediately," Sir Jesper went into elder son mode. "I want someone to get hold of this Janice, and find out where she is. Our father is confused and may be lost somewhere on the grounds. I want the groundsmen and gardeners rounded up to start looking for my father. Now."

The cleaner raced off to follow the instructions.

Freddy turned to his brother. "Where is he?"

Sir Jesper frowned, rubbing his forehead. "He must have got out and gone for a walk, maybe got lost."

"But where's his nurse?"

"She might be out looking for him already, scared to tell anyone she lost him; or maybe she did a runner when she realised he was missing."

"This is your doing – why on earth would you hire a stripper? This wouldn't have happened if I'd been in charge." Freddy regretted the words as soon as he said them – this was no time to score cheap points. And even as he said it he wondered what he would have done with his father. Probably put him in a home.

Jesper opened his mouth to snap something back but paused, taking a deep breath and exhaling loudly. "There is no point in us snarling at each other. Dad has a habit of escaping, you know that. We'll find him, and then we can talk to him. After making sure he's alright."

Freddy nodded, his legs giving way suddenly as he sat on the sofa. He was scared for his dad, he felt powerless.

Sir Jesper turned to him, putting his hands on his shoulders. "I'll find him," he promised, looking him in the eye.

"Right," he told the returning cleaner, mindful of his father's habits of disrobing, "I'll need a blanket and a spare set of clothes: trousers, shirt, socks and shoes."

She nodded her assent and headed for the bedroom.


The staff began to arrive. Gardeners stood at the back, unwilling to leave mud trails on the carpeting, awaiting instructions.

"Our father seems to have had a breakout at some point during the night or this morning, I'd like you to all scour the grounds and find him. As many of you know, he may be confused, so please be gentle; no shouting or anything that might make him scared," Sir Jesper stumbled slightly over the word, suddenly seeing his father cowering naked like an animal, lost, frightened, alone.

Freddy stood up. "Find him. Please."

The staff nodded and walked out, discussing who would look where. The grounds were sizeable, but it wasn't the first time Sir Jesper Senile had escaped and they were confident of bringing him back unharmed.

# CHAPTER 19

Knowing it couldn't last had made it all the sweeter. Sir J's skills in bed were a revelation but just as importantly, they were having fun; he would rise when she entered the room, greet her fondly and whisk her into a waltz or, even better, into his bedroom. But sometimes a whole shift would pass and he would have no memory of her. Then she would follow the usual routine as a carer but couldn't resist sneaking into the ancient four-poster bed next to him as he slept, always remembering to set the alarm on her phone to ensure she was up and appropriately dressed, her charge up and wrapped in his silk dressing gown, before the 8am breakfast was served. Sometimes the alarm wasn't needed and she awoke to find him pulling her towards him for a spot of early morning love-making.

Sir J seemed to understand that their relationship needed to remain illicit. Perhaps he thought she was a long-lost lover. Janice hoped that at some level he knew her, even during those long nights when his behaviour suggested otherwise, but her experience at the home she had previously worked in meant she knew the truth deep down. All those tearful and often shouting relatives who refused to believe that their mum, dad, brother or wife didn't know them, but were somehow pretending; that they could be reminded if only they could say the right thing, show the right photograph or keepsake.

In her most fantastical thoughts, Janice imagined moving in together but her flat was tiny, about the size of the guest suite at The Glades, and she knew part of Sir J's good behaviour was due to his familiar surroundings. The furniture, she knew, had been moved from other parts of the house, specifically chosen by Lady Rose to remind him of his beloved home.

It was easy, then, to be seduced when he matter-of-factly said one evening, "I think we should make this legal."

She was straddling him on his four-poster, her right breast in his hand. She smiled neutrally, blaming her recent exertions for her suddenly hammering heart. Was he talking to her? Or had he flicked back 50 years to the day he proposed to his first wife?

"Okay," she finally croaked, unhooking herself from him and reaching for his silk pyjama top. "I'll run your bath."

He followed her into the bathroom naked. Despite being in his 70s – she didn't want to know exactly where – he really did have an incredible physique. Not for the first time she wondered if what she was doing was wrong. Sometimes she thought the other staff knew what was going on – how could they not? But for most people it seemed age and dementia effectively stripped someone of their sexuality. People simply couldn't imagine that a man with his condition had any sexual attraction.

Her relationship with Sir J would probably get her struck off the nursing register, but she had been reading up on the internet about the sexual needs of dementia patients – there was growing discussion about how often sexual desire came to the fore with this group and some nurses on bulletin boards had discussed why they shouldn't be allowed to satisfy this need, like they did other appetites, with some admitting calling in prostitutes.

"I do mean it, Janice." She loved it when he called her by her name. It felt so intimate, so personal. And it was all the more precious for its rarity. "You name the day, but make it soon, because I'm getting on a bit." He tested the temperature of the water with his hand before nimbly climbing in and lying back.

"Join me?" he asked, eyebrow raised, his cock jauntily rising above the water level.

Janice laughed and began to unbutton the pyjama top she had taken from the bedroom, relieved to be on safer ground.

After taking the breakfast things down to the kitchen, Janice would usually head straight off after her shift. Instead, she decided to do a bit of research, in case Sir J raised the subject of marriage again. She flicked on the kettle and asked Harriet, the cook, if she wanted one.

"Go on then. Everything alright upstairs?"

"Fine."

"He seems to have become really settled recently, much more malleable – happy even – the other staff said."

"Really?" Janice felt pleasure flood her veins. She liked to think she had something to do with it.

"Freddy came to see him recently."

"That's right, I was there."

"Freddy left a bit upset, I think. It always hits the children the hardest."

Harriet was a ruddy-faced round woman, who had been with the family for decades and had worked her way up from kitchen portering to Head of Menus. She was a bit of a gossip.

"He tells some great stories about the two boys," Janice said, "It's a shame he doesn't remember more often when they are around. Sir Jesper's the eldest isn't he?"

"Yes, the two boys are twins – did you know that?"

Janice frowned, "No, no I didn't."

"Hard for Freddy, but that's how these big families work. Jesper got The Glades and the estate and even the magazine company. Mind you, Freddy's never been very successful in business, poor love – or in love, I suppose." She laughed at her barely-there linguistic pun.

"But it does come at a cost, doesn't it? Sir Jesper's responsible for the family now."

"Yes, he's become his father's legal guardian, and he had to find a job for Freddy; you know they call him Fredo next door, like Fredo from *The Godfather*."

Harriet, like the other staff at The Glades, referred to The Lodge as 'next door' despite it being two miles away – it was the closest similar building to The Glades. The small cottages that dotted the road between them were insignificant in comparison to the two grand buildings.

"Guardian? What does that mean?"

"I think it means he's in charge of all of Sir Jesper Senile's money. Not that he ever wants for anything." She gestured towards a shopping list that she would do online later in the day. It included two new pairs of handmade shoes.

Janice smiled and finished her tea. "Right then, I'm off. See you tomorrow – I'm on lates again!"

Janice liked to keep up some pretence about the unwelcomeness of the unsociable hours. Harriet picked up the mugs and took them to the sink. She wondered if Janice had her eye on one of the brothers. Sir Jesper she knew was a bit of a sex pest – he'd even bedded her many years ago – but Freddy, he was a bit different. Turning on the hot tap, she turned her attention back to the menu for tomorrow's ladies charity luncheon. It was an animal welfare fundraiser, so she had better make sure the meat was free-range and there were plenty of vegetarian options.

Now the day had arrived and still Janice wasn't sure what would happen. There had been several clandestine discussions, since Sir J had mentioned it, and he seemed resolutely fixed on the idea. Janice had resisted, remaining non-committal the first few times he mentioned it. But she began to think, *Why not?* Hadn't Mel Gibson got married despite his learning difficulties in *Tim*? She told herself she would go along with it; after all, her job was to make her patient happy – Sir Jesper had been very particular on that subject at her interview. And what else was a wife supposed to do but make her husband happy?

Of course, it wasn't without its difficulties. There couldn't be many brides-to-be who planned a wedding that might never happen because the septuagenarian bridegroom might have forgotten not only his intended nuptials, but also the woman who was walking up the aisle.

First Class train tickets were booked to take them on the sleeper train up to Gretna Green. A one-night stay at the bridal suite at the Grand in Edinburgh – a hotel Sir J had stayed at many times in his younger days – and then back to face the music. Janice had paid for it all herself, maxing out her credit card and putting a dent in her savings – savings she had only managed to accumulate because of Sir J's stock market skills.

She had packed her overnight case, several days before. It was the same case she always took to The Glades when she was on the late shift and expected to stay over. Her wedding dress was a sliver of white silk, its diminutive size as much a practical solution to the smallness of her overnight case as a nod to her taste. She wore white lace underwear and a suspender belt under her smock-like dress, and her work coat had make-up secreted in its deep pockets.

She looked around her little flat, wondering if she would be returning, or if she would be allowed to take up residence in The Glades, as befitting the wife of a peer of the realm. But she wasn't interested in the title, she just wanted to spend all Sir J's days with him, regardless of where, or how many he had left.

# CHAPTER 20

Jack was still angry as he entered the Reel Thing. The pub was a great place to go to be ignored, you never seemed to see anyone you knew – or at least no one who would admit to knowing you. It was probably a great place to meet your mistress if you were having an affair. He headed for the bar, ordering a large glass of red wine and knocking it back without really tasting it. He nodded to the barman for another.

The bar was pretty empty, there was just a blonde sitting at a corner table talking to a man who looked a bit too old and careworn to be her boyfriend. They were talking intently so he left them to their privacy and turned back to the bar. His wedding ring caught the spotlights carved out of the beams above and he pulled it off and threw it at the fireplace. If Lucy was so definite that their marriage was null and void, he was more than happy to oblige.

Last week, Lucy had seemed happy when he suggested a tenth anniversary party, even kind of agreed to the idea of it being a renewal of vows. It had all seemed a bit silly to him, but if it meant she would have new photo albums to remember them by, he was happy to go along with it.

Now she had really fucking done it, though. Why not get divorced then they could have a real dream wedding, she had suggested, stroking his forearm as they lay in bed. Jack had never heard anything so fucking ridiculous. His wife actually wanted to legally separate so she could remarry him a month later, their first wedding forgotten. He didn't even know if that was possible.

He drank down the second glass of red wine and looked towards the fireplace, his ring sitting on the unlit wood. Fuck it. The only thing he wanted right now was to get really, really drunk.

Tory knew she was giving Donovan a hard time. He had come all the way from London, on his day off, to give her an update on the Smith case, and really he had no update to give. She had arranged to meet him late on Saturday, in the Reel Thing, a pub around the corner from her cottage, where she was unlikely to meet anyone she knew. She sat nursing a large vodka and cranberry juice while Donovan was sticking resolutely to soft drinks, arguing he was nominally on duty.

"We matched his hand to the other bits," he said.

"Not difficult considering all the markings," Tory shrugged. The tattoos on his knuckles had haunted her dreams in the weeks since she had found his hand on her desk. In one particularly memorable nightmare the hand had come to life, crawling across the desk and grasping her neck, squeezing it until she couldn't breathe. She had woken up screaming, bringing Janey running from her sofa where she had slept over after a girls' night in. Tory had researched low calorie cocktails and they had stayed up until the early hours of the morning mixing rainbow-coloured mixtures in lieu of dinner.

"Did you know he also had advanced arthritis?" Donovan lifted the drink to his lips.

Tory nodded yes, keen to change the subject.

Donovan continued. "Apparently caused by the knuckle cracking that earned him his nickname."

"What about the men in my flat?"

"Nothing. No record for anything in the UK, but they've only been in the country for a short time. We're checking their information with Interpol to see if they have any information."

Tory raised her eyebrows. "What do you know?"

"Serbian. Not very nice people. We think someone has been back to your flat, a couple of times. Could be them."

"So I do need to stay here?" Tory still didn't know if she had moved out of London because she had to or if she had over-reacted. She knew that Gatsby would have to replace her at the *Post* soon; he couldn't hold her job open indefinitely. The longer she stayed in Cornwall, the more distant life at the *Post* became. The complaints over the vending machine, the hours, the pay, the editorial decisions on stories. Then there was the commute to work through the overcrowded tube. Here she got in her shiny sports car and drove to her named parking place right outside the Grade Two listed building that housed her luxury office.

Donovan broke into her thoughts. "That's up to you, but there's no evidence that the risk to you has reduced."

"Or that there is any?"

Donovan shrugged. "True, but you seem to have settled here quite nicely – I've certainly seen people stuck in worse witness protection."

"But I'm not in witness protection. I left on my own."

"Look, I wasn't sure if I should say, but your neighbour, Mr Brolin..."

"Jamesy?" Tory interrupted.

"Yes. He was attacked on his way home a few days after your flat was broken into."

"Is he okay?"

"Yes. Apart from two broken ribs. I should say, we don't know for sure that it's connected, the attackers didn't say anything, but they nicked his wallet and his mobile. Did he have your new number?"

"No, I haven't spoken to him since I left," she held up her work phone. "Poor Jamesy, is he really okay?"

"He's fine."

"And the *Post*?"

"They had a break in, your computer was stolen."

"Shit. What about my notes?"

Donovan pulled out a raft of printed sheets from his bag on the floor. The type was almost obliterated by scribbled notes in several different hands. "When we first went through it there was nothing that really stood out, but after you mentioned Smith had hinted at some kind of undercover project, I went back through your notes and there's a bit here," he flicked through the annotated pages until he found the one he meant and handed it over. "I wondered if you remembered the conversation and if he said any more."

Tory looked over the page; it had been so long since the meeting had taken place in a greasy spoon café in Hammersmith. She remembered Craig's smile, Gatsby's story about him having the highest missing-teeth-to-tattoos ratio, his order for a skinny latte with caramel syrup and extra whipped cream - seemingly at odds with his hard man reputation which demanded he drink special brew out of cans that he then crushed on his forehead.

She remembered he had thanked her when she had placed the tall glass in front of him and took her own espresso to the other side of the table. They had talked vaguely politely for a few minutes and then she had started asking him for some biographical details; his age, where he lived and his upbringing, where his political ideology had come from.

"My dad had some pretty strong beliefs," he had told her. "He watched the East End change as all these immigrants turned up." He had pronounced it 'm'igrants', she remembered.

Tory had nodded, not in agreement, but to encourage him.

"I remember when you never saw anyone coloured in London.

Now it's spot the white face."

Tory had blanched, hiding her expression of distaste behind her espresso cup, wishing she had bought something larger.

"The thing the government is too politically correct to say is that all these problems, all the sex slave stuff and drug stuff, it's all foreigners. People are coming into our country and taking advantage of our system. Our NHS, our housing. I know people who have been waiting for proper flats for years, and they've no chance while all these foreigners flood into the country and demand houses."

Tory had listened to his tirade throughout two more espressos, hoping those people nearby couldn't hear him, and if they could that they didn't think she agreed with any of it. After a while she had stopped listening, even writing a shopping list in the back of her notebook, as she pretended to take down his every word. Now she wished she had listened more carefully.

She read her notes a few times. She had vaguely thought of creating a story about his setting up some kind of vigilante committee but hadn't been entirely sure that would stand up. He had mentioned the need for the community to rise up and do it themselves if the police were unwilling or unable to for fear of being labelled racist.

She had asked him to clarify what he meant. Was he talking about taking the law into his own hands?

Smith had smiled. "It's down to us to show the police and the government what these people are doing. We need proof."

But he hadn't said any more. And there had been no real suggestion that his comments were anything but empty threats.

"He didn't say any more," Tory eventually said. Donovan was disappointed, but not particularly surprised. "Maybe he simply suggested joining his vigilante committee to the wrong person."

After a pause, she changed the subject. "So what are these new body parts?"

Donovan nodded. "Alongside the hand on your desk, and the foot that was in your fridge, and the torso I mentioned on the phone, we've found a leg and two arms." Donovan didn't want to mention that his colleagues at the station had been taking bets on where and when the head would be found.

"My fridge?"

Donovan realised his mistake. "Yes, erm, we found it by chance.

One of my staff went over to check for any signs of activity, and he noticed a bit of a smell and thought your milk might be off."

"A foot was in my fridge? How do you know it was his?"

"Medical records. He had broken two toes in the past."

"Football?"

"Well, he had been kicking something ball-shaped, but it wasn't made from pigskin."

Tory grimaced. She didn't really want to know any more. "Is anyone else getting these thoughtful little parcels?"

"Yes, but I'm afraid I can't say any more. Just known associates."

Tory took a gulp of air from her now empty cup. "How long had it been there? The foot."

Donovan took out a pad. "Like the hand, it looks like it was removed post mortem. When we found it, tests suggested it was kept frozen and defrosted in your fridge about four weeks ago."

"So it was in my fridge when I packed up and left?"

"Possibly."

Tory finally lost her cool. "Fucking hell, why can't you catch these fuckers?"

Donovan looked over at the only other patron in the pub. The man was heavily immersed in his fast-emptying wine glass but he had looked up from his drink at the sound of her raised voice. He looked legit, his interest prompted by chivalry rather than any particular interest in the participants. Donovan had taken the usual precautions from Paddington just in case someone was following him.

Tory paused, a deep breath. "Am I in danger or not?"

Donovan signed again. "I don't know. Somebody seems to think he passed something they want on to you."

"What?"

"At the moment I would say it was information. There's nothing to suggest Smith was anything but a two-time loser and we could take bets that he would end up dead, but the nature of his demise seems to suggest he had met some very serious individuals. And the men in your flat work for some very serious people."

"But why me?"

"I suppose because it's unusual that someone like him would meet someone like you. Unless it was to pass on that information."

"But it's been a month."

"We've been in touch with all his known associates, identifying any change in his usual patterns of behaviour. We are following up on the idea that he or someone close to him has been gathering information."

"Undercover?"

"Perhaps. Or it might be someone who was in the gang and decided to tell tales. These guys may simply want that name."

"Am I in danger?" Tory repeated. If only she could get a clear answer. One way or another. But as usual the answer was vague, the decision to act left to her.

"Not as much as the snitch, if there is one." Donovan put away his notepad. "While you are here, you are safe. In London, you would be available to capture and question. Over time, as the threat to their operations reduces, so will any potential threat to you."

"So I need to stay here?"

"That would be my recommendation. How is it going?"

Tory shrugged. "Fine, fine. I guess I should think myself lucky."

Donovan stood up. He was hoping to get the last train back to London. "Yes. I'll be in touch."

After he'd gone, Tory stood for a moment, wondering whether to head back to her cottage. Instead she went to the bar, ordering herself a very large vodka and cranberry juice. She drank it quickly. Over her shoulder she saw something glimmer in the fireplace and walked over. A gold ring lay half underneath the unburned wood. She looked over at the barman. He pointed towards the corner seat where a man sat nursing a large glass of red wine. Tory picked up the ring and walked over.

"I'm sorry to bother you, but is this yours?"

Jack looked up at the blonde-haired woman who had been so engrossed in conversation with her tired-looking companion at the other side of the pub. "Not any more," he said, downing the rest of his drink. "Can I get you another?"

He took the ring out of her hand and threw it back into the fireplace so it fell down behind the unlit logs.

"Sure, thanks," Tory said.

Returning with two glasses, Jack sat down. "Your friend gone?"

Tory sighed, picking up the glass. "He's not my friend," she said cryptically.

He held up his glass in salute before taking a generous mouthful, "Cheers."

"You too. So what brings you into a pub on a Saturday afternoon?"

"The drink, what else?"

"Scintillating company?" She looked over at the barman, now engrossed in a copy of *Nuts* magazine.

Jack smiled. "I'm a chef but sometimes I long for a badly poured, over-aired glass of Merlot and a packet of pork scratchings."

Tory laughed. "A jaded palate?"

"My wife has just asked me for a divorce," Jack wondered if he was being disingenuous; after all, Lucy had proposed marriage immediately afterwards. Perhaps he deserved a final fling, though. He eyed up his companion. Her shiny blonde hair hung to her shoulders, a slight curl softening it around her unmade-up face. She wore skinny jeans and scuffed flip-flops, showing off tanned feet and orange painted toenails. A bleached-out t-shirt advertising The Clash clung enticingly to her curves.

Tory was aware she was being checked out and returned the compliment. She took in the tousled dark hair, more a sign of an unsettled mind than the result of artful tossing. She guessed him to be a bit older than her 29 years. He was dressed carelessly in a t-shirt and jeans. His forearms were brown and well-muscled while his hands were slightly paler, calloused in places and adorned with small scars from the nicks and burns that, she supposed, came from spending your working life in a professional kitchen.

"I'm sorry, I'm being rude," he said, indicating her already empty glass. She hadn't even realised she had finished it.

"My round," she said, standing and holding out her hand for his glass, glad she was wearing flat shoes as the effects of her last drink hit her middle ear.

"Maybe just one more." He smiled.

She returned with the drinks, a packet of pork scratchings enclosed in her very white, even teeth. She placed the drinks down and expertly dropped the packet onto the table. It was soon emptied as they talked.

Jack avoided any mention of his impending divorce while Tory was keen to skip any detail about her recent visitor. He seemed to think it was some married lover, which suited her. Instead, Jack told her about his plans to open a restaurant in London and move back to the city where he had been born. Tory talked about moving to Cornwall for her job, of leaving London. Of sometimes being desperate to go back to London, but sometimes wanting to stay; of the attraction of Cornwall, the weather, his favourite beaches, her desire to learn to surf.

Neither volunteered their names.

After an hour and several more drinks, Tory was feeling the vodka sloshing around in her empty stomach. "I think I need to get something inside me." She blushed, realising the entendre too late. "I mean, I'm hungry, and I'm not sure the pork scratchings will do it this time. Perhaps you could come and rummage in my cupboards and cook me some supper?"

Jack smiled. "Where do you live?"

Tory stood, slightly unsteadily. "Around the corner."

Jack followed her out of the pub, his wedding ring, and the fiasco at home, momentarily forgotten. He needed a break.

Over a plate of hastily assembled and quite delicious tomato and pesto bruschetta magically created from a stale baguette, slightly wrinkled tomatoes and a drooping basil plant from Tory's kitchen windowsill, they chatted some more. Jack talked about his enjoyment of creating simple but delicious foods from uninspiring kitchen cupboards. About his desire to inspire people to be more creative in the kitchen. Tory spoke about her move to the country, made excuses for her empty cupboards, and discovering the dangers of running out of milk or wine at 8pm on a Saturday night where there were no 24-hour supermarkets on every – or indeed any - street corner.

The plates were empty and the daylight was beginning to fade when Jack reached out to wipe away a crumb from the side of Tory's mouth as she went to lick it. Her tongue touched the tip of his thumb. He looked from her mouth to her eyes and found himself wondering what her tongue would taste like, unable to stop himself from leaning over the table to find out. Tory stood and leaned further across the table into his kiss, her hands reaching out to feel his body.

Clumsily they walked around from the table, mouths still joined as they explored each other. Tory shed her shoes and pulled at her jeans, the buttons suddenly becoming intricate and unwieldy. It was unbearably slow work to undo them and she finally broke off their kiss to look down and work the fastenings before kicking off her flip-flops and peeling the trousers off. Jack shed his shirt and pulled up hers, revealing a green lace bra. He traced first his fingers, and then his tongue, along the edge of the lace, looking down to notice it was repeated across her hipbone.

He pulled her closer. "Is this okay?" he whispered against her ear.

She responded by grabbing his hand and thrusting it inside her green lace kickers so he could feel the hot, wet warmth of a woman who knew what she wanted. He wrapped his arms around her and unhooked her bra, his hands moving around to feel her breasts drop slightly as their weight was released.

Tory responded by dropping to her knees, pulling his straining cock out of his black shorts and holding it firmly in her hand while she licked the tip, slowly taking more and more of him into her mouth until he had to stop her.

He pulled her up, shed her underwear and his own and pushed her back against the table, thrusting himself deep into her. She gasped at the contact, repositioning herself for maximum pressure on her clitoris. Jack brought his hand down between her legs, feeling the pulse building, his own release mounting. Tory panted heavily, grinding her hips up and into his, demanding more, her quick breath turning to gasps as she felt the delicious flood of warmth spread from her clitoris throughout her body, signalling that it was time for his own desperate release. He came.

They lay together, panting, suddenly very aware of each other, and of their own nudity. Tory realised she was splayed across her dining room table, the darkness her only cover. Slowly Jack stood.

"Bathroom?" he asked.

"Upstairs, straight ahead."

Politely, she looked away while he retrieved his clothes from the floor and she watched him walk out of the room, the streetlight falling on his naked body, describing it. She gathered her own clothes and dressed quickly, unsure if he would come down and leave immediately, or if he would want to stay. She wasn't sure which she was hoping for. Perhaps she should ask him, perhaps offer to make coffee. Her thoughts were interrupted when he returned, wearing only his underwear. Noticing she had dressed, he hastily pulled on the rest of his clothes.

"Do you..."

"Would you…"

They both spoke at once and then stopped suddenly, waiting for the other to finish their sentence, glad they wouldn't have to be the one to speak.

After a pause, Tory decided she would need to break the ice. After all, it was her house and he was the guest. "Coffee?"

Jack looked around, rubbing his hand through his hair again. It had already become a familiar gesture to Tory; she felt she would miss it when he left.

"I should probably go," he said.

Although not sure if he wanted to, the words had just popped out of his mouth. Her lightning-fast dressing while he was upstairs, her silence over whether he could stay, had prompted him to think she wanted him to go. And he probably needed some time to think.

"Okay," Tory unconsciously crossed her arms over her chest, defensive, feeling embarrassed.

Jack nodded. "Lovely to meet you," he grimaced at the false tone of his voice, realised he didn't know her name, and felt it was too late to ask. He immediately regretted the dismissive-sounding parting.

Tory muttered an agreement, fought an urge to tell him her name, even through he hadn't asked, and headed towards the kitchen, leaning against the work surface, waiting for the front door to slam before moving. She headed for the fridge, grabbed a half-open bottle of white wine and took a slug straight from the bottle.

She hadn't wanted to get involved with someone, but still, it wasn't very flattering – the semen wasn't even dry on her inner thigh and he was gone. The wedding ring in the pub fireplace should have been a sign; this had just been some sort of break-up revenge sex. Yet another lame duck fuck, she thought, taking another slug of wine.

Jack stood outside her front door for a few minutes, trying to think of an excuse to go back in. Lost keys? Misplaced cufflink? Offer to make her his famous melting chocolate Cornish salt caramel dessert? No, perhaps not.

With a huge sigh, he gently stroked the peeling green paint of the front door by way of a gentler goodbye, and mentally noted down the address. It was time to go home and deal with Lucy and the divorce papers she had printed out from the internet.

# CHAPTER 21

Albie Pitchfork sat in his newly decorated suite of offices across the quadrangle from the *Compagne* offices, surveying his interior-designed territory. His large office dominated the space that had been created from The Lodge's former chapel. He had overseen its conversion, placing his office to incorporate the large rose window on the East wall. The sunrises were spectacular.

Prior to the walls going up, the architect who had submitted alternative plans expressed concern that Albie's own design would throw darkness onto the remaining space. The council planners had insisted no change be made to the building's exterior and any interior additions would have to be self-supporting to avoid any permanent abrasion to the venerable stone walls of the Grade II listed building.

As a result, the remaining space was kept open-plan and glass doors were inserted behind the old oak doors to provide protection from the winter but let in some much-needed light. The space, which once held family pews, was now populated with rabbit hutches that had been hastily erected for the team of talented and cheap writers who would put together most of the magazine. Albie had combined his office with the conference room, giving him twice as much space while providing a practical reason.

Albie noticed his newly-appointed lieutenant Gus Jacobs had arrived and was unknowingly seated in what was intended to be the receptionist's desk. Having chosen the desk because it provided light and fresh air, Gus had the new computer switched on and was busily creating folders within the content management system for the upcoming issues. He had plugged in a small portable hard drive from which he was downloading the many articles already created for the first issue, as well as a raft of planning documents that he had created from his meetings with Albie while in London.

"You're sitting at the receptionist's desk," was Albie's greeting as he wandered out of his office.

Gus coloured and turned to greet his editor. The red stain on his cheeks was unbecoming next to his red-brown hair. "I'm sorry, I couldn't find my office."

Albie perched on the white gloss desk, purposely invading Gus's personal space and enjoying the discomfort he had caused. "There is no office, there wasn't space. Getting planning permission for this building conversion was a nightmare."

Gus looked over to the white box that dominated the East wall of the chapel, which his boss had appeared from. Albie ignored the intended reproach that his Assistant Editor clearly had no intention of voicing.

Albie had poached Gus from his editorship role at the short-lived *Rosebud* magazine. His official title was Assistant Editor, although Gus was using Deputy Editor in all his correspondence. Gus's role was to deal with the minutiae of the daily running of the magazine, while Albie went out to woo big names for star interviews. From the first, Albie wanted his staff to see him as the figurehead of the magazine and without whom *The MacGuffin* would fail. This talent was about to be demonstrated with the first planning meeting for his inaugural issue.

Albie got up from the desk. "I thought you could sit there," he pointed to a cubicle close to his office, abutted by a wall created from stone memorials. A wall of grey metal filing cabinets provided the only other view.

Gus nodded. Not a very cheery spot, but it would have to do. He recognised that Albie would probably be absent much of the time, freeing up his grand office for him to squat in. "Okay. I'll just finish this and transfer myself over."

Albie nodded. "Shout me when everyone is here. We'll start at nine."

Gus opened his mouth, the meeting had been booked to begin at 10am. "Your will shall be done," he muttered to himself when Albie had walked a safe distance away.

Thankfully, on the dot at 9am, the desks were filled and the slender computer screens glowed as the writers quietly worked their way through the new content management systems, accessing new email, passwords, Twitter and other social media accounts that would be vital to the magazine's success.

On the side of each desk, carefully watched over by their owners, sat fat contacts books, bursting with the names and numbers of agents, celebrities, artists, writers and film-makers that were never shared on computer hard drives. These heavily-guarded and scruffy-looking books were the reason they had been recruited.

Gus stood and caught their attention, and each one filed into Albie's office behind him, their iPads attached to their hands. An interactive whiteboard sat at the foot of the long white table linked into Albie's computer, which boasted a screen almost the same size. On it was a mock-up cover and several dummy spreads featuring planned articles. The donkeys had been busy at work on his behalf.

"Good morning," Albie stood regally and waited for them all to get a seat before continuing. "Welcome to *The MacGuffin*. Our first issue hits the newsstands in twelve days, along with our website and various digital platforms.

"I have already lined up some incredible commissions, kicking off with our cover story - Levi L'Accord, who has finally completed his graphic novel of James Joyce's *Finnegans Wake*. As you know, Joyce spent seventeen years writing his masterpiece and Levi has been working on his version for the exact same amount of time. He's giving us an exclusive look at the first chapter, and an insight into what it was like to graphically translate the imagery of the world's most unreadable book."

Gus Jacobs stared at his tablet screen, willing himself not to snort or make any sound that would give away the fact that he, not Albie, had secured this incredible first issue story. His list of feature ideas had been emailed to Albie as part of the application process and each one had made it onto the planning list for the next six issues, although each was marked down with Albie's initials, denoting that they were his contribution – essentially claiming authorship. Already Gus was wondering what he had let himself in for; the long hours he had expected, but the lack of recognition was already starting to grate. It felt a long time since his lunch with Albie in London, where they had talked about creating great art and the importance of teamwork. As well as a move to Cornwall that would allow finding plenty of time to hit Newquay's famed surf beach at Fistral.

Before his short-lived post at *Rosebud*, Gus had spent almost a decade as an Assistant Editor at *Mankind*, where he had been under pressure to put rippling muscled athletes onto every cover and detail how they achieved their eight-packs in jaw-dropping detail. The truth was he had been bored. He wanted a challenge, and he had to admit life at the helm of *The MacGuffin* was certainly going to be that.

Opposite Gus sat the sales director, Mike Bell, also formerly of *Rosebud*, whose job was to make *The MacGuffin* a success and reap back the spiralling editorial costs. The heavy jowls lined with the daily lunches he enjoyed on expenses as he wined and dined potential advertisers were matched by his deep pockets, similarly lined with his sizeable cut of their cash.

He had followed up immediately on his brief introduction and business card swap with Sir Jesper at the launch of *Rosebud*. Now he would meet Sir Jesper at lunchtime and sign the final agreement. Mike would keep twenty per cent of all the advertising revenue he brought in to the magazine. With that staggering cut and Albie Pitchfork's insistence that he reap ten per cent of *The MacGuffin's* rewards on top of his sizeable editor's fee, *Compagne*'s overstretched finance department was re-reckoning the sales revenues and forecast of profits downwards on a daily basis. But Sir Jesper remained bowled over by Albie's absolute confidence. He remembered their conversation in London with fondness, and the ensuing night with Martine and the little redhead with excitement.

Albie was at his most charming during the meeting. He smiled and took the time to meet the eyes of everyone around the table. "Some of you I am meeting for the first time. You have beaten off competition from hundreds of talented writers to join us here, and I am lucky to be at the helm of such an exciting project. But we can swap CVs later, I've organised some drinks in the boardroom after work." He paused, noting the pleasure in the faces of his new staff. It had actually been Sir Jesper's idea to arrange the drinks party. He had promised to attend.

"You all have access to our planning documents – we want to ensure you know the detail of what each issue includes and welcome any comments. Only Gus and I have permission to edit them, and it will be your responsibility to keep up to date with those changes. Gus?"

Gus nodded, not sure what he was expected to add.

"The documents include deadlines for each individual article and the designer nominated to lay it out," Albie continued, disappointed by his wingman's lack of response. "I expect you all to hit your deadlines and work closely with our team of designers," he nodded down the table where a group of younger men sat. "Gus will be your first point of contact for any problems or questions. I will be looking at the final spreads and will send them back to you with any comments for improvement."

Everyone around the table nodded in unison. They hadn't heard anything that Gus hadn't already told them. Most had copies of the planning documents on their iPads, with alerts set up whenever there was an update. Clearly Pitchfork ran a tight ship, and if they had any chance of staying beyond the first issue and not being replaced by those hundreds of other writers who had applied for a chance to work at *The MacGuffin*, they would need to meet his exacting deadlines.

"Any legal issues will be forwarded on to our lawyer. Lastly we have three rules here at *The MacGuffin:* Firstly, no one talks about *The MacGuffin.* Secondly, no one talks about *The MacGuffin.* Finally, no-one talks about *The MacGuffin.*" He smiled, enjoying the laughter from his underlings as they immediately got the unoriginal joke, despite his poor Brad Pitt impersonation.

Albie waved his hands, "Okay, okay, *Fight Club* jokes aside: I do want to impress that the content of *The MacGuffin* is top secret until it hits the shelves or newsstand app. That means no chatting with peers, girlfriends or best mates from your last job about what you are working on. Secondly, no interviewee gets final cut. This is vital. I don't care who they are. I want to build our reputation as being uncompromising and nobody's lapdog – this is the way we will build our subscribers. Anyone asking for it, tell them no, no matter what the reason. If necessary, we will shut down the interview. When their replacement gets the cover, the agent will have to explain why they fucked up. Finally, this isn't a democracy. It's my name above the masthead, so I have final say. I'm happy to hear suggestions and even arguments, but once I am in possession of the full facts, what I say goes. If I make a decision and find out you didn't give me the full facts, game over."

Albie paused for effect. The writers seemed to be taking it all in. But if they didn't, what he had said was perfectly true. There were plenty of other talented writers out there who would jump at the chance to work at *The MacGuffin*, especially once this group had given up their precious contacts.

"My final point is that you will have noticed we are quite a small team. You are all on freelance contracts – that's because I believe staffers get lazy. And this allows us to buy in talent; we don't have staff photographers, because I want to use the right photographer for every job."

Albie gestured to the coffee pot sitting on the side of the table alongside a selection of current newspapers and magazines. Gus stood and poured a cup for him and took one himself before sitting back down.

Albie took a slow, savouring sip of the sweet-smelling brew, aware that those around the table were hoping to be offered one.

"Right. Next order of business," he felt and enjoyed their collective sigh as their chance for a beverage disappeared. "Our launch is vital – I'm thinking London, we don't want anyone accusing us of having straw sticking out of our ears, but any suggestions for a venue I'd be glad to hear." His tone suggested differently, he had his eye on a new – and highly publicised - art gallery that had recently opened at a former dog-racing track in what was fast becoming a hipster spot in the East End. "The guest list is pretty much set, and most of them will find it easier to be in the capital than down here."

"If we hold the launch here, or hereabouts," Gus spoke up, ignoring Albie's glare, "and get this incredible guest list, it will show just what a fantastic magazine this is, that this calibre of people are willing to travel."

"And if they aren't?" Albie questioned, as those around the table pictured an empty room, filled only with waiting staff carrying untouched trays of drinks and canapés, and all quickly began shaking their heads at the idea. Magazines had been known to fold before they even hit the stands, like a bad play closing on opening night, and none of them wanted to find another new job in the ever-decreasing world of journalism. Talented or not.

"So London it is," Albie took back control of the meeting. "And if no one has any better ideas, I think The Space is the way to go. Classy, arty and witty all at the same time. It's newly opened so garnering loads of attention, the architect who has created The Space is tipped for some international awards and there's a great first exhibition on there at the moment too. I suggest you all go and have a look." He ticked another item from his list with a satisfied flick of his green Mont Blanc fountain pen and looked down at his wrist, pulling up his sleeve slowly and allowing his staff to recognise and envy the Tag Heuer that encased it. It was 10am.

"Right, back to work."

# CHAPTER 22

The day of the September issue planning meeting dawned on Tory with a hangover. After her hour of passion with the man from the Reel Thing – the irony of the pub's name was far from lost on her – Tory had wisely gone to bed. She had spent Sunday on her patio with a chilled bottle of chablis at her feet, going over first Donovan's revelations and then her not-quite-overnight guest. Thankfully Janey had turned up with a bottle of champagne and a platter of locally-made sushi, and a copy of Dick Biggs' latest novel just as she was beginning to annoy herself with sex flashbacks.

Tory hadn't mentioned her lively weekend as they settled in to eat glorious Cornish California rolls dipped in soy sauce and read extracts from the surprisingly well-written homoerotic fiction.

"It's amazing how many euphemisms there are for the act of love," Tory pondered as Janey took the book and read out a particularly steamy session, which saw the hero and his well-hung horticulturalist enjoy a session with the garden hose.

Later, they had discussed plans for a surf lesson the following weekend as they walked along the small harbour that sat at the bottom of Tory's street. The warm wind whipped her hair around her head, scrambling her brain as much as the alcohol she had consumed. The noise of the waves hitting the beach drowned out the gasps of pleasure she kept remembering.

Was it human nature, she pondered as she poured herself a coffee from the pot that had been placed in the centre of the table alongside the customary pastries and fruit, that she found herself more disturbed by the one-night stand with the mystery man than the severed foot that had been found in her fridge? As the room filled and she emptied her coffee cup, she noticed that her desire to create a better issue of *Compagne* was quickly taking precedence over both. The unavoidable protestant work ethic was kicking in.

Nodding to Daniella, who had taken a seat at the end of the table, Tory cleared her voice. "Shall we get started?"

Undeterred, Sophie-Dexter Browning continued her conversation with Pretty McPhail, who Tory was concerned to see looking anything but. Perhaps she needed a mental health day. "Did he receive you in his library?" Sophie was asking about a cancer-ridden newly-made Lord who had agreed to be interviewed about his hoped-for recovery. "Rumour has it he is practically illiterate. Don't be fooled by those impressively filled shelves. He bought those leather-bound books by the yard at Sotheby's."

Pretty was more concerned by the dryness in her throat still lingering from the dusty books she had been surrounded by while interviewing one of Sir Jesper's cronies about the health benefits of hunting. And try as she might, she had been unable to get the grimy ring around the coffee cup he had eventually served her from her mind.

Tory poured out a second cup of coffee and filled her mouth with a croissant, her need for carbohydrates greater than her desire to be graceful. Now wasn't the time for perfect table manners.

"Let's start," she said more forcefully, swallowing the last of her breakfast.

Harry Hampton arrived late from his cigarette break with Jo. He had taken longer than usual, as Jo had news of the new magazine to share.

"Sorry to keep you, darlings," he addressed the table, stopping on his way to his seat to pick up a pastry and glass of freshly squeezed grapefruit juice.

Jo was also well on the way to snagging herself a peer. The wealthy older man she had been seeing was, she was sure, poised to propose. She had wanted Harry to provide some advice on getting a ring on her finger.

Tory smiled at Harry. "As penance, you can hand out these planning documents," she told him.

Harry slapped his right wrist with his left hand. "Naughty Harry," he said with relish, picking up the papers and handing them out.

Tory waited for him to sit down before she began. "Before you are planning documents that will be used each month to give everyone an idea of what they are working on. These are blank pages that indicate approximately what will go where. You can also see that we have already assigned a number of pages for your features. These are not set in stone and the purpose of this meeting is to decide what is going into these pages and if you have enough pages to work with."

Harry flicked through the documents to find the Food pages. "What's this cover here?"

"We are going to try bringing out the sections, by giving some of them a sort of front cover of their own; that way they are easy to find."

"Bring them out? Like wallflowers at their coming out ball?" Harry smirked.

The room filled with the sound of shuffling paper as the section editors identified their own pages and looked for their own front covers.

Pretty McPhail was the first to speak up as her assistant Posy flicked through the pages for her to find Health and Beauty following straight on from Fashion, without its own cover.

"Is Health and Beauty not considered important enough for its own cover?" she asked, her voice layered with frost.

Tory had anticipated that those without section fronts would feel affronted. The only thing worse than having a cover was not having one. "We can't lose too many pages to front covers, but you'll notice that all sections now start on a right-hand page; this allows you to present a really stunning start to your part of the magazine. At the moment we have given Food and Homes and Interiors sections front covers. If it works, it may be rolled out to others."

Lelaina Douglas, who had more pages than most, noticed the Fashion section was placed in the second half of the magazine.

"Why have you put me here?" she asked.

Daniella, who had worked with Tory to put the dummy plan together, had joked before the meeting that she would be off Lelaina's Christmas list for the placement. And oh, what presents Lelaina had in her gift. Her office looked like a high-end designer boutique.

"Fashion sits after the middle of the magazine, as it provides a really lovely place for the magazine to fall open. At the moment it tends to move around the magazine, and we know that many readers want to turn to Fashion first." Daniella hoped the compliment contained in her comment was subtle enough. "This way they will always know where to find it."

Lelaina nodded her agreement and turned back to the pages, mollified.

Harry Hampton noticed his section was bookended by Max Mullen's review pages and a new section had been added, headed 'Sommelier?'.

"Victoria darling, what's this for?" Harry tapped the page with his pen.

Tory looked over. "We have a few new suggested pages, I think there are a few gaps in coverage of the core areas of interest of our readers and it strikes me that wine is one of them. Harry, I know you already have plenty of work to do, so I have taken the liberty of asking the sommelier at Clancy's to pen a column for us, I understand he has worked in some of the best restaurants in the world."

Harry smiled behind his pastry. Malcolm Tullen was a well-known wine buff, but he was also a raging alcoholic. Should he warn his editor before letting him loose in some of the land's finest wine cellars? No, he decided. Victoria's probationary period was over. Let the players take to the stage. The truth will out and it was likely to be more entertaining if it unfolded *au naturel*.

"Splendid. Malc is very knowledgeable," Harry agreed.

"Are you happy to take it into your section? Can you go and chat over word counts and possible content with him?"

Harry thought of Clancy's well-tasted wine cellar and Malc's willingness to share a bottle at any time of day. "Absolutely, why not? I shall arrange to pop in and see him at lunchtime."

Tory removed the question mark from the page and added a 'C' for confirmed.

"Okay, next. You'll notice we've put all the Social pages together, instead of using them to fill gaps at the last moment."

Sophie Dexter-Browning was happy with the change. Tory had already run through it with her in her office that morning. She recognised her Social Editor's ego was sledgehammer-proof, but she needed to keep her onside to avoid wallflower status for all those social events she was expected to attend.

Tory had also taken up her Homes and Interiors Editor's suggestion of employing Lodd McPherson. Tory had asked Betsy if she would discuss the subject of her penning a regular column about making the move from London to a country idyll. Betsy had agreed enthusiastically and yet again she was setting off to an interview on the day of the monthly magazine planning meeting.

Tory had sent out invites to a series of planning meetings to everyone's calendars and a quick check had confirmed the worst. Betsy had organised shoots on pretty much every single one of them. Thankfully Tory hadn't taken it as evidence of how little she valued good planning, but as evidence that she was already a relative master at it.

***

Betsy's role as Homes and Interiors Editor had gained her entry into some of the most beautiful houses in the country but it never ceased to amaze her how few of her interviewees thought to offer her so much as a cup of tea. In an earlier career as a newspaper crime correspondent she had found herself in some of the worst homes in the country, often facing families in desperate circumstances, and tea was always offered. She had rarely accepted, not wanting to delay getting her story and also not wanting to deprive people of so much as a teabag but over the months she had learned that refusing was often an insult and accepting often code for becoming one of them, leading to more candid responses to the difficult questions she had been dispatched to ask, of a tear-stained mother: "Do you think your son killed him?" or broken-hearted parents: "What were your murdered daughter's plans for the future?"

It was these homes that came back to her as she stepped over the threshold of yet another over-priced and over-designed home. The subject today was a revered stage actress who was using the article to build her profile to secure more 'telly roles to get more bums on seats in the theatre', as she had put it during their preliminary telephone conversation some weeks before.

It was a sad day. Dame Juliet Logan was one of the country's richest theatrical treasures. She had won Olivier awards, been given a damehood for her services to theatre, and yet she was angling for bit part roles in primetime soaps to remind people who she was so she could maintain sell-out theatre performances.

Of course, none of that would appear in the interview, as Betsy explained to Dame Juliet. "Call me Jules, darling," was the response.

On her arrival, Betsy noted Dame Juliet's house was a mass of neutrals. Beiges, off-whites and antique whites all managed to clash with each other without actually being there. The Dame's main accessories in the living room were her awards, which sat gleaming and carefully placed around the room. Fortunately the PR had warned Betsy about the home's lack of substance and she had arranged to meet a freelance set designer at the house to bring some colour into the rooms. After all, this was the home of the greatest living stage actress of her generation. People would expect a bit of drama.

Lotte the set designer got to work on the rooms, with strict instructions not to touch the barely-there living room which would work well as a stark contrast to Dame Juliet and her dramatic life, especially with the Dame encased in one of her wonderful vintage formal evening gowns.

Betsy got to work on Dame Juliet. Heading for her bedroom, she pulled open her dressing room and went in search of the famous red dress she had worn for her last Olivier. Covered in crystals, it was loud and brash and would work brilliantly well posed against a more natural environment such as the flowering apple trees in her small courtyard garden.

Dame Juliet expertly applied her own make-up, "Do you want somewhere between everyday and stage?"

Betsy nodded. "Think TV make-up: heavier than you would normally wear, but not visible from the cheap seats."

Juliet went back to her mirror, lit up by rows of bulbs. "I stole this from my dressing room when I was in *Cat on a Hot Tin Roof*. I thought it might be the only chance I got to remember being on the stage. I've kept it with me since – I got my first nomination in that play and this has become a kind of talisman."

"Can we use that? I think the Statute of Limitations is long gone on petty theft." Betsy had already written it down. In the margins she scribbled down another idea. *The Three Dames* – a photo fashion feature with the three great ladies of theatre.

The following day was a rare day in the office to write up her notes. Betsy's heart sank as she saw her desk was again teetering with post. It was funny how most of her colleagues were bemoaning bursting email inboxes, and jealously eyed up her mountain of jiffy bags and boxes, while she had come to hate the post. When she had first started, she had been so happy to get the little freebies that came with being Homes and Interiors Editor for *Compagne*. The PR companies got little notes of thanks and a promise to consider their items when any suitable feature came up. However, word quickly got around that sending in freebies got you the ear of the queen and soon Betsy was drowning under the weight of the emails and phone calls from account directors keen to get on first-name terms with the woman who could justify their outlandish fees with the click of her mouse.

She had learned her lesson quickly. Today emails and phone

calls went unanswered. Her assistant, Jess, happily gathered together all the necessary items for any shoot and her reward was to keep unsolicited samples, which quickly found their way onto her internet seller page.

Once Betsy had done the same and had started to make almost as much money from her marketplace account as she did from her job, her PayPal account balance looking like you might expect a Swiss bank account to. But now her office and home were filled with stuff. Bed linen sets, home and garden accessories – even furniture found its way to her. She had half planned charity auctions and giveaways to good causes, but had yet to organise anything. Sometimes she felt like putting it all out in the street for people to help themselves to – if only it wouldn't fill up again with more. She wondered if there was an Interiors writer over at *The MacGuffin* who would appreciate some of it and dropped a quick email to Gus Jacobs, who replied enthusiastically, promising to stop by and collect any unwanted goodies that would suit their more men's-themed interiors.

***

His meeting over, Albie noticed the new receptionist in The Lodge was bare-legged and that her red hair was escaping down her back, as the pins proved insufficient to hold her very clean hair at bay. She was one of the Flowers of Medieval, apparently. The name sounded more exotic than copy typists, ad bookers and secretaries, and they positively encouraged it. So far he had exchanged eye-meets with around half of them, and swapped phone numbers with a handful. This one was currently at the top of his mental to-do list and he paused to pass the time with her. His success with women, he liked to think, was less about his celebrity status and more to do with his skills at seduction.

Within a few minutes he discovered she was a journalism student, aged 22, and hoping her job as an ad booker and receptionist would bring her a chance for a try-out in the editorial team of one of the magazines.

"Why not let me take you out to dinner and we can talk some more about expanding your experience?" he said, smiling at the intended innuendo.

She smiled back, agreeing with a nod that caused her hair to finally escape its pins completely and cascade down her back. She looked every bit the medieval maiden, her long tresses grazing the top of her buttocks.

Awaking the next morning, the same tangle of red hair on the pillow simply served as an annoyance. She had stayed over. This was one of the downsides to inviting them back to his place, but he had felt he should christen his new bedroom as soon as possible. Now he was nearing 40, he preferred to awake alone, slowly. His morning grooming now took longer. Once he would go days without shaving, throw on crumpled clothes for several days in a row, and the result was devilishly dishevelled. Now in the mornings he was the one who looked crumpled, his bristles leaving an unappealing grey stain across his cheeks. She slept on. He wracked his brains for her name, but mentally shrugged. He wouldn't need to know it. She wouldn't be staying again.

Albie got up and headed for the bathroom down the hall. He had installed a dressing room in the next-door bedroom. At least that meant he wouldn't need to emerge until he was fully bathed and dressed, by which time she would be gone, or at the very least sufficiently disadvantaged by her state of undress to allow him a swift exit.

*Pitchfork 1, Flowers of Medieval 0*, he told himself, turning on the power shower and adjusting the temperature before stepping under its needle-like jets. He didn't want to emerge flushed.

His next accomplishment would be the blonde-haired ad setter with the discreet but still occasionally visible tattoo of a *fleur de lis* above her right shoulder blade.

# CHAPTER 23

"How's the Naked Diet going?" Tory pulled up a chair in front of Janey's giant screen, which she used to help her spot any imperfections in the pages as the staff completed spreads. It was the day after print day; always a relief, with staff taking time to clear their desks of unnecessary paperwork and unwanted press releases, while chatting and catching up on internet shopping and bill paying. For Tory it was quickly followed by a tense wait for the actual magazine to arrive on newsstands when the mistakes that had been invisible during the proofing process magically appeared, bringing with them a slew of letters and emails, asking how on earth such an obvious thing could have been missed; the magic ink theory proving a less successful defence than the magic bullet one.

Janey looked up from the screen. "Done with it when I realised I was eyeing up the man who fries the bacon in Rhubarb, wondering whether, if I took him home to bed, he would let me lick the grease from his face and other body parts."

Tory grimaced involuntarily at the idea. The bacon fryer made a mean breakfast baguette, but he had skin like the surface of the moon. "Good."

"But I have had this great idea," Janey pulled out her folder used for collecting ideas and notes on magazine spreads and fashion shoots. "It's called the 'All you Can Read Buffet'."

"A buffet? Isn't that when you can keep going back to pile up your plate?"

"No, that's an all you can *eat* buffet, mine is *read*."

"Read?"

"It's really simple – when you get hungry, you read this inexhaustible list of food. Recipes, menus, whatever, and trick yourself into feeling full."

"Does it work?"

"Well I started off really hungry and wanted to order everything on it, but then I got through about six pages of menus and I got a bit sick of food to be honest."

"Is it a diet book?"

"No, it's my own diet. I was thinking of seeing if I could drum up some publishing interest, though."

"Why not? I've heard stupider ways to lose weight."

"Talking of stupid, I've got something to show you."

Tory pulled her chair closer to Janey's screen as her friend's fingers flew across her keyboard. She opened up the pages dedicated to wedding announcements. Scrolling down to the third page, she tapped the screen with her index finger. "Look at that!"

Tory squinted at the screen, "Is that Lucy?"

"Yes, your Weddings Editor has announced her wedding, to her husband of ten years, in the social pages of *Compagne*," laughed Janey.

Tory had never seen Lucy smiling, certainly not so radiantly or with such shiny hair. "But isn't this for recent announcements of engagements and weddings?"

As she spoke, Tory turned her attention to the husband. She had heard a lot about his kitchen skills, had even tasted them a few times, but Lucy rarely mentioned him.

"Fuck!" The exclamation came out as a whisper. The man standing next to her smiling Weddings Editor was intimately familiar. It was the man from the Reel Thing. But Janey's next comments vindicated him to some extent.

"Lucy came up with this great plan to divorce him and re-marry him but this time with a wedding befitting her social standing."

The stupidity of the statement drew Tory's thoughts away from her own problems. "She's what?"

"She's come up with this mad idea of divorcing Jack so she can remarry him and have the wedding of her dreams." Janey's voice was thick with contempt.

"And he's happy about that?" Tory remembered his comments in the pub that afternoon: his wife had just asked him for a divorce. Clearly he had some misgivings.

"I'm not sure anyone has bothered to ask. This is the *Everybody Loves Lucy Show*." Janey clicked away from the page. "I think it's a tenth wedding anniversary present, Harry told me that Jack had suggested a big party, something she could attend and feel like a beautiful bride as she hadn't the first time around. But it seems our Lucy wasn't listening."

Tory remembered the story about the Fashion Editor who had ended up doing PR for a cheap supermarket clothing line. She thought of Janey and her diet fads. Perhaps Lucy's idea was in keeping with the place. Maybe she would be better off returning to London.

While her thoughts of the *Post* were fading, there were plenty of magazines there that might employ her now she had the experience. She made a mental note to email Lyle to see if he had heard of anything. After his first flush of emails for lunch and dinner, he had gone quiet. She wondered if she had insulted him with all her refusals, but it had been a difficult time when she had first started – and it still was.

"I wonder if we will get an invite," Janey pondered, clicking back to her fashion spread. There was definitely some muffin top to be Photoshopped off the male model. She'd thought the super skinny trousers had been a bit castrating at the time, though he had insisted in a slightly high voice that he was perfectly comfortable.

Tory muttered something non-committal and headed back to her office, she had meant to ask if there were any hot rumours flying around, particularly about her, but Lucy's impending wedding pushed it out of her mind. Shit, she had shagged her Weddings Editor's husband. Or was he an ex-husband now? That sounded better, but only marginally so. She remembered her reaction to meeting Matt again at her interview, her misgivings that in Cornwall you bump into one-night stands all the time. Fuck, she didn't have time for this. She was a grown-up and if she fancied sleeping with someone that was her choice.

Tory clicked on her emails, reviewing the details of that day's event, and noticed one from Sir Jesper that had announced Jack Ramsden of the award-winning boutique restaurant of the same name would be preparing the menu for *Compagne*'s Food and Drink Awards.

She closed her eyes and sighed. "Fuck," she muttered to herself.


Sir Jesper was in his element. His beautiful wife was by his side and his most important magazine advertisers were arriving in their best suits to enjoy a rare afternoon away from the office. More than donating money, Sir Jesper enjoyed distributing largesse – and he was good at it. There was also the bonus that he had managed to inveigle an invitation for Martine, who was now standing on his lawn in a kingfisher-blue dress, her matching stiletto heels sinking noticeably into the ground. He hoped to find a few minutes alone-time with her, but she was beginning to get less then patient at her lack of appearance in *The MacGuffin*.

After the hunt for their father had failed to find any sign of him, Sir Jesper and Freddy had searched his rooms, finally unearthing a letter written in Sir Jesper Senior's instantly recognisable slanting hand. They had read it in silence.

*Darling boys, I have run off to be with my love – we will be married quietly in Scotland and return after our honeymoon. Who would have expected so much happiness at my time of life?*
*My darling Janice sends love, see you soon. Father.*

"He's what?" Freddy was struggling to take anything in since it had become clear his father had disappeared. Jesper was clearly still in charge.

"Scotland, that means they'll be at the Grand," Jesper had pulled out his phone and requested the number, asking to be put through immediately.

"Yes Sir, I'm delighted to say we do have a Mr and Mrs Donaldson staying with us in our bridal suite," the receptionist had answered suavely.

"When did they arrive?"

"Yesterday evening, late, I believe. Mrs Donaldson said they were married this morning."

Sir Jesper closed his eyes. They were too late. "And when are they expected to leave?"

"They are checking out later today. I believe they will then be heading for his country seat in Cornwall."

There followed for the two brothers one of their longest nights since the one in which their mother had died. Freddy watched as Jesper did the older brother thing, taking charge. For the first time since his father had cast doubt on their inheritance, Freddy wondered if he would actually want to be head of the family.

Deep in thought, both sat, barely speaking, simply waiting for their father's return. Freddy eventually went to sleep on the sofa, while Sir Jesper quietly called the brunette to apologise for standing her up and to indulge in some fairly one-sided phone sex from his father's four-poster bed.

By early morning, he'd had enough. He stopped in at the kitchen below for coffee and toast, ordering some breakfast to be sent up to his brother when he awoke and took off in his car, heading for the train station. Arriving before the London train, he sat in the car and closed his eyes. Despite his worry he was tired.

"Jessie, dear boy, how marvellous of you to meet us!"

Sir Jesper woke with a start at the sound of the car door opening and his father's still powerful voice in his ear. He rubbed his eyes, pulled his stiff body from behind the wheel of the car, and stood before his father. Waiting for him to explain himself.

"This is the new Lady of the House," his father gestured with a flourish to the woman by his side, now demurely dressed in a navy-blue tailored trouser suit, the high-necked white silk blouse beneath it hiding any hint of the cleavage Sir Jesper had been so impressed by when he had employed her.

"Over my dead fucking body," Sir Jesper whispered so only Janice could hear. More loudly he said, "Excellent, Dad. Why don't you get in the car, while the new Lady and I go in search of your luggage?"

Sir Jesper Senior assented and got into the car, allowing his son to grasp his new stepmother by the elbow and march her out of his sight.

"What the fuck is going on?" Sir Jesper wasted no time in asking.

"We got married." Janice had thought carefully how she would handle her shocked and probably not too happy stepsons. "We love each other."

Sir Jesper's face went the colour of boiled pork, but he managed to respond at a normal volume. "You are sacked. I'm his legal guardian, he can't get married, and he doesn't have any money."

Janice nodded. "I know. I just wanted to make him happy. I don't want his money. I just love spending time with him."

Sir Jesper's grip on her elbow tightened. "But he has dementia, he's almost 50 years older than you."

"I don't see him like that. He's a funny, intelligent and sexy man."

Sir Jesper visibly winced at the word 'sexy'. It was true his father was a warm, funny and smart man. That was one of the reasons he inspired such loyalty from those around him. But this money-grabbing whore wouldn't be able to see any of that.

"What do you want?" Jesper knew it was going to cost him to make all this go away, but it would be his father's money really.

Janice shrugged. "Just give me my job back."

Sir Jesper was speechless. He looked into her heavily kohl-ringed brown eyes. Saw tears welling in them, being bravely held back as she faced his onslaught.

Janice nodded. "I want to continue to care for him as I do now, but I will share his bed with him when he's willing and remembers who I am. Otherwise I will take on the role I was employed for, that of his nurse."

Sir Jesper let go of her elbow and walked away, looking over at his father sitting, docile but happy, in the back of his car.

Janice followed him, rubbing her arm where his hand had bruised it. It was vital that he let her be with her new husband. She tried to keep any sound of desperation out of her voice. "I will give up the lap dancing and take up residence in his suite, in the spare room. You can explain that I am becoming a live-in nurse, I won't tell anyone else. You don't even need to pay me."

Sir Jesper watched his father get out of the car, walking towards them.

"Well, Jessie?" the old man asked, face expectant, waiting for an answer to a question only he knew.

Sir Jesper watched Janice move to his father's side, putting her hand in his.

"Let's all go home, shall we?" Sir Jesper Senior patted her hand fondly. "We've had quite an adventure."

Sir Jesper followed, not sure what else to do. His father's live-in nurse. He supposed he could live with that.

"Just don't expect me to call you Mother," he had hissed in her ear as he helped her into the back of the car, shutting the door with some force.

# CHAPTER 24

Sir Jesper and Freddy had eventually left the newly-weds in peace. Their father had insisted on champagne, but by the time it arrived he had forgotten what they were celebrating.

Janice had taken it in her stride. "Both of your sons are here, Sir Jesper – that's a good reason for celebration."

Her words had an immediate calming effect and as Jesper and the equally shocked Freddy sat and gulped at their glasses, they saw how Janice easily dealt with their father's confusion, how she was able to turn her conversation and tone to suit his. Perhaps they would never understand the attraction between them, but it was impossible not to see that they seemed to make each other happy.

Now Sir Jesper felt he was back in control and could turn his attention to pressing work matters. The annual Food and Drink Awards celebrating good food had begun as a small event but over the years, as interest in British food had increased, the quality and quantity – and sponsorship interest – in the awards had grown. They had gone from having a negative impact on *Compagne*'s balance sheet to become one of the magazine's most lucrative ventures.

Now top chefs who had become household names longed to add a *Compagne* to their awards cabinets. The rest of the press was happy to cover the event, helping to put the magazine at the top of the newsstand. And this time around, the new Managing Editor had worked with Harry Hampton to orchestrate a thirteenth issue to come out a week after the awards, dedicated to the nominees, the winners, and the event itself. Tory had outdone herself, with four photographers in charge of covering every angle of the event; some pictures would appear online, some would be included with press releases going out to other media, but the best would feature in the magazine.

Harry, who was loved universally by advertisers and restaurants alike, was key in making their thirteenth issue one of their most successful. Sir Jesper made a note to himself to speak to Harry about increasing the page count for next year, or even putting together a food magazine. Adding *The MacGuffin* to his stable had helped to increase his interest in the business.

The event organiser had planned for very short speeches, recognising that each guest would only be interested in their own category, but had made an exception where Sir Jesper was concerned. She wanted the gig next year and this, along with the blowjob she had given him under his desk that morning as they had gone over the final plans, would help seal the deal. Jo had neatly typed his scribbled notes in a semblance of order and they now billowed from his jacket pocket.

This year, instead of the usual venue of The Glades, Cornwall's famous Botanical Gardens would play host, for free, in return for extensive coverage in the special issue of *Compagne*. Guests would enjoy a pre-lunch cocktail while wandering the grounds learning more about the gardens, the plants that lived there and how they could help support the work of the charity that owned it. Then they were to head into the marquee for a three-course luncheon prepared by the Weddings Editor's husband – or ex-husband.

Harry had convinced Jack to do it. The fee had also been enough for Jack to buy the mobile kitchen he needed to prepare the food. The heat of the day meant he had been happy to play with his menu, the entrée was fairly traditional; seared locally-sourced scallops, followed by a rack of lamb, while several helpings of elderflower gin sorbet would leave guests pleasantly cooled and relaxed for the awards themselves.

The *Compagne* marketplace was also new for this year. Stallholders had paid a premium to set out their very best produce to entice the very important guests to buy for their restaurants, shops and cafés. Boutique gins and *pastis* were being enthusiastically tasted, while nearby stallholders struggled to keep their gourmet cheeses, fish, meats and pâtés sweat-free in the shade.

For Sir Jesper it was win-win: the fees from the marketplace alone had paid for the whole event, including the meal, and the production costs of the extra magazine. All of this made him very happy.

Sophie Dexter-Browning had again been put in charge of the guest list, outside of the nominees. Each table had been carefully created to include at least one ancient family name, a senior member of *Compagne*'s staff, and a celebrity.

While guests gathered around the gin stall, with its fast-diminishing stock, waiters began to serve summer cocktails in vibrant colours.

In the makeshift kitchen, tempers were getting frayed and the temperature was rising. Jack wondered again why he had agreed to do this. At the beginning of the year, when Harry had first mentioned it, Lucy had made it sound like an incredible opportunity – but that was before things deteriorated at home. In the brief meeting with Sir Jesper that followed, he had been charmed. Since then, the event had changed venue three times, he had met with *Compagne*'s frightening Social Editor to discuss the intimate eating habits of the country's landed gentry, and argued out menus with half the staff of the magazine. Even the Flowers of Medieval had added their requests for vegan, macrobiotic and fruitarian menu variations.

The only saving grace had been Harry Hampton. At the point of walking away from it all, a week before the event, and wondering what he would do with ten kilos of fresh elderflower berries, never mind how he would cover the £35,000 bill for his new pop-up kitchen if he returned the substantial fee, Jack had obeyed Harry's command to down tools and head for what he promised was the best Full English this side of the Channel.

"Although I still maintain the best *Boudin Noir* is to be found in Marseille," Harry had insisted.

Leaving L'il in charge, Jack had grabbed his jacket and left his staff to it.

At Baker Bob's, which sat in an unprepossessing former garage forecourt, Harry and Jack both ordered man-sized plates and dug in.

"The thing that really pisses me off is that they seduced me into doing it by sucking up to my talents as a chef, and ever since then they have questioned my every decision. I thought my days as a commis chef were long over," Jack complained.

"Darling boy, it's not personal," Harry had helped himself to a third piece of fried bread. It was incredibly light and golden brown.

Jack, shovelling in forkfuls of lightly fried field mushrooms that tasted as though they had been foraged that morning, had already decided to have a chat with the chef with a view to offering him or her a job at Ramsden's.

"The key to being successful is hiring talented people. But it's also about trusting them to do the job well," Harry asserted. "That's where the problem is at *Compagne* at the moment."

"And what's with that Sophie bird?"

"She's so far round on the circle of *sine nobilitate* she's actually an equal opportunities snob. She only really hates the gold-tap brigade, the nous-nous as she calls them. I hear she's working her way through *Debrett's* looking for fakes at the moment."

Jack sipped his now lukewarm but refreshing Tregothnan tea. "I didn't know people like that existed. I always thought Lucy exaggerated."

"She does," Harry confirmed unapologetically. He had heard about Lucy's madcap plan to divorce and re-marry her lovely husband. "But the thing to remember is that Sophie Dexter-Browning and Timothy Cornell-Johnes hate each other. If he says green she says pink."

"Who is Timothy Cornell-whatever?"

"Royal Editor. Total dick. There's a rumour a Royal once called him an arsehole, quite loudly at a shooting party. I'd believe the story, except everyone needs their arsehole, and no one needs Timmo. But it's worth remembering that if she hates something, tell her he said the same thing and watch her change her tiny mind."

"Lucy was right about you."

Harry crinkled his eyes momentarily. "That I'm dashingly handsome?"

"That you have exceptional people skills." Jack gave a slow, wicked grin as he took the last piece of toast. "You're not bad to look at either."

Heading back to the kitchen an hour later, Jack watched unnoticed from the door as his staff stirred, chopped and snarled at each other. One of his old head chefs had once said that the taste of the food served in the dining room reflected the mood of the kitchen. If this was true, the dessert would be overly tart and the sauce to accompany the scallops would curdle.

"Everyone stop what you are doing and come over here," he called.

When they had gathered around, most enjoying the slight breeze emanating from the door more than the impromptu break, he continued. "There's no denying this is an important job for me – for all of us – and we need to do it well. And we will do it well. We now have a final well-planned menu, we have planned and prepped much of it in advance. Service is in 180 minutes, but first I want everyone to sit down and taste it."

He grabbed clean kitchen whites, stripped off his shirt, and headed for the burners. Showing his staff that he could single-handedly cook the menu for a team of six within a few minutes would make them feel more relaxed about preparing it for 240 people.

A team of waiters and waitresses had arrived an hour before and were now standing in ranks waiting for the guests to arrive to be plied with cocktails and *hors d'oeuvre*, which featured caviar on blinis at Sophie's insistence. Jack had been unconvinced; it felt a little obvious, but he'd had his revenge. The menus printed for each table which also listed him as their author had accidentally-on-purpose missed off the *hors d'oeuvre*.

The elderflower and gin sorbets were ready and plentiful, the scallops ready for searing and plating up on their bed of puy lentils, and the racks of lamb were being sent out whole to allow each table to carve – Jack thought it would taste better and make a great ice-breaker for the guests to argue out who would carve. The accompanying vegetables were cooking and would be served in large platters, which would help keep them warm, although with temperatures reaching 26°, today wasn't the day to worry about cold carrots. The waiting staff had been paired up and assigned tables to ensure food was delivered to diners at the same time. Victoria had arrived early, checking her table number and memorising the names of those she was sitting with. She noticed Lyle was on her table; a welcome relief, and he was bringing a guest. There were a frightening number of people with letters after their names but a quick Google on her iPhone had reassured her of their meaning and importance. As the table's *Compagne* representative it was really down to her to ensure every guest had a good time and was suitably delighted by the event – she had impressed this on all *Compagne* staff invited to attend at the previous day's editorial meeting and could only hope that Janey didn't decide to bore her table with her latest diet fad or that Timothy Cornell-Johnes didn't place peas under any seat cushions.

Tory had spent some time giving herself a lecture on staying away from Jack Ramsden but during a quick hello to Sir Jesper he had suggested that it was incumbent upon her position to wish the chef and his team luck, as well as pass on the many accolades his menu was bound to garner.

*It's not a problem,* she kept telling herself as she walked towards the portable kitchen. Jack had his hands full with his impending wedding, while *Compagne* remained a stopover in Tory's career, and while she had made friends worth taking with her, a romantic entanglement with a married-divorced-engaged chef wasn't going to help.

"This is like a culinary Tardis," she exclaimed, walking into the shiny silver environs of the pop-up kitchen, a wide smile plastered on her face.

Jack smiled before looking up. "More like a double-wide," he added.

He did a less than subtle double-take as he recognised the mystery woman from the afternoon Lucy had dropped her bombshell. He had spent many hours since thinking about her. He had even driven past her house, thought of going in. But what would he say? "Hello, fancy another shag? My name's Jack by the way."

No, it hadn't even just been about the sex. The conversation had been pretty good too; what he could remember of it, anyway. He had returned home afterwards and Lucy had been asleep, piles of wedding magazines surrounding her. He had headed for the bathroom for a shower, regretting the need to wash away the evidence, somehow feeling much dirtier when he emerged clean.

"I'm Victoria Manders, *Compagne*'s Managing Editor." Tory covered her embarrassment by moving forward with her hand outstretched. She looked along the row of staff at the burners, searing scallops and plating up with military precision, seemingly unaware of the heat.

Jack got the hint. "Hello," he smiled and grabbed the hand, adding softly, "again."

His whisper brought a rush of heat to Tory's lower extremities, quickly followed by a wave of shame that flushed her face. Fortunately the heat in the kitchen, and some expensive BB cream, covered the worst of it.

Noticing her discomfort, he gestured to the door. "Outside?"
She nodded and followed him.

"I'm sorry," Tory decided to speak first. "I wanted to introduce myself somehow. That afternoon, I had no idea who you were..."

Jack looked at his feet, embarrassed. "I'm not someone who does that sort of thing," he smiled. "Obviously I am, because I did, but I haven't before."

*Or since*, he silently added with a sense of sadness. She was just as beautiful as he remembered, though today she was more formally dressed in an ankle-length silk sleeveless dress printed with large orchids, her shoulders bare and sun-kissed. A waft of her perfume hit him, making his senses reel slightly.

Tory, unaware of the effect she was having on him, made it worse when she gently touched his upper arm, giving him a little electric shock. "It's okay. Let's just forget about it, shall we?"

Jack nodded, hiding his disappointment. If she could give him up that easily, maybe it hadn't meant anything to her. He felt a little silly. He wondered if it would be inappropriate for him to mention how good she looked.

"Your table will be served in T-minus 15 minutes," he replied.

Tory nodded and walked away. His dismissal had been both funny and final.

Her table was empty, but there was a swell of guests in the scent-filled rose garden. Filled with hues of reds and yellows formally laid out against box hedging, it was a natural gathering place, and offered some shade from the increasing heat. The lawned area was laid out with tables by the terrace of the glasshouse; huge yacht sails that had been secured to the ground using nautical rope and cleats had supplanted the usual marquees. It looked amazing. She watched as the photographers split into those creating the overly arty and unusable style shots within the tabled areas, and those being herded into photo-op groups by Sophie Dexter-Browning to ensure everyone who should be was appropriately captured, names correctly spelt and titles accurately recorded.

It was these times that made Sophie's position at *Compagne* – and her ludicrous demands – worthwhile. Who else knew a Smythe from a Smith? More to the point, who actually cared?

The tables were filling up but sitting off to one corner, although he was smiling at his table's guests, Malachy Drummond's mind was on other things. The middle of a novel was always a tricky thing. What Dick did next would decide the direction of the book. He wanted to ensure he made the right choices. *That wasn't a bad title for his next book*, he thought, scribbling 'What Dick Did Next' on the back of the cloth napkin by his water glass. In doing so, he was reminded of the awful management event Fredo Donaldson had organised during his brief stint as Managing Director. The day had entailed writing personal development plans on paper tablecloths with coloured felt tip pens. Sir Jesper had since moved his little brother on to another post, followed by another one, and one more after that. Malachy had lost track of his actual title.

Nearby, Gus was standing in a cream linen suit bought specially for the occasion. Following his visit to *Compagne*'s offices to relieve its Homes and Interiors Editor of some of her unwanted samples, he had been unable to stop thinking about her. They had chatted for a few minutes and he had been caught by her glorious smile. Since then he had seen Betsy a couple of times but other than smiling at him, she showed no signs of wanting to get to know him better. He, on the other hand, had been caught gazing at her byline photo in *Compagne* several times by Albie, who was quite capable of competitively chatting her up. Gus had made up his mind to at least try and get to know her, starting now.

He headed purposefully towards her. "Hi," he said, handing over a gin and elderflower pressé that had been sweating in his hands while he mentally prepared himself.

"Gus," he reminded her, when she looked at him slightly blankly; her mind had been filled with her latest interview.

She accepted the drink with a shy thank you.

"How are you?" Gus carried on. His carefully-rehearsed lines sounded anything but as he looked into the face he had been dreaming about.

"Good, are you after more samples?"

Gus shook his head. "Not for *The MacGuffin*, although I've just moved into a new place down here. Awful mess, I don't think it's been decorated for some time." Gus smiled, glad he'd managed to get out that key line.

"Really?" Betsy took a sip of her drink and felt a drip of condensation fall from the bottom of her glass onto the skirt of her silk dress. Shit, it would leave a stain if she didn't get it sorted.

"Yes. I thought perhaps you could come over for dinner sometime and perhaps give me some advice?"

Betsy was watching the drip on her silk dress flower as he spoke. She needed to get it under an air dryer quickly.

"Will you excuse me?" she said, walking away and leaving Gus with his mouth half open, forming his next sentence.

Albie sauntered over, having watched the whole exchange including the accidental soiling of Betsy's dress that had caused her to withdraw so suddenly. He chose not to share this knowledge with his Assistant Editor.

"Oh dear, Gus 0, Albie 4," he said, winking at his latest conquest, the blonde Flower of Medieval, who blushed as she walked by, accidentally-on-purpose catching his eye.

Gus took a gulp of his drink to cover his embarrassment. "It's not a contest," he muttered. "Anyway, I think its time to find our tables."

"Not one you can win," Albie retorted to Gus's retreating back.


"Did you get the invitation?" Lucy had been walking on air since, as she kept calling it to herself, Jack's proposal. The question had been directed at Jo Caruthers as she wandered around the Botanical Gardens and the impressive palm tree collection.

The guest list for Lucy's big day had leapt to 350 but the Maracks were happy to oblige, particularly for the £12,000 fee they were being paid simply to allow the use of Tremere Castle. They had even been invited to the event itself.

Behind closed doors the cash had elicited excited conversations among the ancient peers, not only about the much-needed new boiler the £12,000 would fund, but also the possibilities of opening up the house for other weddings. Only the most exclusive ones, of course, and the Maracks had agreed they wouldn't advertise as that would be vulgar. But coverage of this wedding in *Compagne* was bound to bring in a few discreet enquiries. Calculators had been busily consulted to get an idea of how much extra income could be expected.

They had lived in the same spot for ten centuries and the Maracks were doing okay, having amassed several fortunes since Domesday. The substantial house and lands those fortunes had bought had been signed over to the current owner when he was eighteen and his father just 38, thanks to a hereditary disease which seemed to rob the male heirs of their old- and occasionally middle-age. In a family with a few million in real estate, a life-threatening genetic disorder led to fatal financial disarray.

Lucy had also paid to use an ancient drawing of the castle as the centrepiece of her handmade invitations, on exquisite embossed linen paper. Her instructions to the designer had been simple: "I want people to frame these invitations because they are so beautiful."

Looking at her watch, Lucy saw she still had a few minutes before it was time to be seated. Her intention was to go directly to Sir Jesper and plea for space in the magazine to cover her wedding while he was enjoying the fruits of her husband's kitchen labour. She wasn't a celebrity but Jack was heading for his first Michelin star and he had been on *Saturday Kitchen* a couple of times. Also, surely their readers would want to know how a professional Weddings Editor would organise her big day.

But she was too late. "Ladies and gentlemen, welcome to *Compagne*'s Food and Drink Awards 2015," Sir Jesper spoke loudly, commanding their full attention.

Lucy headed for her seat. There would be plenty of time later to convince him.


Tory had headed back to her seat after a few turns around the gardens and after giving herself a good talking to. She didn't have time for romantic entanglements, she told herself again. Jack Ramsden clearly had his hands full with his ex-wife-bride-to-be, and she of course was still planning to return to London.

She smiled at everyone before turning to Lyle, sitting on her left. She was looking forward to a good gossip. She had hardly spoken to him since buying him lunch.

"Hello darling," he said, following enthusiastic air kisses. "Have you met my girlfriend, Lodd?"

He turned to the auburn-haired woman sitting on his other side.

Tory's smile widened. "Lodd McPherson?" She shook hands with her new columnist. "It's great to finally meet you. Betsy has been telling me all about you. I didn't know you knew Lyle?"

"She didn't. I guess I have you to thank for that – we met on the photo shoot for the October issue last month."

Tory sat back in delighted surprise as waiters laid linen napkins across their laps.

"You always did have the best celebrity gossip," Tory told Lyle as their first course was served.

# CHAPTER 25

Despite *Compagne* print deadlines, Sir Jesper had issued a three-line whip to everyone from his wife to the Flowers of Medieval to attend the London-based launch of *The MacGuffin*. He wanted wall-to-wall people there to hide any shortage of other guests.

Other than a quick handshake and attempted eye-meet at the Food and Drink Awards, Tory had rarely seen and had not spoken to Albie Pitchfork. He was either ferreted away in his posh offices, or attending events in London to raise the *The MacGuffin*'s, or his own, profile. Janey and Jo had already gathered that he was working his way through the Flowers of Medieval, who seemed to be living down to their Baudelairian nickname.

Every time Tory went down to the post room, one or other of them seemed to be getting ready for a date with the great man. Surprisingly, there hadn't been many tears and tantrums as a result yet. It seemed they were perfectly happy to each enjoy their one night of passion without expectations. Clearly he had a rare ability to reject without rancour.

Arriving home to her still-bare cottage, Tory had precisely eight minutes to get ready before the taxi arrived to take her to the train station. Fortunately the ever-dependable Jo had made the arrangements, so Tory assumed there would be a comfortable hotel room waiting at the other end of the journey. She threw a dress, shoes and clean underwear into her case and ran to the bathroom for her make-up bag – she could travel in jeans, put her make-up on during the train journey, and get changed at the other end. What she wasn't going to be able to do at any of those points was wash her dirty hair or shave her legs. She chose a long emerald-green diaphanous dress that would cover up her legs. She'd have to make do with her slightly greasy hair.

It was a punishingly hot day and the streets around her little cottage were filled with tourists. The 'For Sale' sign that hung in the small front garden was attracting a lot of attention and much pointing of smartphones from potential buyers. But she couldn't worry about that now. Tory pulled out high-heeled sandals in hot pink and a black crocheted shrug to complete the look.

The rush at least kept her concerns at bay about returning to London. She had called Donovan to warn him that she would be fleetingly returning to the city, but as she had promised not to visit her flat or make contact with any of her colleagues or neighbours he had been unconcerned. She agreed; she would be in the capital, in a completely different part of the city, for less than 24 hours. What could go wrong?

The honking of a car horn outside her front door brought her back to the current crisis, as she zipped up her jeans and shuffled her feet into a battered pair of flip-flops. Maybe she would get time to paint her toenails on the train, she thought, pummelling her way through the tourists to get into the waiting car.

The launch date had been chosen by Sir Jesper to fit into his calendar. He remained rather smitten with Martine, despite his attempts to disentangle himself, and had spent a pleasurable afternoon in his Chelsea flat with her wonderful lips attached to his favourite appendage. She brought a whole new meaning to the term 'deep throat'. Now dressed to impress, Martine headed out of the door for the party. Sir Jesper would follow in his car after a suitably long break.

The venue for the launch was aptly named. The new building was a cavernous space that stretched up to a ceiling several storeys above. If you could have stacked people vertically you could probably have got 100 times as big a crowd into The Space but the launch of *The MacGuffin* was already pretty busy.

Arriving only 40 minutes later than Sir Jesper had demanded, Tory stored her case with the check-in girls, grabbed a cosmopolitan from a waiter and downed half of it; partly from thirst, partly to make it look like she had been there since the requested 9pm.

She had to admit it was an inspired choice for a magazine launch. The exhibition, by an artist curiously named Flow, was like an IKEA showroom for giants. Some critics had seen his or her work as a commentary on the cavernous space itself. But the artist's intention was more about illustrating capitalism's grip on people to constantly demand bigger and better things — and how this consumerism was diminishing humanity. At least that was according to the artist's statement Tory had read online during her train journey.

Tonight The Space was home to huge sofas that easily sat twenty and which people needed to use specially-placed stepladders to climb onto. There were pairs of bunk beds that sat close to the ceiling, and coffee tables that guests could quite comfortably stand beneath.

"It looks great, but it was a fucking nightmare to sort out the Health and Safety of holding the event here," a deep drawl in her ear sent a shiver down her spine.

She turned, smiling politely. Albie Pitchfork stood, dark hair artfully tousled, dressed in a slender-fitting light blue designer suit. The shirt was open at the throat. He looked more like a Hollywood icon than a magazine editor, or at least someone not out of place on the front cover.

"I can imagine the fun of getting out of one of those sofas after a few drinks, especially in heels," Tory agreed, wondering if he knew who she was. "I'm amazed these celebrities turned up for an exhibition designed to turn them into Lilliputians."

"Can I get you another drink, Victoria?" So he did know her name.

She looked around for a normal-sized surface to put her empty glass on and settled for the tray of one of the waiters now wandering around serving *hors d'oeuvre*. It had been a long time since lunch so she snagged him, swapping her empty glass for a few bites of rainbow-coloured sushi. Despite the size of the exhibits, the finger food was minuscule. She piled up most of the contents of the tray onto a black napkin.

"I've been wondering when we'd get to meet properly," Albie returned as she was finishing the last of her sushi bites. "So what do you think?" he asked, his eyes staying on her face, giving no clues as to what he was referring to.

"The magazine looks great, from what I've seen of it so far." Tory decided to ignore the transparent sexual undertones. She looked over to where the first issue's cover had been blown up to match the size of the exhibits. There were also similarly scaled-up versions sitting on the coffee tables.

Already the sofas had filled up and from below it made a comical sight: lines of women in silk dresses, legs swinging with heeled shoes at their ends.

"I'm not sure I want to stand underneath those sofas, one of those stiletto heels could have your eye out." Tory looked around for another waiter. The sushi snacks had only served to highlight her hunger rather than satisfy it.

Albie noticed her distraction. "Hungry?"

Again the husky voice. Tory nodded, striding purposefully towards a table laden with food. A few people were inspecting the dishes – Harry Hampton had already secured a plateful, which was always a good sign. She picked up a napkin and grabbed a few more pieces of sushi. It was addictive stuff, and easy to eat.

Albie had followed her over. "I can take you out for dinner when all this is over. Where are you staying?"

Harry looked over and smiled at her and moved away, without comment – but not too far out of earshot, so he could hear how the Young Turk would play it.

Tory shrugged. She hadn't caught up with Jo yet to find out where she was booked.

"I've got my little place in the Barbican," Albie said.

"Wow, I thought they were dead architect's shoes," she joked, referring to the preponderance of architects living in what was considered one of London's most important abodes.

"I moved in not long after my book became a best-seller, it wasn't quite so fashionable then. I think the overflow have now moved on to Trellis Tower."

Tory nodded to several of the Flowers of Medieval, dressed to impress and not looking too happy that she was dominating the star attraction.

"I'd better let you mingle," she said, nodding towards his fan club. "It looks like I've had my five minutes of favouritism."

Albie smiled and watched her walk away.

She headed towards Sir Jesper and Lady Rose before being stopped halfway by a vision in red. Janey was deep in conversation with Betsy, her missing-in-action Homes and Interiors Editor, who was wrongly but none-the-less elegantly dressed in a simple cream linen suit.

Betsy noticed her looking her up and down. "I know, I know, it should be evening wear. But I couldn't find anything. My wardrobe is currently hanging silk wall covering samples, and I've had to empty my downstairs closet to fit in samples of tiling. I'm lucky I didn't end up accidentally wrapping myself up sari-style in a Terence Conran throw."

Tory and Janey laughed. "You look wonderful, very elegant. Besides, at least you got time to wash your hair, which is more than I did – and thankfully this dress hides my hairy legs."

Janey and Betsy rushed to tell Tory she looked gorgeous.

"But I do have some dry shampoo in my case, if you want to freshen up," Janey, ever the perfectionist, had spotted a glistening at Tory's scalp.

"Lead the way," Tory was happy to head to the cloakroom under her Art Director's expert gaze.

The night was going less well for Gus. Reporters looking for a quote from the editor were less than enamoured at getting his not so glamorous assistant. Albie kept disappearing and the press had a terrible habit of shooting the messenger. Gus knew this wasn't going to help him find another job, which by now he was beginning to think was a necessity. Being deputy to Albie was like parenting all four of the bad kids in *Charlie and the Chocolate Factory* at once. By turns he was lazy, greedy, avaricious and shallow. Albie expected Gus to keep up with his demands no matter how unreasonable and unattainable. It was proving impossible. And, like all narcissistic people, Albie accepted the successes without thanks while failures were taken personally, sharply reprimanded, and never forgotten.

They had spent a long time going over the guest list for the evening. Gus wanted to invite more people than there was capacity for, recognising not all would turn up. Albie refused to believe anyone would turn down his invitation and wanted more precise numbers.

Gus spotted *Compagne*'s Managing Editor talking to a petite woman in a red dress and the beautiful Homes and Interiors Editor.

"It's rude to stare," Albie appeared at his left shoulder, eyeing up the trio of totty before them. He had already decided to bed Tory that night; a wonderful way to celebrate his success. So far the two magazine teams had been working as pretty much separate entities, but there was scope for closer working relationships. Albie was planning to get very close, and decided that the two editors should lead by example.

However, watching his Assistant Editor gaze forlornly at that short-haired blonde, he wondered if he should go for her first. He needed to keep Gus's mind on the magazine, there was no time for love-sick leave.

"So how's it going?" he asked. He grabbed Gus's elbow when he felt him involuntarily move forward as Janey led Tory off to the cloakroom, leaving the blonde alone and ripe for the picking.

Gus turned his attention away from Betsy. Knowing Albie was doing it on purpose didn't reduce his sense of professionalism but nobody's timing could be so consistently awful. Every time he was working on something for himself, be it personal or professional, his boss would suddenly appear and demand attention.

"Really well, the press boys and girls are asking for some of your time. We've got two social photographers here for *Compagne* – they've kept a spread open for October's issue which should all have gone to print tonight, so they can cover it. Our pics – I've briefed the photographers to give us something a bit more celebrity-focused – will go online at midnight. The snapper," he pointed out a young man in scuffed converse baseball boots, skinny jeans and a pinstriped jacket, who was just the right side of shabby chic, "needs to get some group shots of the staff, it's such a great setting. So can you help me round them up?"

Albie nodded vaguely, noting the blonde was still standing alone.

"Of course," he agreed then abruptly turned, heading towards Betsy and grabbing a couple of drinks from a passing waiter.

"Hello, I thought you might like one of these," he handed the surprised woman a drink. "I'm Albie, Albie Pitchfork," he told her redundantly, but with transparent humility. "You're Betsy?"

Betsy nodded, taking the drink. "That's right."

"And you are the fantastic Homes and Interiors Editor that I've been warned against poaching for our magazine."

Betsy smiled; his charm was transparent but no less welcome.

"How long have you been doing it for?"

"My job? About two years. Retrained from newspapers. I was a crime correspondent." Betsy enjoyed the surprised look.

"Really? Quite a change."

"It was."

Betsy looked over Albie's shoulder, noticing Gus, his dark red hair falling over his forehead as he ran around the hall gathering people together while a photographer stood patiently by. She wondered if Albie would introduce them, not knowing that they had already met, but he was too intent on sharing his own story, of his plans for the magazine and introducing the possibility of poaching staff from *Compagne*, especially talented interviewers that were languishing in Homes and Interiors. Betsy nodded and smiled at the right moments, happy to release him when demands were made that he meet new arrivals.

"Excuse me?" he said.

Betsy nodded. "Gladly," she told him and moved away towards the outsize sofas.

Gus watched her, having seen Albie move over to charm the latest gaggle of celebrities who had turned up in time for the all-important photo op. He nervously tugged at his hair. He'd had it cut and styled for the event, and his hands got caught up in an unfamiliar crust of wax and hairspray, which had failed spectacularly in keeping his fringe out of his face. He pulled his hand down and wiped it on the back of his self-consciously skinny jeans then moved towards Betsy, determined to try again. But he was too late. Betsy was now surrounded by women. Gus recognised the *Compagne* editor in green silk, then there was Lodd McPherson the former WAG, and the petite redhead once more. He stuffed a hand into his pocket and changed direction, heading instead towards Albie who had been imperiously beckoning him.

Betsy found her attention wandering from Lodd's story about how she had hooked up with Lyle.

"He called me the next day, to ask if he could meet for lunch," Lodd was telling everyone. "And we met up in London and didn't part for about three days. Imagine me ending up with a member of the paparazzi!"

Madly in love, Lodd was quick to spot the symptoms in Betsy who, unaware of her feelings, still found her eyes seeking out Gus. She was wondering if she should go and speak to him, aware that she had been rude to him at the Food and Drink Awards, and suddenly wanting to explain.

In the end, Betsy went home alone. Gus followed her in a taxi to Paddington, heading for the sleeper train that would reach Cornwall in the early hours, but his vague plan to buy a drink for her in the train's bar was mooted by the classic lack of catering staff.

Instead he sat alone, while Betsy slept fitfully in one of the sleepers, unaware that the man who was keeping her awake was sitting in the next carriage.

Tory never did find out which hotel she was booked into. In the middle of Sir Jesper's speech welcoming guests and thanking all those involved in the magazine's first issue, Albie had leaned over and whispered an invitation too good to pass up: Chinese food and cunnilingus, not necessarily in that order. The journey to the South Bank and Albie's designer pad had been too far in the end and instead they had headed for a hotel.

The following morning Tory headed for the bathroom, stood under the shower, and finally washed her hair. Her lips were slightly bruised and her eyes told her she needed at least another six hours' sleep. But smearing on a splatter of BB cream and a swipe of mascara, she pulled on her travelling jeans and headed back out. Albie was still sleeping. In the daylight he looked a little crumpled, his hair swept back to reveal a high widow's peak and cheeks flecked with graying stubble. She smiled, reaching for a pen and a piece of hotel paper.

The slam of the hotel room door woke Albie, who rubbed his face with the palm of his hand, enjoying the sandpaper sound of his stubble, in an attempt to wake up. He turned to see if his overnight guest remained, and breathed a sigh of relief at the empty space next to him. Sex was one thing, but sleeping together smacked too much of intimacy. He would gladly forgo morning sex if it meant sleeping – and waking – alone.

His eyes finally focused on the note pinned to the crumpled pillow beside him. He pulled the bent safety pin that had been holding it in place out first and silently congratulated Tory for finally finding a use for the sewing kits that could be found in all hotel rooms. A phone number, he suspected, feeling his heart sink, perhaps preceded by a 'thank you for a great night, let's do it again soon'.

He squinted at the sheet, his eyes slow to focus on the few words on the paper. There were just five words, and no phone number. *You owe me dim sum*. He smiled and crumpled the paper into a ball.

Overall it had been a great night. Interest in *The MacGuffin* had been immense; the combination of the exhibition and the artist giving his first ever interview in the magazine had demanded more column inches than it would otherwise have been given. By now Gus would be back in the office compiling the cuttings from today's print and online reviews. He lay back on the goose down pillows.

And he had got to fuck his rival. And she hadn't been half bad.

# CHAPTER 26

Godfrey Cleaver adjusted his tie and headed into Claridge's dining room to meet Lady Rose. Through membership at his club, he had heard hints that the government was clamping down on sales from country estates where tax was due to be paid. There was even talk of a special hit squad. It was time, he decided, to foreclose on their lucrative partnership. But there was no need for Lady Rose to know just yet.

During the course of their 'special' friendship, Cleaver had netted fifteen per cent of her earnings, and had occasionally boosted his percentage where private sales meant he could be a little vague about the final price paid. He was dishonest, after all, and that was really the only thing she could trust.

An unpromising start in life meant Cleaver had always chased after money. Recognising that class was one of the most important of commodities, he had learned to dress well and speak even better. Finding himself in the world of art and antiques, he found the value that something seemingly insignificant could be worth simply through age was fascinating.

"This pen," he was fond of saying to his clients, pulling out a cheap pen from his pocket kept there for the occasion (in reality he favoured a Mont Blanc fountain pen). "This worthless, cheap, mass-produced pen will become unimaginably valuable simply through time. As its identical millions are used and disposed of, its age and its rarity will fetch thousands, and even hundreds of thousands, of pounds with people wanting to buy a slice of a time they never knew."

And while experts could use all kinds of means to discover many arts and antiquities there were more than enough grey areas for him to operate in quite successfully. There was no lying involved, it was purely a question of embellishment.

"You could add several zeroes onto the value of this pen," he would continue, "if it was used or once owned by royalty, perhaps even a great writer. Imagine owning the pen that Shakespeare used to write *Romeo and Juliet*."

With his own going concern, he was making quite a good living when the opportunity arose to help create a catalogue of the Donaldson treasures. And meeting Lady Rose had been a meeting of minds; she saw his value at once.

Now it was time for him to find out hers.

"Lady Rose," Godfrey entered the lobby where she was sitting leafing through a magazine. He allowed his voice to thicken with pleasure at the sight of her. Lady Rose stood and accepted his hands in greeting. "I've organised a private dining room, so we can discuss business without fear of being overheard."

"You do think of everything." Lady Rose smiled and allowed him to lead her off to a private room, already set for two.

He held out her chair and waited for her to settle before taking his own place opposite her. Lady Rose hid a slight smile behind her water glass; Godfrey always laid on such heavy compliments, it was impossible sometimes to take him seriously.

She chose a cold consommé and grilled sole to follow while he, mindful of being on expenses, and despite the heat, chose seared scallops and roast duck. The two had agreed to continue their official business relationship as an excuse to meet and communicate, with Lady Rose on record as seeking advice on insurance, and sending recovered items on to him for repair or renovation as needed. They had agreed on a regular monthly lunch engagement to catch up on this official work, as well as their real business, which was more interesting and much more lucrative to both parties.

Cleaver had earned good money from Lady Rose, and it had helped to ensure his auction rooms stayed in business. *An honest man in this business never makes money*, he was fond of saying to himself. When you factored in the cost of an expensive shop front, appropriately trained and groomed staff, handmade suits and regular trips to his barber, his bootmaker and his bookmaker, he rarely made ends meet.

"There has been some talk of a clamp-down in recent times on sales from estates," Godfrey began after the waiters had presented their starters with a flourish. "The taxman is after his cut on these art and antiquity sales. I've seen a few unlikely candidates hanging around the sales rooms recently, more intent on making notes than bids. We need to be careful."

Lady Rose took a sip of wine. It was something she had known would happen at some point and she was relying on Godfrey's expertise in knowing when it was time to call time. She had already planned a trip to Gibraltar to review her financial standing with a view to possibly dissolving their relationship.

Cleaver had always managed to get her items on sale at the auction house; how he fudged over the ownership paperwork and his own tax returns, she never enquired.

Things were changing anyway, as buyers demanded more evidence of where an item had come from. She didn't blame them. Legal challenges against ownership were getting more common and the laws surrounding buying in good faith were being eroded, thanks to looted art finally beginning to surface as Nazi thieves died off and their offspring presented their family heirloom for sale, often not knowing its dirty history.

Cleaver's expertise had served him very well when he came up against Dougie Lawson, who had presented to him a minor Rembrandt, found in his grandmother's attic. It had passed first tests, but Cleaver had spotted something amiss with Lawson. He admitted he had been trained in art – something that he said had helped him identify the grimy painting when clearing the house of his dead gran. However, further checks revealed Lawson was also a talented painter, and more than able to copy the beautiful brushwork and capturing of light that the Dutch Master was so famed for. Eventually he had admitted the fraud. He had created paint to match that of Rembrandt, and aged his board appropriately, after which the painting, he had admitted, had been 'child's play'.

Instead of calling in the fraud squad, Cleaver had taken him out for dinner. Lawson recognised a fellow scammer, unless the young antiquities expert was giving him a hell of a Michelin-starred last supper before calling in the fraud squad. He had agreed to help Cleaver, and from time to time a genuine painting put up for auction had been replaced with one of Lawson's fakes. Sometimes the fraud wasn't noticed, and the fake was sold.

If it was spotted (and sometimes Cleaver would be the one to spot it; it helped to keep his reputation unspoiled), the owners became the latest in a long line of art collectors who had been duped into buying a fake.

Lawson had got himself into a spot of bother, though; a fight in a pub and a spell in stir, and that line of credit had suddenly closed. Cleaver was left with Lady Rose. For a time he had considered upping his commission, but even that wouldn't be enough.

Lady Rose had begun the partnership without any real idea of how much she would amass and, if she was honest, what she would do with it. Matt wouldn't really need it, and so far she never had. But, like many things in life, it was nice to know it was there.

Cleaver, however, was quite clear about what he was doing with his money. Much of his gains had found their way into the pockets of his local turf accountant, and he had become a firm favourite over the years with the ever-changing and ever younger ladies who worked along the canal near his home. Like many people in his position, he had learned to live up to his income. And he had no intention of stepping it down now. If Lady Rose stopped riffling the Donaldson hoards, he would be back to living off the pitiful profits drawn from his antique salesroom.

There was a time when he would keep accounts, sitting with his calculator at his desk, endlessly doing sums that would give him a retirement nest egg. And as time went on the sums spiralled into fantasy; desperation was a powerful incentive, he knew from experience.

"Do we need to stop?" Lady Rose interrupted his thoughts.

Cleaver felt his fantasy nest egg shrivel. "No, there's no need to shut up shop just yet. What have you got for me next?"

"It's in my room. A drawing."

Godfrey smiled, his juices flowing. "Who by?"

"It's signed by Stubbs, but it looks like one of his apprentices."

"Still, the signature is there?"

"Yes."

"Marvellous. I'll get it down to our lab boys who will confirm that it's genuine and add it to the sales list. Better to get a name like that sold out in one of our Middle East auctions. Anything horse-related is very popular out there. Anything else in the pipeline?"

"Just a few pieces of china. I have them upstairs."

Keen to get his hands on the drawing, Cleaver wiped his mouth with his napkin and stood. "Shall we go and look at them?"

Later he called for one of the warehouse workers he used to collect the works from Lady Rose's suite. Before he left, she again raised the issue of suspending their partnership for a time, or even dissolving it for good. Godfrey would need to find a way to make her desperate to continue.

He headed out of Claridge's, waving away the doorman and the waiting taxi. He needed to clear his head and think carefully about his next move. And there was always the possibility that he would need to save the fare.

Lady Rose sat in her suite, hands resting in her lap, waiting for the drawing and other items to be collected. She had known Godfrey Cleaver long enough to know when he was hiding something. He had been unsettled by talk of ending their lucrative partnership; she knew he had got used to the money they earned. She had always avoided any talk of other scams he might have going, taking the view that it was nothing to do with her, as long as it didn't impact on her business dealings. She knew Cleaver had maintained a good reputation among dealers and buyers, and that reputation was the most important currency in the art and antiquities trade, but it would be naïve to think that she was his only client who sat in the shade. She predicted she would need to get herself free of this entanglement, and soon.

The following day, Lady Rose was in the second kitchen off the hall when her phone rang. The kitchen was originally used to store food. It was several steps down and made of stone, which helped to keep it chill, even on warm days. She was sorting through the cutlery, the bone-handled stuff really wasn't to her taste. But the pretence of animal welfare seemed to have died out, heralding the return of furs to the catwalk, and these things had become increasingly sought after. They were old, but quite common. Still, she was pretty sure Cleaver would find a new home for the set.

She was due to go on a trip to Gibraltar the following week. She would miss Matt, but hadn't really seen much of him since he had moved back home. He had regressed to teenage-like behaviour, spending all his time in front of computer screens in his room with the curtains closed and only coming out to eat. The previous night she had managed to prise him away from his room long enough to sit down to dinner. Sir Jesper was away for the night; some dinner in London, she forgot with whom.

Over the entrée, she had launched into her prepared speech. "Darling, what is it you want out of life?"

Matt had scowled at his plate, his expression nothing to do with the seafood pasta, which was one of his favourites.

"Game designer," he eventually told her.

"Computer games?" she asked. "Those shoot 'em up things that young people seem so enamoured with?"

"No," Matt decided he might as well elaborate, "I've started developing a game that breeds virtual horses. It means people who like horseracing can own and breed and race them – as well as bet on them, of course."

Lady Rose, smiled. "So why are you working at the magazine?"

Matt raised an eyebrow. The answer was obvious. "Dad."

She paused, sighed, and dabbed her mouth with the cloth napkin from her lap. "Did I ever tell you that your father wanted to follow in his mother's footsteps?" Sir Jesper's mother had been a highly successful horse breeder up until the 1980s. She had raced flat.

"No, I didn't know that. What happened?"

"The company needed someone to take over. At one point it was hoped Freddy might do it, but he was clearly not up to the task, so your dad took it on, thinking he could run it until it ran itself and he could leave it alone. But over the years, he found it impossible to leave."

Matt suddenly felt sorry for his father. He had always seemed to like what he did, but knowing something of his father's reputation with other women, he supposed Sir Jesper had found plenty to compensate himself. Not that he would ever share that with his mother.

Lady Rose smiled, guessing his thoughts. "You'd think it would make him understand your predicament more – but now he thinks as a father, not as a son."

Over a dessert of lightest syllabub, she asked him more questions about how the website would work. It sounded as though the only thing holding him back was serious investment. Perhaps she had finally found a good use for her money. She would give it some thought whilst she was in Gibraltar.

The trip was well-timed and it was always good to get a break from all the fawning she suffered under as the wife of Sir Jesper. While abroad she would check on her various accounts. The money she amassed was rarely spent; she self-financed her trips out there, feeling it was wrong to use Sir Jesper's money as it was part of a business trip – in fact it could be seen as a tax deduction, if only she paid tax. She smiled at the thought.

While in Gibraltar, Lady Rose stayed in complete luxury, always at the same hotel, and paid for an almost full-time masseuse, a luxury rarely indulged while living at The Glades. She knew her husband often headed up to London for a massage for his back problems, but it seemed a long way to go, particularly as Sir Jesper generally returned in more pain than he left with.

After coffee, Matt had headed back to his computer screens, and Lady Rose went upstairs to pack. As she was laying dresses on the bed, her private line rang.

She picked up the receiver, wondering who it would be. "Lady Rose?"

It was Cleaver.

Lady Rose's voice was sharp. "Godfrey, had we arranged to speak today?"

"No, but I have a few updates for you."

"Go ahead."

"The vase has sold for £67,000. A good price."

"Yes."

"How do you want the money?"

"The usual way, please transfer to my off-shore accounts."

"Let me check the account numbers I've got with you: 5576998 and 3211345."

Lady Rose silently read them back to herself. "Yes that's right."

"Okay. When are you off to Gibraltar?"

"Two days."

"Well, the money should be transferred before you go."

"Splendid."

"Do you have anything else for me? I wondered if the time was right to dispose of those two old King Louis VII chairs?"

"Perhaps. Let's see when I get back. Is that all?"

"Yes. Have a good trip and we'll speak on your return, I'm sure."

Cleaver replaced the phone and chewed his thumbnail before picking up his phone again. He dialled a number from memory and tapped his finger on the table until it was picked up.

"Yeah?"

"It's me. You need to do it tomorrow."

"Okay."

# CHAPTER 27

Sir Jesper, arriving home the following day, looked around the house and congratulated himself, not for the first time, for marrying so well. Rosie had transformed it from a crumbling stately pile to a statement of stately riches. Not easy in these times, as more and more of the country's ancient family homes went under the hammer. Opening up the house and gardens to raise money for her pet charities had worked out well, the visitors' book bulged with gushing comments.

His wife appeared, having been out to prepare for her trip the following day.

"This came for you." Sir Jesper handed over a thick brown envelope. She could see the start of the letter through the transparent window. *'Dear Mrs Donaldson...'*

*Junk mail*, she thought as she swept it out of his hand on her way up the stairs, "Thank you darling. Will I see you later for the dinner?"

Sir Jesper checked the knot on his tie in the ancient hall mirror that he had looked in every day of his married life. "Yes. I'll be there for about noon to meet the arrivals, are you free to do the same?"

"Yes darling," she called from the upper landing. Heading into her small study, which adjoined her dressing room, she placed the letter on her desk. Sitting down, she weighed it in her hands before placing it underneath the invitations and letters sitting in her in-tray, deciding it could wait.

Matt spotted the waitress with the endless legs over-pour yet another glass of champagne. It wasn't like her mother to allow newbies into the fold; fear of hubby hunters and reporters meant she was always careful and used the same agency for these public events. Perhaps there was an exceptional circumstance. He longed to get back to his laptop. Horseface was in the middle of breeding season and he was keen to see how his virtual breeders were doing. He had high hopes for one of his thoroughbred fillies called Pink Toes, who was in season and had the stallions lining up for a cover. Their owners were currently having closed bids to see who would be successful.

The deadline had passed at midday. He inched out the iPhone

from his pocket, but pushed it back as his father headed towards him, an elderly lady at his elbow. Matt felt assured it wasn't a matchmaking attempt – the woman at his elbow was way beyond childbearing age and even if he could forgive her poor looks, an inability to provide the Donaldsons with an heir would be unconscionable.

Matt half expected that when he made his choice, she would face hormone tests. He put the thought aside. Perhaps he could develop a Horseface for humans. All those unsatisfied dowagers would have great fun testing out their genes against those of other families to find the perfect match.

Smiling directly at his father, he prepared to shake hands, bow to, or air-kiss the elderly stranger. Happily, she settled for a brief hold of her hand.

"This is your Great Aunt Bella, she hasn't seen you since you were about three."

"Great Aunt Bella?" Matt thought he recognised her name. "How lovely to see you. I hope you are well, but I hardly need ask, I can see that you are."

Great Aunt Bella beamed at him. "Well one doesn't like to complain, but when you get to my age, it's a miracle to wake up in the morning."

Her flat delivery suggested she had read his mind and was responding as he had come to expect from old ladies, by complaining about her health.

"I'm glad you awoke this morning," he replied in kind.

She was his grandfather's younger sister, and as such had once lived at The Glades, where she had grown up. *How strange to have to wait for an invitation to your former family home*, Matt thought as he invited her for a walk around the gardens.

"While your legs are still holding you up," he joked. "Do you like horses?"

She nodded, and took the proffered arm. Out in the gardens, they chatted as they headed for a shady seated area.

"So what are you going to do with your life?" Bella asked. "I get the feeling the world of publishing bores you."

Matt laughed at her bluntness. "Don't you want to talk about the weather?"

"At my age, I don't have time for small talk. I might drop dead before I get an answer, or forget what we were talking about."

Matt smiled. "No, I don't really want to be a magazine publisher."

"Neither did your father. But what could my brother do? We all knew Freddy wasn't up to the challenge. Left in his hands, *Compagne* would be no more."

"Uncle Freddy hasn't been hugely successful, but he's very loyal to Dad."

"Hmmm, well never mind that generation; they had their shot, even Freddy, but he muffed it. I want to know about you."

"The thing is, I have this website going that's got the potential to be huge, but it needs some serious investment."

"So tell me about it."

"Basically, it's a virtual horse breeding world; you buy and sell horses, breed horses and race them."

"And where do you make the money?"

"Different ways. When you join, you have to start with buying your basic breeding farm and horses. The game owner gets a cut of any sales or winnings and breeders pay to enter their horses in the race."

"And who does this?"

"Well loads of people bet on horses that don't own them, but this way they can own them. So far I've got 600 breeders, but I can't have any more, I don't have the time to create their horses. I have to create a genetic profile for each one and then create the code that can calibrate the odds on them winning races. But Dad's got me working on the magazines' new websites."

"Have you told Jessie your idea?"

"No. I know what he wants for me. And I know there's no one else to do it. I don't have any siblings and Freddy is childless. It's just me." Matt paused. "Well, it's payback as well. Did Dad tell you? I got into a bit of trouble at university."

"Really? How?"

"Online gambling, I built up quite a lot of debt. Dad eventually agreed to help out, but the payoff was to come and work for him. It's how I got the idea for Horseface though; it's a great alternative to gambling. But I'm not sure Dad will see it that way."

Great Aunt Bella was silent for so long that Matt thought she might have dropped off as she had warned him. But she suddenly spoke up. "Would you consider taking on a partner, someone to invest in Horseface so you can employ people to help you?"

"An investor, you mean?"

"Yes. How much would you need? Are there people you can employ to help you?"

"To really develop it, it probably needs around £200,000; maybe less if we find a cheap office."

Great Aunt Bella looked vacantly ahead for a moment. She came to and patted Matt's hand. "Let me see your business plan and I will let you have a cheque."

"Business plan?"

"I'm not a charity, Mathieu, and this isn't your inheritance. My accountants will need to see some figures then the money is yours. Once you've got it off the ground, we can agree how to approach your dad. If there's one thing I learned from my elopement..."

"Your what?" he interrupted.

"My elopement." She threw up her hands. "Another story for another day. Anyway, what I learned was that it's always better to present unpleasant news as *au fait accompli*."

"You mean wait until it's a huge success and then tell him?"

"That's exactly it. Now I'm tired and ready to go home, can you let your dad know? I'll sit here for a minute."

"Okay."

"And Mathieu? Make sure you come up with a new name for it." She closed her eyes in the sunshine and smiled. "It's high time a Donaldson heir went a different way."

Matt gave Bella a huge kiss on the cheek before heading back into the room to find his father to arrange her return home. His future suddenly felt more secure than it had for many years and he felt like celebrating. His eyes wandered back to the waitress still pouring champagne. The belt of her black apron was wound twice around her slender waist and her skirt sat six inches above her knees as she towered over the short, squat guests. She didn't look like she really cared. Perhaps he should mention her to his mother or see if she fancied heading off somewhere to celebrate the launch proper of Horseface.

Lily was not enjoying her assignment. Everywhere she looked there were over-bred, stuffy, middle-aged people trying to avoid the D-list celebrities who were trying to pick up tips on how to hold a champagne flute. By the stem? By the fullest part of the glass? Who cared?

And why were the ruling classes so bloody ugly? Maybe it was genetics, all those generations of inbreeding. But the house was unbelievable. It had no right to be owned by one family when it could easily house a dozen. The land around it could be publicly owned and used for something much more meaningful than a statement of wealth.

But that wasn't why she was there. Her role was simple: gather intelligence. Although why going undercover required such a short skirt, she would never understand. Bowers would no doubt have a smart reply about her stature but she hadn't bothered to ask the shortarse, just grabbed the micro-skirt, shirt and apron and headed into the van to change, ignoring his shout to remove all her piercings this time.

She spotted Lady Rose attending to her guests by the grand staircase. Smiling, to everyone the gracious host, but she was a thief. And she was going to get caught.

"The net is closing in," Lily muttered to herself, heading back to the kitchen with her empty champagne bottle.


Malachy Drummond was exhausted. Lady Rose had insisted he be the one to provide tours of the pleasure grounds rather than their talented but rather rough-around-the-edges Head Gardener. His head ached and if one more person confused the hollyhocks with gladioli he would scream and throw himself in the well-stocked and recently filled lake.

Malachy had started life working in gardens; it was in his blood, but not under his nails. His father was a plantsman, as was his father before him. By the time he was old enough to decide what he wanted to do for a living, it felt too late. His life was already mapped out and his skills had been provided for. He had inherited a very successful garden centre in the Cotswolds and his career looked stuck in the mud for life until a chance meeting with Lady Rose out on one of her forages for developing her herb gardens led to his penning a small column in *Compagne.*

The truth was, Malachy hated getting his hands dirty. He hated the messy work behind all of the beauty. It was merely a façade, to be enjoyed at open days by the growing legions of garden tourists, who had no idea and no interest in the colossal amount of work involved, preferring to 'ooh' and 'ahh' over the pretty shapes, colours and smells. But looking at the glorious flowerbeds filled with alcea that led to the more formal rose garden, Malachy knew this was not the natural state of the land, and gardening was a constant battle against the pugnacious mud and weeds which threatened to engulf it all.

He smiled at the next group of guests gathering for a look. He longed to invite them to come along on a freezing cold day in January when there was nothing but dirt as far as the eye could see, the sweet smell of the tea roses replaced by the noxious fumes of horse shit.

"Welcome to The Glades," he began, smiling, hands behind his back. "These gardens have been in existence for more than two centuries, when the famous Capability Brown first advised the second Lord Donaldson on how to lay out his newly-acquired pleasure grounds."

Malachy walked off, carefully picking his way over the lawn in his immaculate and mud-free green Hunters as the group followed.

Watching them head into the shade from the large windows above the hall, Betsy Beaufort wished she could swap places. Even inside the thick-walled old house, the heat was palpable. She had been roped in to provide tours of the public areas of the house, despite knowing very little about it.

She had mugged up on its star treasures using Lady Rose's well-thumbed catalogue. "Don't lose it, it's my life's work," Lady Rose had joked with her when handing it over.

"Is this the original?" Betsy had asked. "Why don't you make a copy? I can photocopy it and get it back to you."

But Lady Rose had forcefully insisted no copy be made, for fear it got into the wrong hands, and Betsy had silently pledged not to get any coffee rings on it.

Her hours of homework had been well spent. It meant she was able to speak with some authority on the hunting tapestries – and more importantly linger in the marginally cooler hallway where they were displayed away from the damaging sunlight. She also slowed down in the bedrooms as she showed off the grand furniture that always drew gasps, especially when she let one of the tour lie on the ancient four-poster that had once encased royalty, while failing to explain that the horsehair mattress which had held the ageing frame of the old king had long since been replaced.

Managing to grab a tall glass of pink lemonade before heading back upstairs to meet the final group of the day, Betsy smiled at a young tall woman in a crisp shirt and black skirt, who was looking intently at the paintings lining the hallway.

Lily had ditched the apron and added some lipstick and small diamond studs into her ears to join the tour of the house. It wasn't really part of her assignment but she enjoyed looking at artwork, even if she thought it belonged in a museum rather than a private home. Trained in Fine Art in London, Lily had found herself uninspired by her fellow students' attempts at conceptual art. Her art school experience reached a real low point when her studio mate won a national award and endless column inches for her show entitled *Empties*. It was an exhibition of blank walls and floor space, where viewers were invited to imagine their own art on the walls. For the unimaginative, prompt cards were provided featuring random nouns.

Lily had headed for the History of Art department instead. After a brief fling at curating, she had found herself consulting with the Fraud Squad, and from there she had joined Her Majesty's Revenue and Customs, helping the tax man collect the right artworks from tax dodgers, and more often from criminals, in lieu of tax owed.

In time she had been asked to join a special taskforce designed to clamp down on antiquity sales among old estates after it had come to the taxman's notice that a large number of goodies were finding their way into the country's auction houses without the proceeds being declared and millions of pounds worth of capital gains tax was being lost. The tax office was indifferent to their sale but, as with any other industry, they wanted their cut. Sometimes she laughed at the irony that she was taking back artworks from the landed gentry in the name of the Queen, whose ancestors must have once bestowed the treasures on them.

Her boss, Bowers, was quite old school. There was no battering down doors and confiscating precious artworks; he favoured a quieter approach. With all but the worst offenders, he would gently explain that although the artworks belonged to the offender and they were free to sell them, if they made a substantial sum of money they needed to pay a percentage to Her Majesty's Government. This could be far from simple because the items in question were often hundreds of years old, and their owner lacked the original sales receipt. His team was often required to enter into a complex and time-consuming negotiation to agree and then recover their share of the profits after working out exactly what those profits were. The record time so far was nineteen years, with a particularly intractable peer. Bowers was convinced the ancient dowager was eking the argument out in the hope she would drop dead before it was concluded so they would need to begin negotiations from scratch with the next generation. As Bowers had said, "Suits us, we'll just get the cash from inheritance tax instead."

As a working class girl who had made it to university only with the help of a part-time job in her local supermarket and an array of student loans that she reckoned she would have paid off just in time to collect her pension, Lily had no problem ensuring that those who could paid their share. Her work with the tax office so far had seen millions of pounds of unpaid tax recouped through confiscated artworks at her recommendation. Long may her work continue.

Looking around at the work on display, she noticed their guide referred occasionally to a tatty leather-bound book; what appeared to be a cheat sheet to The Glades antiquities. What she wouldn't give to get her hands on that.

Further down the corridor, Matt was watching Lily and thinking exactly the same thing about her. He had finally sought refuge from his parents' friends, and their insistent kissing, hugging and even hair-ruffling, and headed upstairs to grab space on one of the ancient seats displayed in the open windows to find out who had won the blind auction to cover Pink Toes on Horseface. He put away his phone and sat watching, wondering if he should join the tour and strike up a conversation with her.

Sir Jesper had returned from escorting his father's sister to her waiting chauffer-driven Daimler on the front drive, her words of warning ringing in his ears. "Mathieu is his own person, as you once were. Don't force him into something he will hate you for."

Sir Jesper had muttered something non-committal and kissed her powdered cheek before helping her into the car. He fought an urge to tell her about her older brother's new 'wife'; an unnecessary cruelty he quickly quashed. Despite her own catalogues of indiscretions in her day, it would probably kill the old girl.

Entering the house, he watched his son chatting to a tall, slender young woman, her hair pinned casually to the top of her head, who looked suspiciously like one of the wait staff. Matt saw his father watching from over her shoulder and gave a brief nod. Sir Jesper nodded back, Bella's warning ringing in his ear, and decided to leave him to it.

"So are you free after this afternoon?" Matt was determined that she wouldn't get away without giving him her phone number.

"I'm just down for a few weeks from London," Lily replied.

There was no guide to dealing with the perp's good-looking son in her investigator's handbook, and he was good to look at. Lily had studied Fine Art and knew aesthetics well.

"That's okay, I'm just asking for an evening, we could have dinner."

Lily sighed. Maybe it would be good to get a break from working on this case. *Yes, to catch his family in a huge tax fraud*, she silently reminded herself. Would he still want to go out with her then?

"Okay," she said, hardly realising she had spoken out loud. She gave him her mobile phone number as he tapped it into the paper-thin tablet that seemed permanently attached to his left hand. She could always treat it as further undercover work.

Matt smiled his thanks. "I'd better get back to work."

Lily smiled in return and wandered back down the corridor to the kitchen. She needed to report her latest find, and pick up her pay packet from the agency where she was moonlighting.

"Well that's never happened before," she muttered to herself and anyone else who might be listening.

# CHAPTER 28

Lady Rose was in Gibraltar for a matter of hours but in that time her whole life changed. Heading straight for her bank, she had given over her memorised account numbers and provided the necessary verbal codes to gain access to her accounts.

The polite bank clerk had smiled as the elegantly-dressed woman had walked confidently through the door. She was used to seeing some odd characters, who used the unusual banking practices on the Rock to store money for ill-gotten or at the very least ill-defined gains. Inheritance, the clerk guessed of the lady before her, perhaps money deposited by a dying relative to avoid tax.

However, as the woman reeled off her account numbers and she entered them into her computer, the clerk, used to seeing large figures flash across her screen, let out a gasp when she saw the size of the figures come up.

She was looking at two accounts, both showing exactly the same sum.

"Would you like to look at the accounts yourself?" she asked, unwilling to call out the amounts in case they were overheard. The bank prided itself on it discretion.

"Thank you."

"Go to Room Three please." The clerk sent the information over to the computer in the small office which was used by banking customers who wanted additional privacy to view their accounts and online statements, as there were few paper trails on offer.  At the same time the clerk picked up the phone on her desk and called her manager from his office; she had a feeling that this lady was going to get a shock when she saw those figures.

Lady Rose headed to the room indicated, first passing through a metal detector and storing her handbag in the locker provided. Inside the small room, a computer sat on a high desk, with a stool before it. She clicked the mouse to clear the screen saver and saw her account numbers come up.

5576998 Account balance €1000
3211345 Account balance €1000

Lady Rose half turned to the door, assuming the account numbers that came up were wrong, before going back to the computer screen and re-reading them. They were correct. She clicked on the first account. Its balance had been £2,960,052 until three days ago. The second account told the same story; this time well over a million had been withdrawn. Where had it gone?

Panic rose as the reality hit. All that work, all that time, and it had been all for nothing. And in that instance she knew who had done it. Cleaver; Cleaver had taken it all. He had set up her accounts and she had all but forgotten, it had been so long ago. Now he had taken every penny, leaving the minimum amount needed to keep the accounts open.

She cleared the screen, pulled open the door and stopped to grab her bag from the locker, almost laughing at the rigid security protocols of the bank. She had lost £4 million, and it hadn't been stuffed into someone's handbag.

The bank manager stood by the desk, his eyes on her, watching, waiting for her to respond. Lady Rose smiled at him and nodded a hello. There was no point asking them, the money had been withdrawn using all the correct security. Just not by her.

She stopped at a bar and sat outside with a large brandy. Her mind was blank. How could she get Cleaver to give her back the money? The police weren't an option, she instantly recognised, and that would mean involving her husband. Her mind flickered momentarily to her son's recent black eye. Jesper had mentioned Matt had got involved with loan sharks as part of his studies. But she had no intention of hiring thugs to threaten Cleaver.

She drained the glass, eyes watering slightly as the raw alcohol hit her throat. For the first time in a long time she was hit with a longing for her mother. Practical and calmly efficient, Lady Margaret would have sat her daughter down, patted her hand and told her, "Rosie, you are far from destitute, you have that glorious home and a very rich husband. You can start again."

Returning home, via flights to London and the sleeper train from Paddington, Lady Rose excused herself from her husband's vague enquiries as to her early return and changed in her dressing room before going back through to her study. Despite the assurances she had imagined her mother giving her, fear had been gnawing away at her since she had seen the figures come up on the screen, the fear she had successfully kept at bay her whole life, of destitution, of that day when all her and her mother's belongings were no longer theirs. She had gradually begun to feel the anxiety born that day was unnecessary but now it had returned. She was eight years old again, homeless, racing around the house and packing up her belongings before the bailiffs arrived, undoubtedly well-dressed, but bailiffs nonetheless.

The brown envelope Sir Jesper had given her was still sitting in her in-tray on her writing desk, partially covered with cream and ivory embossed envelopes, which would contain invitations to that winter's social events.

Perhaps it would tell her more about the accounts, she may have over-reacted and the bank had simply responded to the withdrawal request by hiding the money elsewhere. After all, banks these days put blocks on accounts when you bought anything more expensive than the weekly shopping. This was nearly four million pounds. Her heart lifted and she picked up her silver letter opener and sliced open the envelope. The cheap brown paper tore and its contents spilled out over her writing desk. A booklet entitled *Ways to Pay* sat on the top of the pile. She picked it up with growing fear and saw the letter which sat underneath it.

*It has come to our attention that you have earned income in the amount of £4.6million over the past 22 years, on which income tax is now due. We have calculated the sum now owed is £1.2 million plus interest.*

*As of today you owe £1.4 million for which payment is immediately due. You have 30 days in which to pay the full amount or court proceedings will be brought. In cases of deliberate tax evasion, we may pass on our files to the Crown Prosecution Service to begin legal proceedings against you. This can result in further fines and/or a custodial sentence.*

Lady Rose sunk into the chair by her desk. It had happened. The fear was real. She was beyond destitute. In twelve hours she had gone from a millionaire to hopelessly in debt.

Another large brandy and a rare cigarette smoked in the kitchen where the smell would soon pass were all she needed to come up with her plan of action. All those years of dreary dinner parties where her husband's distant family discussed avoiding land tax, inheritance tax and the horror of tax bills on the pittance they made from their huge estates had given her some insight. A specialist tax accountant would be her first port of call – someone who could act on her behalf and agree to more reasonable payment terms with the taxman.

Next, the money - or at least most of it - would need to be found and paid, and soon. She headed downstairs where Sir Jesper was nodding off on the sofa in the library.

"Darling," she said as he opened his eyes, sleepily. "I'm off to London again tomorrow, must get something for that ghastly wedding we've been invited to."

# CHAPTER 29

The senior partner at Knight, Maxwell and Day came to the lushly furnished reception area to collect Lady Rose in person. She was seated in his office where tea and coffee sat on a silver tray, ready to be served.

"Thank you," she murmured, automatically sipping at the scalding hot drink as she prepared to share the story she had rehearsed. She recognised instantly the impeccably dressed man in front of her was there to make money but, like most men, was not infallible to a hard luck story, not even from a knight of the realm's genteel wife.

He introduced himself as Maxim Day; he was the senior partner in the firm and clearly incredibly successful.

"I'm afraid I've been rather silly," she began when she had drained her cup. "Selling a few antiques and so on from the family attic, it appears they are counted as earnings."

She handed over the letter, which he read through twice in silence.

He looked up and smiled. "You did the right thing coming to see me."

He walked behind his desk, sitting down and pulling out a legal pad and a pen. "Firstly, can I ask, were these solely your assets or shared that were sold?"

Lady Rose paused. She had always considered the antiquities as lost until she unearthed them. *Finders, keepers,* she told herself.

"Mine," she said aloud. "And it's imperative that my husband is kept out of this entirely."

"Is there evidence to suggest that they belonged to you and you were the only one to profit?"

"Not really, these things were bought before people got receipts. But the tax bill is addressed to me."

"In that case we must act fast. The tax office would be quite within its rights to contact your husband to discuss payment if they think he is also involved."

"What do you recommend?"

"I would never recommend handing over such a sum without a fight," he said. "But there is always a risk that HMRC will want to make an example of you and look for a prosecution." He paused. "Do you have the money?"

Lady Rose sighed heavily. "Not all of it, no. In fact it was stolen from me," she paused, debating how much of the story she need tell. She went for a half-truth. "Let's just call it a bad investment. I can probably raise the money eventually, but certainly not within seven days."

He scribbled on his pad. "I would guess that we could spend several weeks haggling over the amount of tax due and reduce your burden considerably. However, a partial payment always helps in calming the waters. Good faith, if you will. Let me give one of my contacts there a call and we'll see what we can do. The most important thing for you is to keep the bailiffs from the door next weekend."

He picked up his phone and requested his secretary put in a call to John Fordham.

"Johnny, dear, it's Maxim here," he spoke into the sleek Bang and Olufsen device after a few seconds. "Yes, how are you? I know, it was a frightful bore wasn't it? She's a good cook though — it almost makes up for her awful husband." He paused and laughed uproariously for a minute before starting again, straight-faced. "Now I hate to talk business on a Friday afternoon so close to cocktail hour, but I have someone here to discuss a very sudden and unexpected tax bill in need of some help." He paused again, looking down at the letter, before reading out Lady Rose's tax number. A pause as the man on the other end typed it into his computer. "That's the one. What we are looking for is a reasonable amount of time to allow her to organise the finances."

He paused again.

"I think it's perfectly reasonable that when someone sells something that belongs to them, they don't expect to give the government a cut." This was said more forcefully, the jolly banter in his voice all but replaced by more steely tones. There was a pause as she heard the man on the line express some incredulity. "She was badly advised on that one, yes. Now if we come up with, say, twenty per cent of the total on Monday, will you be willing to open negotiations to discuss the rest of payment?" Again a pause. "And this interest is a bit steep, don't you think?" Maxim looked up and smiled reassuringly at Lady Rose. "Well that's true, but then neither do you. Marvellous, marvellous. I'll get the money in my hand this afternoon and we can halt all this silliness." He looked up at Lady Rose who nodded her agreement. "Yes, I will vouch for that. Look, ask your gal to call mine and we'll get a meet in the diary – maybe at the club, we could play squash afterwards? Lovely."

Maxim replaced the receiver and clasped his hands together. "It may sound strange, but you picked a good time to get caught. The old taxman doesn't want any wrangles, they just want the cash. Government is on their back about this – then there's all those nasty corporations getting away with daylight robbery. I think they would be very happy to get £750,000 from you, but we are a way from getting that written in stone."

Lady Rose did a few calculations in her head. "So what happens now?"

"We need to pay up £280,000 on Monday and then I'll start negotiations to get the final bill as low as we can. But you can forget the interest to be paid on it for a start."

Lady Rose pulled out her chequebook. She had already moved over a sum of money from her inheritance to the account she used for her everyday expenses. Her mother had left her a few hundred thousand pounds that had never been spent. Or handed over to her husband. She had officially entered the marriage without a dowry.

"Who do I make it payable to?"

Once done, she turned to a new page in her chequebook. "And your fees?"

"My time comes to you at £500 an hour, but you can expect to save a lot more on this," he stabbed the bill with his index finger. "I would suggest a retainer as the way to go – see my gal on the way out. She will fix the sum, usually three days. Expect a call from me on Monday, to acknowledge receipt of this payment, they will want to process it to make sure it doesn't bounce," he smiled, taking the sting out of the words. "Then a final payment request will be sent within the next few weeks."

"Can you ensure that it is sent to you instead of my home?"

"Yes. Let my gal know so she can add that to your file, tell her I said that all your correspondence should come here."

"And I have a number for you to call," Lady Rose handed over a hand-written card. It was for a new pay-as-you-go mobile phone bought from a kiosk at Paddington Station that morning.

She rose and held out her still gloved hand. "Thank you, Mr Day."

"Please call me Maxim. Big fan of *Compagne* by the way. My wife never fails to buy a copy."

Lady Rose smiled and headed to the door, stopping to pass on instructions to his secretary and request that a taxi be called to take her to her dressmaker. After all, she really did need a dress for that ghastly wedding.

Back home, she headed for her study to put away her chequebook. Her account would cover the downpayment and the accountant's fees, but she still needed to find more than £500,000. Her choices were limited; there were some items that could be put up for auction, she could borrow from her husband – the money was there in his accounts for the taking – but somehow she preferred to steal than beg money from him. That way, she felt she had earned it.

# CHAPTER 30

The wedding day had finally arrived. Lucy had spent the final few days in a flurry of activity. Her nails were perfect, her skin had a gentle sun-kissed glow. Weeks of enrichening conditioners had created the kind of hair that models could only dream of. She had to keep fighting the urge to swing her head from side to side every time she passed a reflective surface, telling herself she was worth it.

She had awoken in the turret bedroom of Tremere Castle, greeted by a chilled flute of champagne, its vintage the year of her first wedding, which would also be served in the hall as guests greeted the newly-married couple. On a silver tray there was a light breakfast of warm croissants and strawberry jam made by the castle's ancient cook, who was kept on purely for her renowned powers of preserve-making.

Lucy nibbled on one corner of the buttery pastry, aware that she would need something to keep her energy levels up. Her make-up artist and hair designer were due within the hour; she would dress, and then the bridesmaids would join her for champagne and some informal photographs before the ceremony began.

A card had arrived for her from Jack, which she left on the desk unopened. An anniversary card, she suspected, he was such an old romantic. But she wasn't interested in that wedding and she had no time for his sentimentality right now – his role was to stand at the head of the aisle waiting for her, eyes shining with love, in the immaculate dark grey suit she had picked out for him at Prada. She knew he would play his role perfectly.

The day was warm and sunny, enough for the dowagers below to shed their tweed jackets while standing on the lawn outside the castle. Red-veined faces were tipped towards the sunshine as they hoped to get the ceremony out of the way so they could indulge in some gossip and enjoy the food, which included asparagus and hollandaise, pork loin and fondant potatoes with seasonal vegetables and gravy that was rumoured to have taken ten days to create.

On the other side of the county, Tory awoke knowing something was wrong immediately. A look at her clock revealed she had seriously overslept. The glass of wine with Janey on her terrace had turned into two bottles as she had chatted with her friend about the magazine and the imminent wedding, and later considered life after *Compagne*.

She had taken Donovan's call on her way home from work, eventually having to pull up in front of the harbour where a packed surf school was teaching wetsuited tourists how to balance on surfboards. The sergeant was finally making the call she had been waiting for all these weeks.

"I can go home?" Tory had shouted loudly into the receiver, realising the surf school people had stopped listening to the instructor and turned to her car, where her window was open. She repeated the words more quietly to herself, testing their truth as Donovan continued to talk.

London was no longer a no-go area, he explained. Gatsby and the *Post* were desperate for her return, her flat was waiting for her and she could go.

When she had answered the phone, Tory was so surprised by Donovan's voice that she had failed to recognise it. There had been very little in the news since he had visited her and he had obviously decided to keep the body parts tally to himself. Cracker Smith's grisly death had been long-forgotten by the media – the police had obviously kept out any reference to a journalist going on the run in fear of her life, if there had ever been any threat. As Donovan retold the story, it was easy to see how she might write a film script out of it, maybe ratcheting up the tensions by inventing a meeting between her and her intended assassin.

However, it was someone else who had been killed. The story, it seemed, had ended less well for a 23-year-old called Billy Woodward. Apparently he had started working for the drugs gang a year before, and his death led police to believe the gang had identified him as a snitch. All this meant she was off the hook.

The police would continue to investigate the people thought to be responsible for Woodward's and Cracker's deaths, but with other outstanding crimes against people much more worth the mourning, it was likely the murder hunt would find its way to the police canteen's back burner.

"I can go home," Tory had said again as she had hung up.

Not wanting to be alone with her thoughts, she had called

Janey and invited her round for a glass of wine to celebrate, and discuss Lucy's nuptials. She wondered if she should now tell her friend about the case and how she had come to Cornwall and *Compagne* as a temporary measure. In the end she had said nothing.

Now there was no time for her to think about how she would extricate herself from *Compagne*. She had an important task to perform: the dress and shoes were facing her, ready to throw on, and she had to be in the car in precisely ten minutes. The ceremony was scheduled for midday and it was already getting on for 11am. She knew Lucy had planned her wedding to perfection and certainly didn't want her own absence to ruin the day, even though it was unlikely they would ever see each other again once Tory had returned to London.

A quick shower and hair wash, her overnight bag stuffed with a change of clothes and make-up she could put on in the car, she pulled on the deep red silk dress that had been sent to her the previous day by the wedding's official dressmaker and slipped on her battered Birkenstocks – she would change her shoes after the drive – then into the car for the 40-minute drive to Tremere Castle. She still wondered how she had managed to be talked into being a bridesmaid for the wedding of a man she had slept with. She made the journey in less than 35 minutes, changing her shoes and pinning her hair up as she got out of the car.

With no one to give her away, Lucy was happy to make her entrance alone. The four bridesmaids headed down the stairs first and Lucy followed after a beat of ten. She heard or imagined intakes of breath from the hall below as her guests got their first glimpse of her beauty. It was perfect.

But the bridesmaids stopped as Tory, at the front, turned to one of the guests to ask him to repeat what he had said. Lucy stood on the third step down, a fixed smile on her face, fighting an urge to shout for her to carry on or the moment would be ruined.

Tory turned to look at Lucy, her hands making a shooing movement, indicating she should go back up the stairs. Lucy frowned, then remembering the make-up artist's advice, quickly uncrumpled her brow, choosing instead to glide down the stairs and face Tory.

She turned to the guest who had impeded her bridesmaids'

progress through the hall. It was L'il, Jack's second-in-command at Ramsden's. Lucy referred to him as Jack's best man, although Jack had kept insisting he didn't need one this time around. L'il wasn't his real name, but by now she couldn't remember what it was – his nickname 'Little'; an ironic reference to his hulk - had long ago been bastardised to L'il. And the idea that those who met him assumed his name was Lily or Lillian had yet to cause anything more than a raised eyebrow among new acquaintance.

Such was Lucy's annoyance it took her three times to hear what her bridesmaid was saying. "They can't find him."

"Who?"

"Jack."

Lucy frowned again, then instantly relaxed her forehead. The last thing she needed was a creased face in the wedding photographs later.

"He's probably walking the grounds or nipped into the kitchen to check the food," she said, wondering if she should begin her descent again. "I don't know why you needed to interrupt our arrival like that."

L'il interrupted. "No, he's not here, I went to pick him up from your house and he wasn't there. Car's gone."

"Some sort of emergency at the restaurant?"

"Been there, everything is fine."

"Well I'm sure he will turn up, let's just carry on without him." Lucy nodded, everything settled.

"You can't get married without a bridegroom," Tory said quietly, a look of incomprehensible shock flashing over her face. Her Weddings Editor had clearly lost the plot. She watched silently as the colour drained from Lucy's face. She seemed to be struggling to take in that the chances were she had been stood up at the altar.

L'il seemed to shrink before Tory's eyes. He was beginning to worry that his role as unofficial best man meant he was expected to step up to the altar instead.

Lucy looked from L'il to Tory and to the face of each of her other bridesmaids – who had all been chosen because of their similar height, weight and colouring, as opposed to their closeness to the bride – then finally to the guests nearby who had heard the exchange. They all refused to meet her eyes. She realised she was frowning again, but also that it no longer mattered. There would be no wedding photographs. She turned and raced up the stairs, into the turret bedroom, and headed for the dressing table where Jack's envelope lay unopened.

She ripped it open and pulled out the card. It was padded, two teddy bears holding a big red love heart and the words *'To My Wife on Our Anniversary'* in silver curling script across the top. She opened it and read the brief inscription.

*To my ex-wife on our anniversary.*
*Your ex-husband, Jack*

Beneath it was a lawyer's address in London, accompanied by the words 'for all correspondence'.

Tory had raced after Lucy and stood uncertainly by the bedroom door.

"He's not coming," Lucy said, looking at her through the mirror. She began to rip up the card, turning it into confetti, which she then threw up in the air just as she had planned for the rice that had been dyed the same colour of the bridesmaids' dresses for guests to use after the ceremony.

She turned back to the mirror, slowly pulling out the pins that had been painstakingly placed in her hair only an hour earlier. "I thought I was planning the perfect wedding, turns out it was the perfect divorce."

Tory looked at her, her heart pounding as she tried to think of something she could say. In the end, she picked up the still chilling and slightly flat opened bottle of champagne and poured a healthy slug straight into her slightly crazy Weddings Editor. There was nothing she could say, and she knew it.

Eventually she helped Lucy change into jeans and a t-shirt, cleaning some of the heavy make-up from her face.

"What did he say?" Tory asked, for a moment wondering if he had mentioned his one-night-stand with her.

Lucy shook her head. She didn't want to think about Jack. But she supposed she never really had. "He doesn't love me anymore."

"He wrote that?"

"No. But he didn't need to. I know."

"How?"

"I didn't love him either. All these years writing about the perfect wedding, I became the expert at it. But a perfect marriage? I've no idea."

Tory sat next to her on the bed, pulling the flowers out of her own dishevelled hair. "L'il has gone downstairs to make an announcement to the guests, let's get you out of here."

Lucy nodded. Looking around the room, she saw there was nothing she needed to take with her. She had decided to totally refresh her wardrobe following her wedding. Everything she had brought with her was new for the new Mrs Ramsden.

She paused on her way to the door. "Tory, there's one more thing I wanted to tell you."

Tory's heart knocked painfully as she waited. Did she know about her and Jack?

"I resign."

Tory nodded. It was probably for the best, for her best health anyway. She watched her former Weddings Editor walk quietly down the stairs and head for the back door where a taxi was waiting to take her home. Lucy knew Jack wouldn't be there. And, she realised, it was almost a relief.


Tory headed down the main stairs, feeling suddenly conscious of her silk dress and big hair. Despite removing the pins, the hairspray liberally applied at the last minute by the hairdresser held it in full-bodied position. Guests were circulating, talking much more animatedly than at most wedding receptions she remembered. Most were drinking the champagne that had been sent out along with the news that the ceremony was cancelled. After all, everything had been paid for. Why not just drink up and carry on?

Tory helped herself to a flute from a hovering waiter and took a large gulp, before remembering her hangover and her imminent drive back to the little cottage. She would hang around for a while and head home to bed. And then where? She had a lot of thinking to do.


Matt had been bowled over when Lily had agreed to come to the wedding with him as his date. When he had called her and asked if she was doing anything on Saturday, she hadn't expected him to bring her to a Cornish castle for a wedding.

Now they stood together on the lawn, drinking and, like all the other guests, discussing the non-wedding and what they should do.

"I've never been to a wedding like this," Lily said. She wondered if she should take a tour of their long gallery, but decided to consider herself off-duty.

"Me neither. The groom usually shows up."

"I wonder what happened."

Matt shrugged. He wasn't really interested. He was more interested in finding out about his date. She had told him on the drive over that she had studied Fine Art, and that she had taken waitressing jobs for a bit of extra cash and a chance to spend the summer in Cornwall, home to so many renowned artists.

She was evading his questions, having not picked up a sketchpad for many years. Although she found herself itching to capture his likeness; perhaps he could be her muse.

"Do you have a studio in London?"

Lily shook her head. "No, I work out of a small flat, it's my living and work space."

"I'd like to see it sometime."

"Next time you're in London," Lily said, a safe bet that he would never come.

But Matt already had it planned. His great aunt had come good with the money and he had secured some office space for Horseface in the South Bank on the promise of her investment. He just needed to hand in his notice to his father and he was gone. But that could wait until Monday.

"Great," he said.

Lily drained her wine glass. "I know people are still hanging around, but this is a bit weird, shall we go?"

Matt was voicing his agreement when he heard a phone ring. Lily looked down at her vibrating bag.

"I'd better get that," she said, pulling her phone out and walking away as she answered it.


In the end Lady Rose had worn a dress from her closet, her plans to buy something new for the wedding not having materialised. Shopping was the least of her worries. A few quiet enquiries had shown that Cleaver had disappeared from his home and suddenly shut up shop, presumed living in Thailand. She had no hope of getting the money back. The previous evening she had added the leather-bound book cataloguing the Donaldson belongings to the crackling apple logs in the library fire. It was over.

Sir Jesper, standing by her side, noted it was the third time he had seen her in the same dress recently. It was most unlike her. He hoped she was not exhausting herself with the busy social diary. They had barely a free weekend until Christmas.

"Darling," he began. A thought had occurred to him, as he had watched the shambolic wedding unfold.

Lady Rose turned to him, expectant, ready to leave.

"I've been thinking about something recently. My father, as you know, signed everything over to me many years ago to avoid inheritance tax. But the value of the estate has grown so much under your careful hands, I think you deserve some recognition."

Lady Rose nodded. Wondering what was next. Perhaps he was going to offer her 25 years' back pay for running his home. It couldn't have come at a better time.

Sir Jesper gently stroked her cheek. "I think it's time we captured your portrait for the Great Hall. Matt has been talking about this artist he's with, I thought we could get you two together and ensure that those lucky enough to inherit The Glades in generations to come can look up at your beautiful face and know who they have to be thankful to."

Lady Rose smiled, her smile quickly turning into a laugh, and the laughter into a tear that rolled down her cheek.

"Thank you," she managed to whisper.

Sir Jesper used his index finger to catch the tear before sucking the salty water from his finger.

"Come on, let's go."

Lady Rose led the way, failing to stop and say goodbye to anyone. She just wanted to go home.

# CHAPTER 31

Tory sat down at one of the tables set out in the empty marquee where the happy couple should by now have been cutting the untouched cake. She looked at the intricate icing, wondered what would happen to it, and noticed some wag had removed the groom from the top tier. She thought of the next issue of *Compagne* that was already being planned, her assertion to her team just the previous day that it would be their best yet. Who would take over if she left?

She finished the champagne and fought an urge to take a bite out of the cake. For her adventure to end with a decomposing body in a builder's skip somewhere in Hammersmith seemed, dare she say it, disappointing. But that was the nature of crime, she supposed. People killed each other and priorities changed. Perhaps it was the Hollywood effect that she had expected to be tracked down and threatened and for the mystery assassin to go out all guns blazing. But now this unknown man who had ordered her flat turned over, who had orchestrated all those body parts to be found in and around her home, had murdered a young man, presumably talked into an undercover adventure by the idiotic Cracker Smith and then too scared to make a run for it when Cracker turned up dead.

Now she could return to her life in London. No more spell-checking names of the country's landed gentry. No more tortuously high heels. But there would also be no more lunches with Harry or nights in with Janey. No more Sophie and her endless demands for Valentino on expenses.

Tory's thoughts turned briefly to Jack. Judging by the card and the rumours now circulating the wedding, he had gone to London himself. Maybe she could meet up with him, talk about what happened, and see if they might start something.

Albie, she knew, had also all but returned to his life in the city, interest in his flagship men's magazine waning as the lure of TV punditry had proved too powerful for him to resist, but there was no way she would be dropping him an email.

Matt watched Lily's back as she listened to her caller. It didn't sound like good news.

"So it's over then?" she asked and Matt wondered if it was a boyfriend she hadn't mentioned. "Will she pay?"

Lily had listened to Bowers with growing astonishment. It seemed Lady Rose had lost no time in employing one of London's biggest tax sharks to get out of paying her way. Bowers, used to her outbursts, took it in his stride. "Lily, this is a success story. Someone making money like this has agreed to pay her back taxes. It seemed she didn't think she was doing anything wrong."

Lily snorted. "Of course she didn't."

"The first payment has come in already. The rest will follow eventually, I'm sure. Putting it bluntly, the government needs the money now, not to have it tied up in expensive legal battles."

Ignoring his goodbye, Lily forcefully hit the 'end' button on her phone, momentarily missing the heavy old-fashioned phone her mum had clung onto at home, which offered a satisfyingly heavy slam.

These fucking people always seemed to get away with it somehow. Lady Rose would pay, but she wouldn't *pay* for her crime. Lily stood for a moment looking up at the castle. The owners had apparently rented their ancient seat to the not-so-happy-couple – she wondered if they would declare the earnings and made a note to check when she got back to London.

Matt walked over, "Everything okay?"

Lily looked at him, scowling for a moment. She watched his expression of concern. He really did have a face worth drawing, she thought. Thankfully there was only a passing resemblance to his mother. She finally smiled. "Come on, let's go back to your place."

Matt's frown instantly cleared. "Okay, but I should warn you that I'm back living with my parents again. Only temporarily – I'm starting up my own business and I couldn't afford the rent."

Lily laughed. His mother had screwed her out of a result; it felt only right that she got to screw her son under her roof.

"Come on."

Lily walked away from the marquee and the still milling guests towards the makeshift car park on the castle's polo field.


Betsy had arrived too late to watch the drama of the wedding ceremony unfold. She had spent the previous night filling a skip with all the unwanted house and garden accessories that had made her home uncomfortable. She wore a green linen shift dress and matching shoes and had come alone.

She spotted her Managing Editor sitting alone at a table under the billowing yacht sails that made up the wedding marquee and headed over. "What happened?"

Tory poured her a glass of wine from the selection on the table. "The groom was a no-show."

Betsy's mouth formed an 'o' before she took a drink of wine. "How's Lucy?"

"Gone. Not coming back."

"To the castle?"

"To *Compagne*."

*Shit.* Betsy wondered if this would make her own resignation letter, now sitting in her out tray, bad timing. She had planned to do it on Monday. It was time, she had decided, to get back into real journalism.

Tory sat drinking wine, seemingly caught up in the day's drama. Betsy hadn't realised she was so close to Lucy but she seemed clearly upset.

Letting her eyes wander, she spotted Lyle Taylor and Lodd McPherson walking hand-in-hand, laughing happily. "Back in a sec," she said, getting up to say hello to them.

Lodd air-kissed her new friend as she broke slightly away from Lyle.

"You two look very happy," Betsy said, smiling.

Lodd nodded. "We are. It's weird. Did Tory tell you I took the columnist job?"

"She did. It will be great having you at *Compagne*."

*Even though I won't be there,* Betsy thought. Perhaps she would hand her notice in to Sir Jesper instead.

Lodd looked over her shoulder, spotting someone she knew.

"Come with me," she relinquished Lyle's hand – who demanded a kiss before she left his side – and put her arm through Betsy's. "There's someone you simply must meet."

She marched her across the lawn, her high heels seemingly no impediment, to the man standing looking into the lake which sat outside the castle.

"Gus, meet Betsy," Lodd said loudly, dragging his attention from the carp. "Betsy, meet Gus."

She put Betsy's hand in his outstretched one. "It's time you two got to meet each other properly."

Betsy broke into a smile as Gus reddened slightly.

"Fancy a walk along the beach?" he asked, his hand still clasping hers.

Betsy nodded, giving his hand a squeeze. "Let's go."

Tory didn't remember the journey back to her little cottage but when she got there she changed clothes, leaving her bridesmaid's dress lying at the foot of the stairs, and headed for the kitchen where she pulled out a half-empty bottle of vodka from the freezer.

"I'm going home," she said to herself again, looking around her. She looked fondly at the French windows that opened out onto a little terrace where she had sat many times in recent weeks and drunk wine with Janey, and beyond it the small, slightly overgrown garden. Sitting on the floor, she knew that if she opened the doors, she would faintly hear the swell of the Atlantic Ocean, imagine the wide beach filled with late afternoon surfers and smell the slight salty tang of sea air that had played such havoc with her naturally wavy blonde hair.

She thought of her flat in Hammersmith, the dusty offices of the *Post,* her desk teetering with press releases and the spike that had been used in such a grisly way. Gatsby's grubby little glass box and the ancient vending machine that spat out instant tea that could remove the enamel from your teeth with one mouthful.

And she finally began to get that excited feeling in her stomach. *I'm going home.*

She would email Jamesy about her flat and she needed to arrange to see her parents; she had avoided them in person, unwilling to put them at any risk, with only semi-regular phone calls to update them on her glamorous new life.

An editorship on a national magazine had been a sojourn, an adventure, she reminded herself. She had saved money for the first time in her life – and she could keep the wardrobe.

And you never knew – maybe she would return one day.

# CHAPTER 32

Sir Jesper looked aghast. He had come to rely on Tory to keep everything ticking over. Since her arrival he had been able to launch *The MacGuffin,* which was showing every sign of being a huge success. Albie remained its figurehead, although he now spent most of his time in London, the kudos that he was getting from the magazine was incredible. There was even talk of an award.

"You can't leave." It was a statement of hope, not fact.

"This was only ever temporary. I have a life in London. I had to get away and this is where I've ended up." Tory paused, realising she was being unnecessarily rude. She took an invisible breath and started again. "I've loved it here, it's been an incredible experience, but I am a newsman, not a magazine editor. I love the smell of newsprint in the morning."

In the end Sir Jesper had no choice but to let her leave.


Matt had been the next person to enter his office. He had written a letter of resignation and had included a cheque for the outstanding amount owed to his father – which he was secretly hoping he would refuse.

Sir Jesper had guessed his reason before he had opened his mouth.

"You're off, are you?" he had said.

Matt looked surprised. Had his mother spoken to him? "I've identified someone from the IT department who can work on the websites until you find a new Digital Editor. I don't mind helping you recruit, but I've written down some good IT recruitment consultancies if you get stuck," he handed over his carefully-written handover notes.

"When do you want to go?" His father ignored the printed sheets his son had dropped on his desk.

"Two weeks."

Sir Jesper sighed, stretching his hands out on the desk in front of him. Matt handed over the cheque. "I know I haven't worked off the money I owe you, but I can pay you back."

His father looked at his son as he explained his plans. Perhaps it was more important to let him go his own way. After all, hadn't he wanted the same thing at one time? The games software company

Matt was setting up could turn out to be more lucrative than publishing. And if Matt didn't want *Compagne*, then Freddy's demand to split up the company so he could take his fair share would be less important.

"Consider me a partner," he said, ripping up the cheque.

Freddy had seen Matt go into his brother's office as he had entered the reception area. He and Jesper had hardly spoken since their father's return from Gretna Green. But they would need to settle things. He went in as his nephew left, looking delighted.

"The Managing Editor has just handed in her notice," Sir Jesper said by way of greeting. Freddy shrugged. "The Weddings Editor is also not coming back after her disastrous non-wedding at the weekend. And Matt is off to London to set up a software design company."

Freddy nodded. It would all sort itself out, Jesper had a knack for falling on his feet, what with his perfect wife, the home she had created, and the success he was making of the Donaldson Publishing Group.

"What do you want?" Jesper's question was open-ended. Either his brother simply wanted to speak to him, or he had readied his demands for equal shares.

"I don't want your life," Freddy started. It was the only thing he was sure of. Since his father's elopement, Freddy had realised the responsibility of being the eldest son. He had seen the everyday requirements of being Managing Director of the Donaldson Group. Watching his brother dealing with the stresses and strains of running the company, the packed social diary that required him to spread so much largesse, Freddy recognised he didn't want it. Perhaps if he had been brought up to do it, he would have been equally at home with it. But he hadn't. And he wasn't.

"I'm leaving," he said finally.

"Where are you going?"

"Back to London."

"To do what?"

"I'm thinking of opening a gallery."

Sir Jesper hid a smile. It was typical of Freddy. A new venture, something to occupy him for a few months before he got bored and moved on. He had never fully appreciated the freedom he had as a younger son.

"Okay." Sir Jesper knew what was coming.

"I want money to set it up. I will need around £2 million."

Sir Jesper nodded. This was to be the price of holding onto the empire his family had built up, and which his son didn't want.

Freddy stood, holding out his hand for his brother to shake. "I'm going to visit Dad, and then I'm catching the sleeper to Paddington. "Give me a ring when you've thought about it."

Sir Jesper took his brother's hand, clasping it in both of his.

Freddy turned to leave, and stopped at the door. "I'm going to borrow a couple of the Flowers of Medieval to help get it up and running."

Inspired by his father's lust for life and recent marriage, he had decided the redhead and the blonde should join him on his adventure.

Sir Jesper shrugged. He had lost his brother, his son, his editor and a key member of his editorial team. He could afford to lose a couple of receptionists as well.

***

The morning of the planning meeting for the Christmas issue dawned. It was a hot day, making it hard to think about snow and roaring fires. Ever ahead of the curve, Betsy was already halfway through her spread of the finest country houses across the land bedecked with grand fifteen-foot Norwegian spruce trees decorated with priceless family heirlooms.

She and Gus had arrived early to work, having spent the weekend together. He had been surprisingly willing to help her heave unwanted furniture into her fast-filling skip. Her resignation letter, for the moment, had gone back into her drawer.

Harry Hampton was planning the first of a month-long binge of Christmas lunches as chefs fought to feature in the food pages of this all-important month. Already his diary looked like a Michelin-starred advent calendar with a gourmet treat to be discovered every day. Little known to most, Harry tended to sit down on Christmas day with a simple repast of fresh breads from his local artisan bakery, generous chunks of Melton Mowbray Stilton and Cornish Yarg cheeses garnished with sliced apple, grapes, celery and a bottle or two of Château Margaux.

He considered the menu palate-cleansing and often lived on it for the full holiday season. After a few days he also tended to find a welcome slackening to his waistband. If the average man could consume 10,000 calories on a typical Christmas day, Harry must average that throughout December – although he did what he could; he always passed on the gravy.

Already he had planned the winning meal. He had plumped for a Michelin-starred gastro pub in Hampshire serving roasted goose stuffed with *foie gras*. The idea of a goose being force-fed to expand its liver to get the much-loved pâté only for its brethren to have it rammed up its arse before cooking was intriguing. He scribbled on his notepad a few opening lines.

Further down the table, Malachy Drummond typed in the last lines of his novel on his tablet. Dick Biggs had finally got his man – all eight inches of him. Malachy had already let Sir Jesper know he too intended to leave and that this was to be his final issue. The royalty cheques were flooding in and he felt ready to end his double life.

In a rare moment of equality, Sophie Dexter-Browning sat by Jo, admiring the size of her antique ruby engagement ring. Jo had surprised all but Harry by announcing her engagement to Sir William Northam, a middle-aged childless peer in Gloucestershire desperate to breed to save his land. In the end all she had needed to seal the deal was proof of her fertility.

Now Jo was marrying into the world she and *Compagne* so carefully helped to construct and maintain, Sophie was keen to ensure she not only got an invite to the wedding, but covered it for the magazine as well. With the Weddings Editor post now sitting vacant, Sophie was rather keen to take weddings under her wing; Oscar de la Renta had just revealed his darling winter collection crying out to be worn.

Jo, not one to forget the many slights she had suffered from the Social Editor, was equally determined the invite would not be forthcoming. Her wedding would be small, inexpensive and held in her hometown. It didn't really matter; she was happy. Her husband-to-be had money and a title but, more importantly, he had her heart.


Sitting alone at his desk, Sir Jesper was distracted. He hadn't told anyone but Freddy that the editor had left *Compagne* as he had remained hopeful up to the last minute that she would change her mind. He had sent the latest offer of her permanent appointment by email the night before but it was now ten minutes to the hour and he could hear staff filing into the conference room next door for the planning meeting.

His offer, well, it may have come out a bit like an ultimatum, he guessed had fallen on deaf ears. After letting her leave, he had turned up at her little cottage, offered to buy it for her outright, doubling her salary, and adding several extra zeroes to the limit on her company credit card. Tory had been polite but resolute. It wasn't about the money, she had said. It was about her life.

He would have to run the planning meeting himself and appoint someone as Acting Editor until he could find someone more suited to the role. He wondered if Gus Jacobs was up for the challenge. He thought back to the last time he had seen the promising young editor. Two months under the whip hand of Albie and Gus had aged ten years.

Sir Jesper had been reminded of last year's production of *Waiting for Godot*; Gus had become Lucky to Albie's Pozzo. But, if he remembered the plot correctly (he had been rather distracted by his delightful companion's lips around his cock in the second act), Lucky got his revenge. Perhaps that's all this was, the end of the first act.


The ancient clock in the hallway struck the hour, interrupting Sir Jesper's thoughts. Well, he would worry about all of that later. Jo would help him find a new Acting Editor while he looked for someone to fill Tory's designer shoes more permanently. Of course, he would need to let them down gently later if necessary. He suspected he would have to come up with a suitable redundancy package if he or she didn't get the job permanently, but he could afford it.

In the conference room, turned chilly by an over-active air conditioner – perhaps to get them all in the mood for the Christmas issue – Sir Jesper turned to the large interactive white screen as the possible cover images for the December issue flashed up across it, including one of a sand snowman kitted out in a top hat, monocle and cravat, which had been designed by the donkeys to lighten the mood. "We have a few choices this month, thanks to our former editor, Victoria..."

He paused as everyone gasped at the word 'former'. Sir Jesper had struggled to come up with a suitable way to let the staff know about Tory's sudden departure. He felt a calm approach was needed. Just casually dropping it into conversation was the way to go. Not for the first time he wondered why he had never formalised her contract, locked her in for several months' notice period. But her sudden arrival and the uncertainty about her predecessor's future meant he had wanted only a temporary relief.

Harry looked up from his notepad, where he was scribbling notes for his Christmas lunch feature. He managed to get one word out: "Where…"

"So sorry I am late," a voice interrupted him, breathless, or just out of breath, but bringing immediate warmth to the room.

Standing in a black sleeveless dress, Tory looked towards the head of the table, smiling at Sir Jesper, who was already on his feet and walking towards her, hand outstretched. "Marvellous, marvellous," his reply was all the encouragement she needed as she moved towards the chair he had vacated and sat down.

"I'll leave you to it," Sir Jesper closed the door and practically skipped back to his office, wondering if he would still have to buy her that house. After all, he had put nothing down in writing.

He paused at his office door, remembering his recent acquisition to the team. After Max Mullen had mentioned his intention to quit his food column, Sir Jesper, desperate not to lose all his staff at once, had fired off an email to his favourite chef. He nodded at the man now sitting in Reception and beckoned him towards the conference room.

"Sorry to interrupt," Sir Jesper's head reappeared around the conference room door as Tory was trying to bring the room to order, after Sir Jesper's almost shock announcement. He turned to speak to someone at his side before ushering him into the room. "I just wanted to introduce our new food columnist, Jack Ramsden. He's poised to get his first Michelin star for his Cornish restaurant and will be filing recipes for us from the December issue. Many of you will remember him from the Food and Drink Awards."

Tory's mouth dropped open for just a second before she quickly closed it, instead turning it into a grin directed in Jack's direction as he sat at the end of the table and gave her a wide smile that crinkled the corners of his eyes most becomingly.

"Victoria, perhaps after this meeting, you can take Jack around the building and show him the ropes."

"I'd be happy to," she replied before welcoming Jack in a tone warm enough to lightly toast the bagels, which were sitting on the table surrounded by tiny portions of cream cheese and slivers of smoked salmon.

He nodded back to her, encouraged. Jack had thought hard about taking on a writing role at his ex-wife's ex-magazine, but assurances from Sir Jesper that Lucy had left and headed off to London had made up his mind, as had the chance to work alongside Tory.

"Right," Tory's voice settled back into her normal register as she helped herself to a bagel from the centre of the table and took control of the white screen behind her.

"The December issue," she said, turning with a wide smile. "What have we got?"

www.ingramcontent.com/pod-product-compliance
Lightning Source LLC
Chambersburg PA
CBHW021011120726
47905CB00009B/2952